Her pulse accelerated along with her steps.

I can't face him now. I'm not ready.

Sam touched her shoulder. Ruth shrugged him off and stepped into the street.

A horn blared. She turned her head in time to see a car bearing down on her. Then someone yanked her back onto the boardwalk. Only after her heartbeat slowed did she realize that the arm wrapped around her waist belonged to Sam.

"You could have been killed." His voice shook.

She was only aware that he still held her. "Please…let go."

He released her. "Where are you going in such a rush?"

She could not look at him. "I suppose I should thank you for saving my life." But she did not feel thankful.

"Didn't you hear me? Didn't you see the car? You acted like you were running away."

I was. But she couldn't say that. "I'm in a hurry."

"I can see that, but nothing is worth risking your life."

My heart is.

Books by Christine Johnson

Love Inspired Historical

Soaring Home
The Matrimony Plan
All Roads Lead Home
Legacy of Love
The Marriage Barter
*Groom by Design

*The Dressmaker's Daughters

CHRISTINE JOHNSON

A small-town girl, Christine Johnson has lived in every corner of Michigan's Lower Peninsula. She loves to visit historic locations and imagine the people who once lived there. A double-finalist for RWA's Golden Heart award, she enjoys creating stories that bring history to life while exploring the characters' spiritual journey—and putting them in peril! Though Michigan is still her home base, she and her seafaring husband also spend time exploring the Florida Keys and other fascinating locations.

Christine loves to hear from readers. Contact her through her website at christineelizabethjohnson.com.

Groom by Design

CHRISTINE JOHNSON

HARLEQUIN® LOVE INSPIRED® HISTORICAL

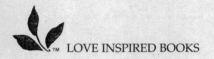 LOVE INSPIRED BOOKS

ISBN-13: 978-0-373-28271-5

GROOM BY DESIGN

www.Harlequin.com

Printed in U.S.A.

To give unto them beauty for ashes...
—*Isaiah* 61:3

To God, the Author of everything,
belongs all the glory.

Chapter One

Pearlman, Michigan
July 1923

"No, no, no. I won't do it." Ruth Fox glared at her younger sister Jen. "We have enough to do without chasing after rich men." She glanced at the dress shop's clock before pressing another seam on Mrs. Vanderloo's tea gown. The wealthy client wanted her dresses by five o'clock, and Ruth was running late.

"But think how it would help Daddy." Jen, perched on a stool at the worktable, twirled a pincushion between her hands while their youngest sister, Minnie, hung on every word. "Three daughters at home costs money. If even one of us married a wealthy man, we could help Daddy get the treatment he needs."

"Yes, we could," Minnie echoed. Ruth's baby sister would go along with anything Jen suggested, no matter how ridiculous, and this went far beyond ridiculous.

Ruth finger-pressed the next seam and reached for a hot iron off the old stove. On hot summer days, she wished for an electric iron, but those cost money, and every cent was needed for the hospital. "You could best help by basting that blouse for me."

Naturally, Jen ignored her request. Of all the sisters, she possessed the least skill and interest in sewing. Her dreams leaned more toward the adventurous, like flying airplanes.

Jen plunked the pincushion down on the worktable. "You heard the doctors. Daddy needs that electrical treatment."

"Electrotherapy."

"Whatever they call it. The point is it'll cost more. After this latest episode..." Jen's voice drifted off in concern. "Did you see the look on Mother's face? And then she left for the sanitarium that very afternoon. It's bad, isn't it?"

Ruth had to stop this conversation from escalating into hysteria. "We don't know that."

"Because no one tells us anything." Jen crossed her arms. "Do they think we can't figure it out? We're grown women. Tell me the truth, Ruthie. Mother left you in charge. I saw you looking through the ledger last night. We don't have the money for the treatment, do we?"

Ruth hesitated. It hadn't taken her long to discover they were deep in debt, but revealing that fact would serve no good purpose. "I'm sure Daddy and Mother have taken care of everything."

Jen looked doubtful.

"Even if they haven't," Ruth added before Minnie picked up her sister's pessimism, "it doesn't mean we need to hound rich men. There are more reliable ways to make money."

"It would take twenty years to earn it on our wages," Jen countered, "and Daddy needs the money now. That's why marrying into wealth is such a good idea. You heard the story of Nurse Walker when we last visited Daddy.

How her patient Mr. Cornelius fell in love with her and paid off all her debts?"

Ruth hated to admit the story had tumbled around in her head, too.

"He was rich." Minnie's eyes lit with excitement. "From oil."

"Automobiles," Jen corrected. "But it doesn't matter how he made his money. What we need to do is find our own Mr. Cornelius."

Ruth shook her head. "That was just a story. Even if it is true, that sort of thing only happens once in a lifetime."

"No, it doesn't." Minnie fairly quivered with excitement. "I know someone just like Mr. Cornelius. Mr. Brandon Landers helped Mrs. Simmons when he fell in love with Anna."

"That's not the same," Ruth said, though in some ways it was. The man had given Anna and her mother a home when they lost theirs. In time, he fell in love with Anna and married her. Anna's mother still lived in the guest cottage on the Landers estate right here in Pearlman. "He married Anna for love, not money."

"I love his brother, Reggie, and in time Reggie will love me," Minnie insisted. "It'll be just like Mr. Cornelius and Miss Walker."

Ruth would never understand her baby sister. After initially shying away from the college man, she had developed a crush on him. This plan of Jen's provided just the vehicle to encourage Minnie's fancy for a man who didn't deserve her.

"Mother and Daddy would never let you marry at your age," Ruth cautioned.

"Eighteen is old enough. Plenty of girls my age are engaged, and some already married. I wouldn't want to wait forever, like..."

Groom by Design

Though Minnie stopped before uttering the hurtful words, Ruth knew her sister meant her. Ruth had never had a beau, never danced with a man and never experienced a romantic kiss. Oh, she longed for it all. A home. A family of her own. A good Christian husband, poor but hardworking. A man who wouldn't mind a plain wife with poor eyesight. Countless tearful prayers had been sent heavenward, but at twenty-six, she was a spinster.

Minnie was right about girls here marrying young, but she didn't understand that a man didn't love you simply because you loved him. That applied doubly to rich, handsome men. The wounds they inflicted lasted a lifetime.

Ruth attacked the seam with the iron.

"I'm sorry, Ruthie," Minnie said with a sob. "I didn't mean anything by it. But can't you see? Daddy needs our help, and this is the perfect solution."

"We are already helping by taking care of the shop and house and praying for him." Yet as Daddy's heart grew weaker, Ruth feared the small contribution they made would never be enough. But marry for money? That road led to nothing but heartache, as their oldest sister could testify. Beatrice had married the heir to the biggest fortune in town, yet she'd confided to Ruth that her marriage was struggling.

Jen drummed her fingers on the tabletop. "Any little bit would help. Even if we can't marry into wealth, at least we wouldn't be living at home anymore. Daddy wouldn't have to feed and clothe us. Any decent husband would help pay for the treatments."

As Jen ticked off the benefits of her idea, Ruth paused in her pressing, iron held high so it wouldn't scorch the delicate georgette crepe. Her sister had a point. None of them brought in much from their part-time jobs. The dress shop had lost clients. Maybe marriage was the only answer.

Unfortunately, no man would look twice at plain old Ruth. Jen dashed around in trousers half the time, discouraging all but the most forward-thinking man. That left Minnie, and Ruth couldn't abide the thought of her baby sister marrying that idler Reggie Landers.

Ruth pushed up her spectacles and set down the heavy iron. "There must be a better way to help Daddy. It's not as if we can walk up to a man and ask him to marry us."

Jen tossed her head. "Don't be ridiculous. We'll come up with a plan of attack."

"A plan of attack? You make it sound like a military maneuver." Ruth shook her head. Sometimes Jen behaved more like a boy than the lady she ought to be.

A scorched smell tickled her nostrils. The iron! In her inattention, she'd set it down. She jerked it up. Thank goodness, the silk hadn't burned.

"I made a list of eligible bachelors." Jen produced a crumpled piece of paper from her pocket. With a great show, she smoothed it out on the tabletop.

Ruth fought a wave of panic. "No man wants to feel like he's being hunted."

"But it's all right for them to pursue us," Jen pointed out before addressing her list. "Gil Vanderloo is home from college. He asked me to dance once. A definite possibility. You could ask about him when you drop off the dresses."

"I will do no such thing." Through the open windows, Ruth heard the church bells ring the five-o'clock hour. "Oh, dear. Mrs. Vanderloo wanted her gowns before five so she could dress for her garden party. You've made me late with all this silly talk."

She finished the last seam and slid the dress onto a hanger to cool. She plunked a plain straw hat on her head and jabbed a hatpin through the loose bun of fine blond hair at the nape of her neck. Gloves, gloves… Where were her gloves? She dashed around the shop looking for them while her sisters reviewed Jen's list. If she weren't already frantic, the whispers would have driven her mad.

"I don't have time for this nonsense." Ruth grabbed the pasteboard carton she used to protect garments against dirt but hesitated. Even this short distance could wrinkle the gowns, and Mrs. Vanderloo didn't have time to iron them out. Considering the weather had cleared after this morning's rain and few clouds now graced the sky, she decided to risk going without. What could happen in a few blocks?

She grabbed the hangers and held the dresses high so their hems didn't brush the ground. Once out the door, she'd loosely drape them over her other arm and pray they didn't crease.

Before leaving, she directed her sisters to close the shop. Without waiting for confirmation, Ruth pushed backward through the door, turned and crashed into something very solid. The impact staggered her, and in a desperate attempt to regain her balance, she dropped the hangers.

"Hello, there." The rich baritone voice came with strong hands that caught her by the shoulders and prevented a spill.

She'd run into a man—a very tall man. A stranger, no less. An extremely handsome stranger who at that very moment still held her shoulders. Ruth swallowed hard as she looked up at his impressive height. Goodness! He practically scraped the sky, but the effort was worth it. He looked as if he'd stepped out of a moving-picture show in his meticulously tailored suit. Clean-cut and dark-haired, he exuded the confidence and charm of the fashionable set. From the expensive silk necktie and jaunty fedora to the polished black shoes, every inch of him advertised his wealth.

And she'd just plowed into him.

"Are you all right?" His voice did sound kind.

Ruth drew in a shaky breath, far too conscious of the hands he'd just removed from her shoulders. My, he was handsome! An exotic yet comfortingly familiar scent enveloped him. She breathed in deeply. Bergamot. That was it. The scent reminded her of a steaming cup of Earl Grey tea. Who was this man, and why did his touch send a shiver down her spine on such a hot day? He must think her either careless or a fool. Or half-blind. As she adjusted her glasses, the taunts of her childhood schoolmates came to mind. *Goofy Ruthie. Frog eyes.*

"I'm sorry." She averted her gaze. "I wasn't watching where I was going."

"The fault's mine. I wasn't paying attention."

He was apologizing? She risked another glance at the exceedingly handsome man.

His lips curved into a wry smile. "Sorry about your dresses."

Dresses? She smoothed her skirt. Oh, dear, she'd worn a plain old dress that was years out of style and fraying at the cuffs. "I'm all right."

"I meant the ones you dropped." He bent, and she followed his outstretched arm to the horrifying sight of Mrs. Vanderloo's tea gowns floating in a mud puddle.

She clamped a hand over her mouth, but it couldn't stop the strangulated cry that shot up her throat. Already she was late, and now Mrs. Vanderloo's expensive dresses were ruined. This could cost the shop dearly.

He lifted the gowns with one hand and brushed at the mud on them with the other.

"Stop!" she cried. "You'll only make it worse."

"I'm afraid it's too late." He turned the dresses so she could see the damage.

Her eyes blurred with tears. The ivory georgette bore a

streak of dirty brown, and the mint-green lace gown looked as if an entire pot of coffee had been dumped on it. For years Mrs. Vanderloo had been one of the shop's best customers, but lately she'd gone from ordering new dresses to bringing in ready-made frocks for alterations. Each time she complained about the bill. Each time she threatened never to bring another gown to them. This would be the proverbial last straw. The shop couldn't stand to lose more customers.

She gulped. "They're ruined."

"They're just dresses."

"Just dresses? They're not just dresses. They're tea gowns. Expensive ones. What will I do?" She pressed her hands to her face, nauseated at the thought of how much this would cost.

"I'm sorry," he said more gently. "I wasn't thinking of their value. Let me help. Since the whole thing is my fault, I'll replace them. Is there a store in town that sells comparable gowns?"

Ruth shook her head.

"Then let me bring you some catalogs tomorrow."

"No!" Even though Mrs. Vanderloo had bought these from a catalog, she would insist Ruth replicate them exactly, using the same or better materials at no charge.

His forehead furrowed. "I assure you that the catalogs are from the finest stores. Select any gowns you wish. Cost doesn't matter."

If cost didn't matter, then he must indeed be rich.

"I couldn't."

"Nonsense." He held the unmarred sleeve of the georgette gown next to her arm. "If I may make a suggestion, I'd choose a different color. Ivory doesn't suit your fair complexion. Rose would better bring out the color in your cheeks."

"But—" Ruth began to protest that the dresses weren't hers when the peculiarity of his statement struck her. Few men could tell rose from blush. To most, both were pink. Yet this stranger clearly knew the full range of colors and hues. "Are you an artist? It's not every day that I meet a man who understands color."

He laughed. "Who doesn't like a little color? Don't worry. I'll set things right. What do you say? Will you let me buy the dresses?"

The offer was incredible, especially when Ruth was to blame. "That's not necessary—"

"Of course it is. We'll get two that highlight your fine features."

"But you don't understand. The dresses aren't mine. You see, I'm a seamstress, and these belong to a customer. I was supposed to deliver them before five o'clock so she'd have them for her garden party tonight." Ruth broke off, acutely aware that she'd started blathering.

The man glanced at the Fox Dress Shop sign over the door, and a look of dismay crossed his face before he reined it in with a taut smile. "Then I'll let your client choose the replacements."

"You would do that?" Ruth tried to wrap her mind around such generosity. "But it isn't your fault, and Mrs. Vanderloo is quite particular."

The corners of his eyes crinkled in a way that suggested he smiled often. "Of course she is. But together we can persuade her that it's to her best advantage to accept the replacements."

Together? He was going to go to Mrs. Vanderloo's house with her?

She must have been standing with her mouth agape, because that smile of his turned into a grin.

"I ran into you," he said. "It's only fair that I offer the apology." He extended an arm. "Shall we?"

Ruth couldn't breathe. This handsome, wealthy stranger wanted to escort her down Main Street in front of everyone. No man had ever done that, and this one didn't even know her. Such a thing was not done. Tongues would wag. Ruth pressed her hands to her hot cheeks and pretended to check her hat in the window. Behind her, the stranger still held the dresses, and inside the shop her sisters grinned like monkeys.

They thought she was flirting.

She whirled away from the window and straight into the arms of the handsome man. Oh, no! She'd done it again.

"I'm sorry." She backed away, her face blazing hot. "I didn't realize you were standing so close. I—I was just checking my hat." She patted it for emphasis.

The elegant suit, the gold cuff links, the silk handkerchief. A man like him would never be interested in a wallflower like her.

"You look quite presentable." His easy smile warmed her in the most unnerving way.

It was just a compliment, she told herself. Nothing more. She was the one who'd let reason fly away on the wind. No doubt Jen's ridiculous marriage idea had precipitated such lunacy. He just happened to match her criteria exactly. What if…? Ruth shook her head. Instead of fantasizing about relationships that could never happen, she should concentrate on the business at hand.

Mrs. Vanderloo was her customer. Ruth should handle the situation alone, but the man's offer of two new dresses might appease the difficult client. The dress shop couldn't afford to lose her business. Ruth had no choice but to accept. Of course, she would pay him back for the gowns. That should settle the matter.

"All right. I accept." She might have to concede that point, but she didn't need to take his arm. "I'd better lead the way."

Sam Rothenburg's day had progressed from bad to worse. First, the train had been late. Then he'd arrived at the store to find construction days behind schedule. When Miss Harris, the secretary, told him that his father was threatening to make a progress inspection, he had to find a way to spur the out-of-town crews to work faster, or Father would yank him off the project. Sam had proposed this store. He had to make it work.

He'd promised the work crews a bonus for finishing early, and they'd sped up. Then three crewmen dropped an expensive display case, shattering the glass and snapping the oak framing. Sam had left rather than lash out at the workmen. Head down and boiling with frustration, he never saw the shy, delicate creature step out of her shop.

She looked a few years younger than him. She was slender and rather plainly attired, and her gaze fluttered this way and that but never directly at him, rather like a frightened bird. Sam had never considered himself intimidating. The thought almost made him laugh. If she only knew how powerless he was. But she didn't know him. No one here did. Per Father's orders, no one would until after the store opened.

So he withheld his name and hoped she hadn't seen his dismay when he learned she was a dressmaker. The moment Father realized a dress shop stood next to the future site of Hutton's Department Store, he would crush it. Sam felt a little guilty. This lovely woman would soon find herself out of a job. That was why he'd offered to replace the gowns. It didn't cost much to ease his conscience.

She hadn't accepted his arm, however, showing an independent streak that impressed him.

He hurried to catch her. "You're quick on your feet."

She ignored his comment. "I suppose I ought to know who you are." Her gaze never left the boardwalk ahead.

Sam swallowed his initial concern. This lady couldn't possibly know who he was or what type of store would soon open next to hers. Father would not have given the Pearlman city council the Rothenburg name, thus no one could know a Hutton's Department Store was opening in Pearlman. Father liked to make a spectacle of every grand opening. That was why the store windows were covered and an out-of-town crew hired. He even went so far as to use a holding company to purchase the property. Well before the Hutton's Department Store sign was revealed, people's curiosity would be piqued. It was a marketing ploy that had worked well in the past, and Sam expected it would generate the same response here. For now, no one must know the Rothenburgs were involved, including one lovely dressmaker.

"You can call me Sam." No last name just yet. When pressed, he'd use Roth, but the shortened version of their name that they'd adopted during the Great War never sat well on his tongue.

"Sam." On her lips his plain name soared. "Samuel. Like the Old Testament prophet." Faint pink still tinged her fair cheeks. "I'm Ruth. Ruth Fox."

Fox Dress Shop. With dismay, Sam realized she must own it. The unease returned. The arrival of a Hutton's Department Store tended to drive local clothing stores into extinction. His family's stores gave the common man or woman the chance to improve his or her station in life by providing fashion at affordable prices. Thanks to Hutton's, a housekeeper could dress like a Vanderbilt at a fraction of the cost. In the past, only the well-off could afford to hire a seamstress or tailor. Those wealthy clients could continue with their hometown shop, but they usually abandoned the local tailor for the quality and value of Hutton's merchandise. Progress was inevitable. It could also be painful.

"Ruth." Repeating her name distracted him from the guilt. "Like in the Old Testament." He could use biblical references, too.

"I was named after her. Ruth left her homeland to remain with her mother-in-law."

"Did you do that also?"

She blushed. "I'm not married. No mother-in-law."

"Yet." He loved the rosy color that infused her cheeks. "If I remember correctly, the Old Testament Ruth didn't stay widowed."

A faint smile graced her lips. "Naomi did arrange for Ruth to meet her kinsman, Boaz, and he did marry her."

"Don't I recall that Naomi had to use a little inventive persuasion to get Boaz to notice Ruth?" Sam glanced over to see this Ruth's cheeks ablaze. With such an alabaster complexion, every flush showed. A wisp of her honeyed hair floated free from the knot at her nape and streamed onto her shoulder. He wanted to tuck it behind her ear, an urge he hadn't felt in eight years. Since Lillian…

Ruth ducked her head. "Perhaps."

For some reason that he couldn't discover, this conversation embarrassed her. He shifted to another topic. "Ruth's a pretty name."

"It's plain, just like…"

Though she didn't finish the sentence, he could guess what she'd intended to say. *Just like me.* But she wasn't plain, not in the least. If only she could see how lovely she was, not in the gaudy manner of socialites, but in a natural, God-given way.

"Hello, Ruthie, dear." A short and rather round older woman hobbled up to them with the assistance of a cane.

"Mrs. Simmons. How are you?"

Ruth addressed the woman with so much warmth that Sam took notice. Was this how small-town people treated each other? Fragments of a childhood memory came to mind. A pretty little town blanketed in snow. The glow of lights. The cheerful greetings of shopkeepers. Father laughing, holding him up to a shop window. Sam had felt loved, wanted, as if he belonged. Maybe Pearlman was like that.

Ruth stooped to embrace the older woman. "Is your knee bothering you again? I thought it was healed from your fall last winter."

"Oh, it is. It is." The woman chuckled. "You know how it is with rheumatism. Sometimes the old legs don't work quite the way they ought. But enough of me. How is your father doing?"

Ruth's smile faded. "We haven't heard from Mother yet. She left for Battle Creek on Monday."

Sam pretended to examine the merchandise in the drugstore window.

"Do you know when he'll be coming home from the hospital, dear?"

Ruth's father must be very ill if he required hospitalization. That meant the family needed the dress shop's income even more. Sam shoved aside the guilt. It wasn't his problem.

Mrs. Simmons grasped Ruth's hand. "I've been praying for him."

Prayer? Sam shot a sideways glance at the woman, whose round face glowed with hope and compassion. That was exactly what his mother would say.

"Thank you." Ruth ducked her head, something she did

far too frequently. "Daddy can use everyone's prayers. We hope to get a wire from Mother soon."

If Ruth were waiting for a wire, then they didn't have a telephone yet. Incomprehensible. How could a business operate these days without telephone service? He shook his head. If the Foxes didn't step into the twentieth century, their dress shop was sure to fail, Hutton's or no Hutton's.

"I'll be sure to let you know," Ruth continued. "We're hoping for good news."

"I'm sure you'll get it," Mrs. Simmons said. "I understand the sanitarium has exceptional treatment for his condition."

Sanitarium? Mrs. Simmons must mean sanatorium. A sanatorium meant Ruth's father suffered from a contagious and life-threatening illness like tuberculosis. He might never come home. Each word the two women uttered made his stomach roil more. Father's marketing ploy hung over the Foxes like an invisible weight. When the department store opened in two weeks, their livelihood would be hopelessly crippled.

That wasn't his concern. He was here to open a store. Provide quality clothing at an inexpensive price. Hutton's brought economic benefit to the masses. It gave people more for their hard-earned money. He couldn't let one little dress shop derail progress.

Chapter Two

Once Mrs. Simmons left, Ruth had to face Sam and the uncomfortable knowledge that he now knew her father was in the Battle Creek Sanitarium. True, perfectly healthy people visited the famed health institution, but they had money to waste in the vain pursuit of youth. Her father obviously did not fall into that category. Sam probably figured he suffered from tuberculosis or mental illness. Neither was true, but she could not share her father's dire prognosis without breaking into tears. Talking with Mrs. Simmons had been tough enough, but a perfect stranger? Never.

So she averted her gaze and urged him to hurry along with her to Mrs. Vanderloo's house. Again she walked ahead, trying to ignore the knot tightening between her shoulder blades.

To his credit, he didn't say a thing.

At first she was grateful for the silence, but then it gnawed at her. What did he think? Did he regret his offer to replace the dresses? She ought to tell him that she would pay him back, but every time she opened her mouth, a sob threatened. Finally, she gave up and plodded onward.

He matched her stride, a distinguished presence that drew

the notice of the people they passed. Eloise Grattan, even more a spinster than Ruth, halted in her steps and stared in disbelief, as if she could not believe such a handsome man would ever walk with plain old Ruth Fox. Sally Neidecker tilted her head to best advantage as she paraded in front of them.

"Well, hello," Sally purred, her sleek bob gleaming in the sunlight.

If Ruth had the gift of speaking her mind, she would ask Sally how her beau was faring.

"Good afternoon, ma'am," Sam said and nodded.

Ma'am. Ruth could have laughed. Sam had assumed Sally was married. And she would be if she hadn't broken her engagement to Reggie Landers.

Sally pursed her lips into a pout. "*Miss* Neidecker, Miss Sally Neidecker. And you are?"

"Late," Sam said as he skirted around Sally. "Miss Fox?" Once again he held out his arm for Ruth.

Though she could not accept his escort, joy welled inside her. He had sidestepped Sally in order to stay with her. Though he must have acted purely from a business sense, hope fluttered to life that he might actually prefer her company.

Or he was married.

Ruth glanced at his hands. No ring, but then, not every married man wore a wedding band. That would explain his lack of interest in Sally, however. With each step, the need to know grew stronger. Was he married? She couldn't just ask. It had to come out naturally in conversation.

Her pulse pounded in her ears, and her mouth felt dry, but she managed to get out a simple question. "Where do you hail from?"

If he was surprised by her sudden question, he didn't show it. "Lately, New York."

"The city?"

"That's the place."

A well-off New Yorker. He could be among the country's elite. That thought put her even more on edge. She instinctively checked her hat and hair.

When he offered nothing more, she hazarded a glance. He caught her gaze and returned a lopsided grin that sent a bolt of heat straight to her cheeks. She turned quickly, but he must have noticed her blush. "My, it's hot today. I don't suppose it's ever this hot in New York."

"More so. The tall buildings and paved streets hold in the heat."

His casual manner put her a bit more at ease, and she recalled that not all New Yorkers acted superior to country folk. "Mariah and Pastor Gabe—they're sister and brother—are from New York City. Maybe you know the family. Meeks?"

"The name doesn't sound familiar." He glanced across the street. "How far is Mrs. Vanderloo's house?"

"Just a couple more blocks." The knot between her shoulders tightened. He was anxious to get this over with. How tedious her company must be. "They live on the hill."

"The hill?"

She pointed to the rising terrain to the left. "The hill is where the wealthy live." She struggled to keep frustration from her voice. Families like the Neideckers, Kensingtons and Vanderloos had been customers for decades, but they'd gradually stopped coming to the dress shop. Didn't they realize how much her family depended on their business?

"The unfeeling rich, eh?"

She felt a pang of guilt. He must think she detested anyone with money. This was not going well.

"I'm sorry," she murmured. "That's not what I intended."

He chuckled. "It's not the money that causes the problem—it's what people do with it."

"I suppose you're right." But money *could* cause problems, especially when there wasn't enough of it.

"At least you concede some aren't half-bad," he said. "Take your Old Testament hero King Solomon. He was rich beyond measure and just as wise."

"Until he allowed his wealth to corrupt him."

"Then you don't think it's possible for a wealthy man to be good?"

Ruth knew she should hold her tongue, but for some reason, she couldn't stop speaking. "God gives us all that we need. Those who accumulate more are taking it from others."

He looked startled, and she regretted her words. What had gotten into her? She never spoke her opinions to anyone outside the family, especially not to handsome strangers.

His initial surprise soon melted back into the easy smile. "Would you forgive a man his wealth if he uses it for philanthropy?"

She had to concede that point. "Of course. I should never have said what I did."

"I happen to like honest, open expression. Do go on."

Ruth had already said too much. "I don't usually state my opinions. Now, my sister Jen would tell you exactly what she thought." For a brief moment Jen's preposterous marriage idea flitted through her mind. What if? She eyed Sam carefully. He might be just the type to tame Jen. He certainly had the wit to match Ruth's wild younger sister. If he had any patience at all—and their brief time together suggested he did—he could mold Jen into a proper lady. Perhaps Ruth should introduce them.

"Jen is your older sister?"

Ruth tried to guess Sam's age. He looked to be around thirty. Perhaps he wouldn't be interested in someone several years his junior. She mustn't mislead him, though. "She's next youngest after me. Twenty-four this year."

"Next youngest? Then you have more than one sister?"

"I have three. The oldest is Beatrice. She married Blake Kensington four years ago. The Kensingtons are more or less the town fathers." She noted a flicker of recognition at the mention of the Kensington name. Who wouldn't notice? It was plastered on half the businesses in Pearlman. "I'm next, then Jen and last of all Minnie, but she's just out of high school." Ruth did not want Sam to get any ideas about Minnie. Fighting her baby sister's attraction to one wealthy man was difficult enough. Two would be impossible. So she pushed forward the sister of choice. "Jen is quite…spirited." That seemed the most positive way to describe her sister's disposition. "She definitely speaks her mind. She's probably the best conversationalist of us all." She hazarded another glance, hoping to see a spark of interest in his expression, but instead his brow had furrowed.

"You have all sisters?"

Odd that he would pick up on that. "You think that's unusual?"

"I suppose not. In my family, it's just boys, though there are only two of us. I would have liked a sister. You must be a fine one."

A sister. He thought of her like a sister. She supposed that was a good thing, seeing as she wanted to introduce him to Jen, but disappointment still blanketed her.

They walked on in silence. She couldn't think of a thing to say. Crickets trilled and playing children shrieked. Motorcars putted past. All normal, yet today each sound reminded her that she was a plain country girl who couldn't ever hope to interest a handsome man like Sam, no matter how much sisterly help she received. Each silent moment made her feel more and more awkward until she couldn't stand it any longer.

"Are you the older or younger?"

His eyebrow quirked at her abrupt question. "The older. Harry is several years younger than me."

That made Sam the heir. Even more impossible, but maybe Jen stood a chance. If the Lord wanted them together, He would make the seemingly impossible possible.

She swallowed the growing lump in her throat. "Did your brother come here with you?"

"No. He's in college."

"During the summer?" The handful of collegians from Pearlman always returned in the summer months.

"He wants to finish his graduate studies early." Again he cast her a smile that melted her determination to stay reserved.

"I see." She looked toward the passing storefronts so she wouldn't have to see that unnerving smile. "When did you arrive in town?"

"This afternoon. The train was late. I should have known then that everything was going to go wrong today."

Everything. Such as their collision and his resulting offer to patch things up with her client. "You must be terribly busy. You don't need to come with me."

"Don't think you can get rid of me that easily, Miss Fox. I'll have you know that I'm more stubborn than the proverbial mule. Besides that, I can't get much done with a shattered—" He suddenly stopped, as if he'd just remembered something. "There was a little accident, and I need to find a good carpenter. I don't suppose you know one."

"Peter Simmons is the best in Pearlman. He made the bookshelves and counter at the bookstore."

"Peter Simmons," Sam repeated. "Related to the woman you spoke with earlier?"

She nodded, pleased that she could help the orphaned boy. "You won't be disappointed."

"I'll take your word on that."

Ruth allowed a brief smile while she considered how to get Sam and Jen in the same room. A simple introduction would tell if they were compatible. They would certainly make a fine-looking couple. Ruth's energetic sister was the only one of them with Daddy's dark hair, and Jen wouldn't disappoint Sam in the honest-expression department. All Ruth needed was a reason to bring them together.

The church secretary stepped out the front door and waved. As Ruth waved back, she realized the answer was right in front of her.

"Would you care to join us for Sunday-morning services? We attend the church across the street."

Sam glanced at the prim white building with its plain glass window. "I don't know...."

"I could introduce you to everyone in town. As a newcomer, you'll want to meet people."

If she weren't mistaken, he looked decidedly uneasy. "I'll have to let you know tomorrow."

That was a quick side step if she ever heard one, and she wasn't about to get Jen involved with someone who wasn't a Christian. "Not a churchgoer?"

"On the contrary. I simply don't know how long I'll be in town."

"But today is Friday and you only just arrived. Surely you wouldn't have to leave tomorrow."

His cheek ticked. "You're right, of course." A pause. "I'd be glad to join you."

"Good." Ruth breathed a sigh of relief. Her plan would

still work. "You can meet us in front of the dress shop. The service starts at ten o'clock."

"Fine, but if something comes up, don't wait for me."

Before she could continue the conversation, he started whistling a tune. At the end of the street, they turned left and wound up Elm Street into Kensington Estates.

She pointed to the ocher-colored Victorian with dark green trim that was half-hidden behind a tall cedar hedge. "That is the Vanderloo house."

She stopped at the gated walkway, intimidated as always by the turreted three-story home. Already cars lined the lawn, meaning Mrs. Vanderloo's party was under way. This would not be pleasant.

"After you." Sam opened the gate and motioned for her to precede him.

She summoned her courage and stepped ahead. In passing, his hand brushed her sleeve. A thrill ran through her, like one got from going too fast in a motorcar or running the rapids in a rowboat. She gasped at the unfamiliar sensation.

"Is something wrong?" he asked.

She swallowed hard and shook her head.

"Don't worry. I'll handle everything. Let me do the talking." His casual smile would have set her at ease if not for his hand on the small of her back. "I know how to smooth things over with irate women."

Women? Plural? How many women had he managed to infuriate and why? Maybe it wasn't such a good idea to introduce him to Jen after all.

Sam couldn't help noticing that Ruth's eyes were the most delicate shade of blue, like winter ice. If she hadn't lifted her gaze in surprise, he would never have seen how perfectly they matched the blue of her hatband. Her pale brows arched above her glasses, and her lips pursed into a question that was never uttered.

When she again ducked her head, he realized he'd put that badly, made it sound as if he was a scoundrel around women.

"I meant female customers," he added hastily. "In my business I often deal with complaints."

Her brow only furrowed deeper. "Are you in sales, then?"

It was the question he'd been dreading and avoiding. He refused to outright lie, and since Father insisted no one know that a Hutton's Department Store was opening in town, he'd avoided all but necessary contact with the locals. Crashing into Ruth had ended that tactic.

So he rushed past a full answer. "I do have a lot of experience working with customers. Please, allow me to take the lead."

The question mark vanished from her lips and the furrows from her brow, replaced by determination. "Thank you for your offer, but Mrs. Vanderloo is my customer."

"And this—" he waved at the dresses "—is my fault. I trust we don't have to go over that again."

After a brief internal battle that played out on her lovely face, she acquiesced with a quick nod. They set off for the house. For such a small town, the home was fairly sizable, rather like a country house for a wealthy New Yorker. A circular driveway cut through the lawn, and several automobiles lined its edge, their headlamps and windshields reflecting the late-day sun. Tall oaks and maples dotted the property while crimson geraniums spilled from large clay urns on either side of the front door.

He let Ruth drop the heavy brass knocker against the thick oak door. Once its dull thud faded, the faint clink of glasses and murmur of voices drifted past on the afternoon breeze.

"She must be in the garden," Sam said.

"Her housekeeper should answer." Ruth knocked again.

Sam's arm had begun to ache from holding the dresses for so long. He draped them over his other arm, drawing a critical look from Miss Fox.

At last the door opened, and a trim socialite stared up at him. The perfectly coiffed hair and expensive summer suit left no doubt he was looking at Mrs. Vanderloo.

"I'm sorry. It's an inconvenient time." The woman began to close the door.

She thought he was a peddler, a door-to-door salesman!

Sam caught the door before she fully closed it. "I beg your pardon, Madame." He swung the dresses before him with a flourish. "I'm afraid there's been an accident."

"I'm so sorry, Mrs. Vanderloo." Ruth's voice shook, only making the situation worse.

That was when the woman noticed Miss Fox, and all the venom that might have been directed at him spewed instead on Ruth. "What have you done to my gowns?"

Ruth flinched. "Th-th-there was a little accident."

"Little? It looks like you threw them in the mud and trampled on them. What were you doing? You were supposed to bring them before five o'clock."

"Yes, I know." Poor Ruth's complexion got blotchy. "I would have been here if I hadn't dropped them—"

Sam was not going to let her take the blame. "The only reason she dropped them was because I ran into her. The fault is entirely mine and so is the remedy."

Mrs. Vanderloo didn't seem to hear him. "I trust you'll make this right, Miss Fox, or I'll have to take my business to a more reliable establishment."

Sam clamped his jaw shut so he wouldn't speak his mind. He would like to tell the woman that she'd have a tough time surpassing the excellent stitching he'd noted on these gowns, but Ruth rose to the occasion with surprising grace.

Calm as a pool at nightfall, she expressed her sympathy and regret, ending with "Of course, I'll compensate you for your loss."

She would compensate Mrs. Vanderloo? It took all of Sam's will to hold his tongue. Ruth had claimed the credit, when he was paying the bill. Part of him wanted to correct the record, but another part remembered that Ruth's father was in the hospital with a serious illness. Justice against charity. In the end, charity—and the lovely Ruth Fox—won out. It wouldn't hurt his pride too much if Mrs. Vanderloo thought that Ruth was paying the full cost.

He shot the socialite his most disarming smile. "Not only will she make it right, but Miss Fox has promised to buy you two new dresses to replace those that were ruined. That's quite a generous offer."

As expected, Mrs. Vanderloo's ire diminished. "I, uh—"

He lifted an arm of the ivory georgette dress to drive home the point. "Considering how outdated these frocks are, you're making quite a bargain of it. Two new gowns in the latest fashion. You won't find that guarantee elsewhere. Miss Fox can drop off some catalogs tomorrow." He'd make sure Ruth had those catalogs before they parted ways tonight. "Make your choices at your leisure. We don't want to keep you from your guests any longer."

The woman seemed placated, until one last burst of petulance sneaked out. "But it doesn't help me tonight. I'd planned to wear one of them."

"That would have been a dreadful mistake." Sam snuffed out her objections with the kind of observation that had won over reluctant girls in his college days. "The color and style are all wrong for you. Mint-green? Ivory? Not with your complexion. And the length. They must come to the ankle. Not at all stylish these days. In my opinion, that delightful navy suit brings out the copper in your stunning auburn hair."

Mrs. Vanderloo primped with a girlish giggle, and Sam knew the battle was won.

Until he looked at Ruth. Miss Fox's lips were pressed into an expression of undeniable displeasure. Now what had he done?

Chapter Three

That evening Ruth tried to keep her attention on the stack of bills piled on Daddy's desk, but her thoughts kept drifting to Sam. When he'd suggested a rose-colored dress would suit her complexion, she'd foolishly thought he saw something unusual in her, but apparently he said the same sort of thing to every woman. A charming smile came in a salesman's box of tools. It meant nothing.

Moreover, he'd abdicated his offer to buy the dresses, instead placing that burden on her. How would she manage to scrape up enough to pay for two new gowns capable of meeting Mrs. Vanderloo's standards? She'd already spent her meager savings reducing their debt at the mercantile so the store would extend them credit again.

Ruth sighed and opened an envelope from the Battle Creek Sanitarium.

The figure on the invoice made her heart stop. How could they ever pay this, not to mention the additional treatment? Yet the doctors had made it clear that without that therapy, Daddy would not survive the year.

Ruth's hand trembled. He couldn't die. All her prayers and pleadings must count for something. She would do anything to save him. Anything? Jen's bold idea came to mind. Would she marry for money? Ruth didn't contemplate the answer for long. No matter what she would do, no man of means would marry her. Jen, on the other hand, could captivate someone like Sam. Perhaps Sunday would initiate the most unlikely of Jen's many ideas.

Ruth smiled at the thought and reached out to touch one of the miniature stuffed elephants that stood on the shelf above the desk. She'd made them for her father when she was much younger. Red, green, purple, gold, blue. She'd been so proud of them, and he'd treated each like a priceless jewel.

"Exquisite," he'd said after receiving every one. "Perfectly stitched."

He'd encouraged all of them in their talents. Never once did he criticize her shyness or Jen's poor stitching. He didn't push any of them into the dressmaking business. Ruth couldn't spend enough time in the shop. She loved the feel of the different fabrics, the satisfaction of the perfect pleat, the hope that sprang to life with each new dress. She loved to sketch new designs and dream one of her creations could turn a goose into a swan.

She picked up the first elephant she'd made, a pathetic calico creation with uneven stitching. Only her father had recognized that it was an elephant. He gave it a place of honor. She wiped away a tear and set the elephant back in place. Her father had taken one of her elephants with him to the sanitarium, along with Jen's tattered baby blanket, photographs of Beattie's babies and Minnie's copy of *Little Women,* which he'd promised to read. He'd insisted those treasures would heal him more quickly than any doctor.

Yet he was still sick.

"Get well, Daddy," she whispered.

In the meantime, she had bills to pay and no money with which to do so. Mother had told her which accounts to pay and which could wait. Daddy's care came first, followed by the dress-shop bills. She had assured Ruth that the merchants in town would extend credit a bit longer, but the drugstore had insisted on cash for a single box of aspirin, and the mercantile had refused any credit until the account was paid down. Considering her oldest sister's husband managed the mercantile, it was a slap in the face.

Now, as Ruth stared at the ledger, she could see disaster looming. Paying the sanitarium would nearly empty the family's bank account. She'd have to short the shop's fabric supplier in order to buy Mrs. Vanderloo's dresses.

"It's bad, isn't it?" Jen had crept up so softly that Ruth hadn't heard her.

Ruth slammed the ledger shut. "Nothing to concern you."

Jen pulled up a chair. "Just because Mother put you in charge doesn't mean you're the only one who knows what's going on. I can read a ledger, too. I keep the accounts at the airfield." She tapped the ledger cover. "I say we ask Beattie for help."

Memories of Beatrice's whispered fears swept over Ruth. "We can't."

"Why not? Blake might be tightfisted, but she'll get it out of him somehow."

Ruth couldn't tell Jen that their oldest sister's marriage was struggling. Her husband, Blake, gave her only a pittance to spend on herself. Beattie used every cent for the children. Moreover, Blake's lack of leniency at the mercantile showed he would give his in-laws nothing. Beatrice had confirmed Blake went through money at a frightening rate. She feared gambling—or worse. No, Beattie couldn't help.

Neither could Ruth betray a confidence. "I could never ask Beatrice to part with money intended for her children."

Jen dismissed that excuse. "They won't suffer. They're

Blake's kids, too. Beattie's our sister. She'd want to know we're having financial trouble."

But Beattie did know, and not being able to help pained her. "Maybe she can't."

Jen frowned, her eyes darting between Ruth and the ledger. "What's really going on?"

Ruth folded up the sanitarium bill. "I've already said more than I should."

"If you mean that Blake's being a cad, I already know that."

"Jen!"

The girl shrugged. "Everyone knows it. Pearlman's a small town. There aren't many secrets here."

Ruth felt sick. Beattie would hate that her marriage was the talk of town gossips. "We shouldn't pass along rumors."

Jen snorted. "I'm not the one doing the passing. If you ask me, Blake Kensington was always a cad."

Ruth rummaged through the bills to hide her distress. Aside from the problems in Beattie's marriage, Jen had struck too close to the painful secret that Ruth had kept for over ten years—a secret that must never see the light of day.

"Are you all right?" Jen asked. "You look pale."

"I'm fine. It's just a headache." Her head did throb, though that wasn't the only reason she felt ill. "I'm just a little worried, is all."

"That's why I suggested one of us marry into wealth." Jen's voice lowered. "That man you met earlier looks promising. Nice suit. Nice smile. Rather handsome. Is he married?"

"Jen! I would never ask a stranger such a thing." Though she had wanted to.

"You don't ask directly." Jen rolled her eyes. "You ask if his wife came with him."

"I didn't think of that." Ruth straightened the stack of envelopes. "He's not wearing a ring." Perhaps Jen was already attracted to Sam. Ruth played up the point. "And he does act like a bachelor."

"How does a bachelor act?"

Ruth felt her face heat again. "They flirt with pretty women."

Jen laughed. "You do like him!"

"I do not. I simply find him interesting."

Jen's laughter came out in a snort. "Interesting? He's unbelievably handsome. The man could be a moving-picture star. Maybe he is. Did you ask what he did?"

"He's a salesman."

"Oh." Jen considered that a moment. "Maybe he sells moving pictures. What do they call that? A promoter?"

"I don't think he has anything to do with moving pictures."

Jen's eager smile turned into a frown. "Did you at least get his name?"

"Sam."

"Sam what?"

Ruth had to admit that she didn't know. As far as she could recall, he'd never given his last name, though she'd told him hers. How peculiar.

Jen gave her a look of thorough exasperation. "How could you spend an hour and a half with a man and not ask him anything important? What *did* you talk about?"

"Business. Mrs. Vanderloo's dresses."

"Dresses. Of course, you'd talk about dresses. If you're ever going to find a husband, you'll have to learn to talk about things that interest a man."

"We had business to address. Nothing more."

"It wouldn't hurt to learn a little more about the man."

"One can hardly ask a stranger personal questions."

"There are other ways of getting information." Jen looked as though she was about to burst. "Unlike you, I happened to ask around."

"You did what?" Ruth tried to look horrified, but she was curious. Still… "That's gossiping."

Jen rolled her eyes. "How else are we going to know? You didn't learn anything, and you had the perfect opportunity. Business. What woman talks business with a handsome bachelor?"

Ruth wasn't about to divulge the little he'd shared about his family or the unnerving way she'd felt when he touched her.

"Well, do you want to know what I heard?" Jen's smug smile told Ruth she'd heard plenty.

"I'm not listening to gossip," Ruth said, knowing her sister would spill the news anyway.

"It's not gossip. It's fact. He's working for the new store that's opening up in the old carriage factory next door. You know. The store that everyone's wondering about. I heard they're going to sell automobiles."

"Another one? There's already the place selling Cadillacs. You'd think one would be enough for such a small town."

Jen grinned. "Maybe he's rich like Mr. Cornelius, and he'll sweep one of us off our feet. Then all our troubles will be over."

Ruth couldn't believe Jen was still stuck on that patient-nurse romance she'd heard at the sanitarium. Such a fortuitous occurrence couldn't happen again, or could it? "If you're interested in Sam, you'll have to move quickly. It doesn't sound like he'll be in town long."

"Me?" Jen squeaked. "Why would I be interested in Sam? You're the one he was doting on."

"Doting? He helped me after we collided. Any gentleman would do the same. I'd hardly call it 'doting.'"

"It looked like doting to me." Jen crossed her arms. "I'd say he's already sweet on you."

"I'd say you're talking nonsense, just like that idea of yours." Ruth pulled the stack of unpaid bills closer. "Besides, Mother will be home Tuesday." Jen would never pursue her ridiculous plan in front of their mother.

"No, she won't." Jen withdrew a crumpled envelope from her pocket and handed it to Ruth. "She's staying two more weeks."

"Two weeks?" Ruth yanked the letter from the envelope and scanned her mother's sprawling writing. Jen was correct. Two more weeks. The family couldn't afford the costs that had already piled up. If Mother knew they were in such dire straits, she would never have decided to stay in Battle Creek. But Daddy had always handled the bookkeeping. After he went to the sanitarium, Mother had tried to manage, but judging from the lack of ledger entries and number of addition errors, she had no head for figures.

"So you see, there's plenty of time," Jen said as she headed to the door, "for you and Sam."

Before Ruth could scold her, Jen ducked outside.

Ruth lifted her glasses and rubbed the bridge of her nose. Her head pounded, and she still had to finish opening the bills. She halfheartedly leafed through them until she got to the last. From Kensington Bank and Trust. Her heart stopped. If the ledger was correct, Mother hadn't made a payment on the dress shop's loan in months.

She ripped open the envelope and unfolded the letter. A single sentence greeted her: *We request your presence the morning of Monday, July 23rd at 9:00 a.m.*

Her stomach dropped. What if the bank demanded they bring their payments current? She couldn't scrape together enough for a single payment, least of all the total owed. It was impossible.

Panic raced up and down her spine. What would she do?

She stared at Mother and Daddy's wedding photograph. They looked so young and solemn on their happy day. She pressed a finger to the handmade frame.

"What do I do, Daddy?"

He couldn't possibly answer, but an idea sprang to mind. The bank wouldn't expect her to do anything in her parents' absence. Any paperwork would require Daddy's signature.

She took a deep breath. All would come out well. She would simply go to the bank Monday morning and listen to what the banker had to say. Then she would convey his message to her mother, who would tell Daddy. That would settle the matter.

Though Father would not approve of hiring a local, in the morning Sam approached young Peter Simmons about repairing the display case. Considering the job did not require Peter to enter the store, Father shouldn't fly into a rage. The town fathers already knew he was opening some type of retail establishment. One display case wouldn't give away that it was a Hutton's Department Store.

Sam stood inside the garage watching Peter assess the damage to the case. The lad looked rather young to be an expert carpenter, yet his blackened mechanic's hands tenderly stroked the oak framing. His solemn, almost reverent expression contradicted the cowlick springing from the crown of his head. Tall and beanpole-thin, he looked like a boy trying to be a man.

"That's a pretty bad split," Peter said slowly as he pointed out the worst of the fractures. "It's at the joint. I'd hafta replace three pieces. Here, here and here." He indicated each one. "But this is old oak. I can't match it."

Father's sharp eyes would notice the repair unless Peter could make it seamless. "What can't you match? The color?"

"I'll try, but it'll be tough."

Sam chewed on that. "Can you get close enough that people won't notice?"

"Can try."

Apparently that was the best Sam could hope for. He'd checked out the shelving and counter at the bookstore and found the workmanship first-rate. If Peter met those standards, he just might pull this off. "And the glass?"

"Got some out back that'd do. It's not quite this clear, though. If you want the same kinda glass, we'll hafta order it."

Sam didn't have the time or money to order new glass. He was going to have to pay for the repairs himself. Father didn't accept additional costs. Period. "We'll use what you have on hand. Your rate?"

Soon enough they settled on a reasonable fee. Sam paid half in advance, but Peter seemed less interested in the money than the work. Soon he resumed running his hands along the breaks and examining the joinery.

"I saw your work at the bookstore," Sam commented as he tucked his wallet back into his suit jacket. "You planning on going into carpentry? You're young. What? Twenty?"

"Eighteen."

Just a boy. At eighteen, Sam had been ready to conquer the world. College and sport beckoned. Girls flocked to his side. Those were carefree times. He'd made friends, garnered accolades and met Lillian. Again he shoved away the thought. "So why work at the garage?"

Peter's attention never left the display case. "It's the family business."

"Ah, I understand." All too well. Families could be both a blessing and a curse. Like Peter, Sam was tied to the family business. His brother was champing at the bit to join the Hutton empire, and his father loved to pit the brothers against each other. Survival of the fittest, Father claimed. Fine. Sam would prove he deserved to inherit the business. He'd make his mark with the Pearlman store.

Ruth Fox had it easy. Sisters had to be kinder than brothers. Her father wouldn't force the girls to fight for survival. They'd be expected to work together to make the dress shop succeed.

"Do you know the Fox family?" Since that walk yesterday, Sam had been unable to get Ruth out of his head.

Peter looked up. "Why?"

"I met one of the daughters yesterday."

Peter stiffened. "Which one?"

"Ruth."

"Oh." Peter's shoulders relaxed, and he went back to his examination of the case. "She runs the dress shop down the street."

"Then it's her business."

Peter's brow furrowed. "She tell you that? I didn't take her for one to put on airs."

"No, no." Sam quickly backtracked, feeling as if he'd betrayed her. "I assumed she owned it, because she seemed to be in charge."

"It's her pa's."

"I see. So she's managing it for now." Sam couldn't bring himself to say aloud that he'd heard Ruth's father was in the hospital, even though Peter no doubt knew it. "She seemed nice."

Peter shrugged. "I suppose."

That was just the sort of answer he should have expected from an eighteen-year-old, but Sam wanted to learn more about Ruth. "She has pretty features. Probably draws a lot of attention at dances and church suppers."

"We talkin' about the same woman? The Ruth Fox I know don't go to dances. I ain't never seen her with a fella, neither. Maybe you mean one of her sisters. They're all friendly as can be."

"And Ruth's not?"

He shrugged. "Jess quiet, is all. Kinda hard to get to know."

Sam couldn't deny that. He'd sensed her reserve, and the one time she'd stated her opinion, she'd quickly retreated behind self-deprecation. Why? What held her back? Why didn't she trust people? Of course, if she knew who he was, she'd have good reason not to trust him. But she didn't know, and he'd done everything he could to charm her. He'd even given her his most expensive catalogs for that Vanderloo woman's replacement gowns. Yet she'd acted as if they were coated in curare, dropping them on the dress shop's worktable without so much as a thank-you.

Well, if that was what she thought of his generosity, why did he bother?

"Something wrong?" Peter was staring at him.

"No. No." Sam patted his jacket as if he'd forgotten something. "I should get back to work."

"Yeah, me, too."

After one last handshake, they parted. Nice, clean business deal. Exactly the way he should be dealing with Ruth Fox. But her face kept coming to mind. Those pale blue eyes, the translucent complexion, the honeyed hair. The worry creasing her forehead.

Sam hurried his step. He needed to stop thinking about

her. She wasn't his problem. Her father wasn't his problem. Their dress shop wasn't his problem.

He barreled down the boardwalk. Unfortunately, he had to pass the dress shop to get to his store. Despite it being a Saturday, Ruth was hard at work, her back to him as she pieced fabric at the large worktable. He slowed to take it all in: the dress form draped in voile, the bolts of fabric piled on shelves and sketches tacked to the walls. He slowed when one drawing caught his eye. He'd never seen such an exquisite gown. Who had drawn it? Ruth? Or someone else in the family? He had to know. Whoever it was, he or she displayed remarkable talent.

His fingers grazed the door handle. Her sisters weren't there. Just Ruth. If she'd drawn the sketches, the compliment might bring her out of her reserve. His gaze flitted to the sketch of a stunning peacock-inspired gown. Ruth would glow in such a dress. He envisioned entering the finest ballrooms in New York with her on his arm. Heads would turn. The grand dames would wonder who she was. The younger ladies would ask where they could purchase such a gown.

Sam sucked in his breath. This was lunacy. He needed to get control of himself.

"Oh, good. You're back," called out a female voice.

Heels tapped the boardwalk, punctuated by breathless gasps.

Sam dragged his gaze away from Ruth. "Miss Harris."

The store's secretary hobbled toward him gingerly. Each step brought a grimace.

"Mr. Roth—"

"What is it?" he snapped before she blurted out his whole name.

She patted her bobbed brunette hair. "Your father is on the telephone. Long distance."

Of course it was long distance. Father was in New York. At least Sam hoped he was. "What does he want?"

"I don't know." She shifted her weight from one foot to the other, wincing with each movement. "He wouldn't tell me anything except that he needs to talk to you right now."

"All right." He motioned her ahead. "Let's go."

"You go ahead." Again she winced. "I'll follow in a bit." She grabbed the frame of the dress-shop window for support. The poor woman must have developed blisters.

He sighed and offered her his arm. "Father can wait a minute or two longer."

"Thank you." Miss Harris offered a teary smile. "You're a real gentleman."

Then why did he feel like a heel for wishing it was Ruth's hand on his arm? Though pretty by conventional standards, Miss Harris didn't inspire the slightest interest. Ruth, on the other hand...

He glanced one last time into the dress-shop window, only to see Ruth staring at him, a stunned expression on her face.

Sam had a wife. Or a girl.

Ruth looked away the moment his gaze landed on her, but she'd seen his dismay. Not only was he married, but he also didn't want her to know about it. If he hadn't wanted to keep his wife a secret, he would have told Ruth about her. He'd had ample opportunity. He might have mentioned he was married when she invited him to church. Any decent man would, and she'd thought him thoroughly decent.

Maybe she was wrong. Maybe he wasn't married. Maybe that woman was a mere acquaintance. Except she didn't look like an acquaintance. The pretty woman hung on his arm, her head practically against his shoulder.

Feeling slightly nauseous, Ruth sank onto her stool. What

had she been thinking? Daydreaming was more like it. She took a deep breath and chased away the disappointment. Rich men did not look twice at poor, plain women. This incident proved that fact. At least she'd discovered the truth before introducing him to Jen. No wonder he'd hesitated to accept her invitation to Sunday worship.

With a clatter, Jen and Minnie burst into the shop.

"Did you see that?" Jen said as she plopped onto one of the wooden stools opposite Ruth. Minnie took the other.

Ruth couldn't discuss this calmly, so she began pinning together the panels of the blouse that she had just cut. "I can't imagine what you mean."

"Your Sam helping that woman."

"He's not *my* Sam," Ruth said. "He's simply a new acquaintance."

"He's more than an acquaintance, silly goose. He looked for your approval before helping her."

"What he does or doesn't do is none of my concern." Ruth smoothed the tricky voile before matching edges and pinning.

"I thought you liked him," Minnie said.

"He's a pleasant gentleman."

"Pleasant?" Jen snorted. "That's not going to get his attention. If you like him, you have to go after him. Let him know how you feel."

"Go after him? You must stop listening to this modern-girl nonsense. Nice women do not chase after men."

Ruth reached for another pin, but Jen yanked the pincushion away. "She's not his girl."

"Who's not whose girl?" Ruth motioned for the pincushion.

Jen moved it farther away. "That woman. She might like your Sam, but he's not the least bit interested in her."

Ruth dropped her hand to the tabletop. "How do you know?"

Jen grinned. "He called her 'Miss Harris.' He was only helping her because she'd hurt her feet in those ridiculous shoes. If you ask me, anyone who wears such impractical footwear deserves to get blisters."

Ruth felt such relief that she didn't bother to scold her sister for her lack of compassion. Sam had addressed the woman formally. That meant… "She must work with him."

"That would be my guess." Jen leaned forward to whisper. "It leaves the door open for you."

As always, heat flooded Ruth's cheeks. "I am not pursuing a man. I—I couldn't."

"That's where we come in. In fact, we've already set things in motion."

Ruth stared at Jen. "What have you done?"

"Nothing much." But Jen's impish grin said otherwise. "We just talked to Beattie and came up with a plan. What you need is a pretty new ball gown, one that will catch Sam's eye."

"A ball gown? For me?" Though she secretly longed to someday wear a fancy gown, the stack of unpaid bills came to mind. "I'd rather spend the money on Daddy's treatments."

That sobered Jen for only a second. "We'll use leftovers, scraps. You can work miracles with fabric. You design the gown. We'll help put it together. But we have to do it quickly."

"Why?" Ruth wasn't sure she wanted to know the answer.

"There's a dance at the Grange Hall next Friday," Minnie replied.

"A dance?" Ruth did not dance. "I couldn't."

"Dances are the perfect place to meet men and get to

know them," Jen insisted. "There are lots of people around, so it's not at all risky."

That might be the case for Ruth's sisters. Every one of them danced beautifully, even Jen. Of course! Jen. Ruth's clumsiness could provide just the excuse to bring Sam and Jen together.

"I'll go if you go," Ruth said.

Jen paused. She seldom attended dances. Minnie was the one who loved them. "Me?"

"Yes. All of us. If we're going to do this, then it has to be all of us."

Minnie agreed right away. Jen looked uncomfortable but made the sacrifice. Now all Ruth would have to do was get Sam and Jen together on the dance floor. Her job would go easier if they'd already had a chance to talk. The hubbub following the church service might not be the ideal time. She needed another venue.

The Highbottom family walked past the shop carrying a heavy basket. The children raced ahead, eager to get to their destination. Judging from the blanket Mrs. Highbottom carried and the basket in her husband's hands, they were headed for the park. Perfect.

Ruth gave her sisters an encouraging smile. "Tomorrow would be a good day for a picnic, don't you think?"

"A picnic? Why?" Jen stared at Ruth as if she had lost her mind, but then her lips slowly curved back into a grin. "You invited Sam, didn't you?"

"Not yet. But I will at church."

"He's coming to church with us?"

"I hope he is. He said he would try to attend."

"Perfect." Jen set down the pincushion. "You can ask him to the dance then."

"Ask him?" Ruth's plan had just backfired. "I can't do that."

"Don't worry. We'll be right beside you, won't we?" Jen glanced at Minnie, who nodded.

"A woman does not ask a man to a dance."

"Then suggest it. Talk about it, leave him the opportunity to invite you." Jen leaned forward and rolled the pincushion between her hands. "Don't worry. Sam likes you. He'll take the bait."

Panic coiled around Ruth's rib cage and squeezed tight. Ask a man to a dance? How? She'd stammer and blush. What if he said no? What if he laughed? What if he confirmed what she'd heard for years, that she was too plain to ever attract a man? Her only hope was a humble man who valued the inner woman more than superficial beauty. Certainly not one who was dashing and wealthy. Once Sam met Jen, he'd see that she was the better catch. But to get the two of them together, Ruth had to play along with Jen for a little while.

She breathed deeply to steady her voice. "All right, but you can't focus all your energy on me." She hid her shaking hands in her lap. "If one of us is going to marry a wealthy man—" she hated how that sounded "—then all three of us have to try."

Minnie grasped what she was saying at once. "Ruth's right. I'll try for Reggie, and Ruth can try for Sam. Who are you going for, Jen?"

That caught the confident planner off guard. "I don't know. I guess I'll start looking." She pulled her crumpled list out of her pocket. "Maybe I'll begin at the top of the list and work my way down."

"That's no way to find a husband," Ruth pointed out. "Maybe you should see who strikes your fancy—and who fancies you."

"That's what I'm doing." Jen slid the pincushion to the center of the table. "The way I see it, to find a husband, you first have to decide who you want. There might be as many choices as pins in this cushion, but one of them is the right one." She plucked out a pin. "So you try them one at a time until you find that man."

"We'll help you," Minnie added. "We'll all help each other. Right, Jen?"

Her sister nodded.

Ruth was still skeptical. "How?"

"We will solemnly promise to do all in our power to help each other win our chosen husband," Jen said. "We'll promote her to him. We'll find ways to bring the two together. We'll do whatever it takes. Agreed?"

Jen and Minnie shook on it and looked to Ruth. This promise had so many holes that it was bound to fail, but Ruth had to agree to it. If Jen were the right woman for Sam, as Ruth suspected, then the only chance she had of bringing them together was this plan. Once they discovered how suited they were to each other and fell in love, marriage would follow. And Jen was right. That marriage could solve all their problems. Sam had already demonstrated a measure of generosity and compassion. With Jen's tireless prompting, Sam would surely help Daddy get the treatment he needed.

So Ruth placed her hand atop theirs to seal the pact.

Sam didn't bother to sit at his desk. He picked up the telephone receiver and listened as his father got straight to the point. "I want you to look into a property that's coming on the market. It'll be offered at a good price—an excellent price." Sam held the receiver a few inches away from his ear. Father's booming voice carried across the room. Harry always joked that they didn't need telephones and telegraphs. Father could be heard for miles without technological assistance. "If this deal works out, it'll go a long way toward paying for your mistake."

As usual, Father jabbed at Sam's decision to open a store in Pearlman. In Father's eyes, the store had already failed, and when the opening proved his point, he'd hold it over Sam for the rest of his life. No matter what it took, Sam would ensure this store not only opened strong but also thrived for years to come. That meant getting every detail right, including one broken display case. Maybe this crazy property purchase could buy him a little time.

When his father paused for a breath, Sam pulled the mouthpiece close and cut short the directive. "When am I supposed to do this? I'm spending every waking hour getting the store ready. If you send me out of town, we'll have to delay the grand opening."

Father cackled. "I'm not sending you anywhere, boy. You won't have to leave your precious town to look it over. The property's right next door."

"Next door." Sam got a sinking feeling as he calculated whose property that must be. Since the store was located on a corner, that could mean only two locations, and one was a house across the alley.

"*Right* next door." Static crackled the line but it didn't obliterate Father's words. "Why didn't you tell me we're opening up next to a dress shop?"

Chapter Four

Sunday dawned still and sunny, one of those lazy summer days that inspired picnics, fishing and rowing on the pond. The latter was out, since Ruth's family owned no rowboat, but, if Sam accepted their invitation to a picnic, she might be able to persuade him to dip a line in the river. Jen loved to fish. It was the perfect opportunity for romance to flower.

But first Sam had to show up for the church service so she could invite him.

"How long do we have to wait?" Minnie fussed with her hair in the dress-shop window. "The service is going to start soon."

"I know." Ruth bit her lip and glanced left and right to see if Sam were coming. "I told him to meet us here."

Jen grinned. "You like him."

"He's simply a nice gentleman."

The church bells rang. A rooster might as well have crowed, for like the apostle Peter, Ruth had denied the undeniable. She did like Sam. Seeing him with another woman had hurt more than it should.

"*A nice gentleman,*" Jen mimicked, and then both she and Minnie burst into giggles.

"Hush!" Ruth hissed as she glanced left and right again.

He wasn't coming. All those nerves had been spent on nothing.

"We'd better go." She blinked back the disappointment.

Jen hugged Ruth around the shoulders. "I'm sorry. Something must have come up. We can still have a picnic. I'll pack the basket."

That promise would be forgotten as soon as they returned home, but Ruth accepted the offer with a squeeze of gratitude. "Let's hurry. The bells have stopped."

"Wait!" Jen pulled her to a stop. "Here he comes. Ruthie, he's perfect for you. So tall and distinguished, like a congressman or company president. Look at that suit! It must have cost a fortune."

Sure enough, Sam had rounded the corner and was headed their way, his fedora at a jaunty angle and an ease in his step that made Ruth's stomach flutter. No moving-picture actor could look finer or cause such a rush of emotion. He'd hounded her thoughts since they met. She hoped he couldn't see it in her eyes. She ducked her head and pressed a gloved hand to her abdomen to still her nerves.

"And the way he's smiling at you," Jen continued, apparently unaware how far her voice carried. "If you ask me, he's already in love."

"Jen!" Ruth twisted the handle of her bag in consternation.

Surely he'd heard Jen and was just as mortified as Ruth. Yet his gait never slowed and his smile never wavered.

"Fine morning, ladies." He tipped his hat.

Ruth couldn't breathe, least of all say anything. Maybe he hadn't heard Jen after all.

"Yes, it is, Mister…" Jen paused dramatically. "I'm afraid I don't know your name."

Ruth wanted to shrink into the boxwood shrub between

the dress shop and the old carriage factory, but there was no escaping this encounter, especially since she was the one who'd suggested it.

"Sam," she hissed at Jen. "I told you his name is Sam." She mustered a weak smile for him. "Forgive my sister's poor manners."

Sam grinned at each of them in turn, ending with Jen. "Nothing to forgive. We haven't met yet. Mr. Roth, but you can call me Sam."

Roth. Nearly the same as Ruth. Ruth Roth. It sounded ridiculous. On the other hand, Jen Roth had a nice ring to it, confirming those two were meant for each other. Even Jen's despised full name, Genevieve, sounded good.

Sam extended a hand, which Jen pumped vigorously. Considering the way he winced, she'd probably gripped him with her usual enthusiasm.

"I'm Jen, and you already met Ruth. That's our little sister, Minnie."

Minnie grimaced. "Jen makes me sound like a baby. I graduated from high school last month."

If Sam's head was spinning at being surrounded by three women, he never let on. He congratulated Minnie on the accomplishment and turned to Ruth. "Am I late? I heard church bells."

Jen shot Ruth a look that translated "church bells" into "wedding bells."

Ruth tried to ignore her sister. "If we hurry, we'll arrive before the opening hymn."

He extended an arm to her, and a little thrill bubbled up Ruth's throat. Even though she wanted him for Jen, she warmed to the fact that he'd chosen to escort her over her younger sisters. It must be because she was the oldest. Of course. Good manners dictated he escort the oldest sister. That was all. If she hadn't been here, he could have escorted Jen. That could be a problem at the picnic. She hoped Sam liked to fish so she could send the two of them off together.

"Well," Jen said, "we don't have all day. Let's get going." She grabbed Minnie's arm and the pair took off in the lead.

Ruth hesitated. She didn't want him to think she held any affection for him when he needed to fall in love with Jen. So she kept her hands on her bag and began walking after her sisters. "So glad you could join us, Mr. Roth."

Sam frowned before matching her stride. For half a block, silence reigned between them. She looked at the storefronts. He apparently felt no compunction to talk. She fidgeted with the handle of her bag. He whistled an unfamiliar tune.

He was the first to speak. "No repercussions?"

"Of what?"

"Mrs. Vanderloo was pleased with the gowns in the catalogs?"

"Oh. Yes." Ruth couldn't tell him how humiliating yesterday's encounter had been. Without Sam's calming presence, the woman had again threatened to withdraw all business until Ruth threw in a third gown at no charge. How she would pay for that in addition to the other two was beyond imagining, but, as Mrs. Simmons always said, God would provide. Somehow.

"Good." His tone softened and deepened. "Why don't you show me her selections after church?"

Ruth fixed her gaze on her sisters' backs, afraid to look at him. Sam needed to fall for Jen, not her. Definitely not her. In the end, she would only disappoint a man like Sam Roth. Jen was right that he must come from money. His good suit was even more finely tailored than the one he'd worn Friday. The linen appeared to be mixed with silk. Silk. Goodness! Never in all her life would she be able to afford a silk garment. The closest she'd ever get to silk was smoothing her hands over the fabric she fashioned into a client's gown.

"I can stop by the shop," he added, "or your home, if the catalogs are there."

Ruth reined in her wandering thoughts. Sam had presented exactly the opportunity she needed to get him together with Jen. All she had to do was act. No hesitation this time. Once he fell for Jen, she'd be relieved of this terrible emotional roller coaster. "We are planning a picnic this afternoon. In the park. Why don't you join us?"

"Your whole family will be there?" He sounded skeptical, as if he feared she was trying to trap him.

She rushed to reassure him. "Yes, my sisters and I."

He grinned. "Sounds nice."

She took that as acceptance, and her stomach settled back in place. "Shall we say two o'clock? Near the pavilion?"

"Two o'clock."

They'd reached the church steps at the same time as Ruth's oldest sister, Beatrice, and her two children. Upon spotting Sam, four-year-old Tillie planted her hand firmly in her mouth while the two-year-old boy did his best to tug away from his mother's grasp.

"Ruth," Beattie gasped, "I'm so glad to see you. Would you be willing to take Tillie? Little Branford is testing my patience this morning."

Naturally, Ruth agreed. Watching Tillie meant she would have to sit in the Kensington pew. That would leave Sam with Jen and Minnie.

Jen apparently figured that out at the same time. "But you have to sit with us," she hissed, tilting her head toward Sam.

"You'll be fine." Ruth smiled at her sister's panic. "It's only for an hour or so."

Jen's frown deepened as she watched Beattie attempt to calm her son. "Where's Blake?"

Beatrice's shoulders stiffened at the same moment that Ruth's stomach tightened. She could guess. He'd doubtless visited the speakeasy again last night.

Beatrice, her back to them, murmured, "He's not feeling well."

Jen's eyes narrowed. "Maybe he should see Doc Stevens."

"It's not serious." But Beattie's shoulders drooped, and Ruth ached for her sister. In such a small town, people had a tendency to think they knew what was going on and offer unsolicited advice. Ruth suspected this was not the first time her sister had heard such comments, but it couldn't be welcome coming from family.

"Hurry," Ruth urged in order to break this train of thought. "The opening hymn is starting."

Naturally little Branford chose that moment to voice an earsplitting shriek of displeasure. Through the open door, Ruth saw the people in the last pew turn to see who was making such a fuss. Mrs. Grattan frowned until she spotted Sam. Then her displeasure turned into avid interest.

Sam didn't appear to notice. He swooped to Beatrice's rescue and knelt before the unhappy little boy. "Good morning, Master Kensington. What seems to be the trouble?" His calm, respectful tone quieted little Branford at once.

The boy, nose running and hair mussed, stared at Sam.

"Could you show me where to sit?" Sam held out his hand.

Branford took it, still wide-eyed.

Ruth had to admire Sam's calm in the midst of the storm.

By giving the little boy a solemn duty, he'd distracted Branford and elevated him at the same time. She smiled her gratitude.

"Thank you, sir." Beatrice looked from Sam to Ruth and back again.

She looked so worried that Ruth realized her sister had no idea who Sam was. "This is Mr. Roth. He's a salesman and new to town. We met Friday, and he proved most helpful with a little problem I encountered. He agreed to join us at church today."

Beatrice's concern eased. "You are quite the rescuing knight, Mr. Roth. Thank you again."

Sam bowed slightly. "Glad to be of assistance."

The hymn had entered the third verse. "We should find our seats," Ruth said. "Mr. Roth, you can join Jen and Minnie."

Sam tapped the little boy's hand, still firmly holding on to his. "I believe this young man has a duty to perform first. He agreed to show me to my seat."

"Please join us, Mr. Roth." Beatrice looked so relieved to have Sam's assistance that Ruth couldn't very well drag him away from her. "You already know Ruth, and little Branford seems to have taken a liking to you. It would be a big help."

"Then how could I refuse?"

Ruth tried hard to swallow as Sam showered her with one of his oh-so-charming smiles. As if released from indenture, Jen and Minnie scurried to their regular pew, leaving Ruth with Beatrice, the children…and Sam. Her perfect plan had failed.

Sam heard little of the sermon with Ruth and a squirming toddler nearby. When he wasn't prying the boy from under the pew or blocking him from shooting out into the aisle, Sam peeked at the fair beauty beside him. More than once he spotted a delightful flush on her cheeks.

Any interest on her part would vanish the moment she discovered his father was buying her family's shop. The points he'd gained by helping her sister with her rambunctious boy would vanish. Sam found himself in a pinch. Father would never allow a dress shop next door to Hutton's. He would raze the building and extend the department store. If Sam hoped to win Father's confidence, he had to facilitate the purchase. But what would happen to Ruth?

He mopped his brow. All around him, women fanned themselves and men undid the buttons on their jackets, but his discomfort came more from dismay than the heat. Four women and one sick father would soon lose their livelihood, thanks to his insistence the company open a store in Pearlman.

It's not my problem. He'd repeated those words often the past two days, but it sounded even less convincing in church.

Sam was never so happy to rise for a benediction. He'd barely heard a word of the sermon. Something about doing unto others. Standard material. The moment the benediction ended, the congregation headed for the doors, where the minister greeted them before they scattered for the shade. Sam waited in line behind Ruth and her older sister, exuberant toddler still in hand.

"I can't thank you enough," Mrs. Beatrice Kensington sighed as she reached for her son. "I can take him from here."

She'd have a struggle. The boy had found his legs and wanted to run.

"Let's wait until we're outside." Sam kept hold of the squirming toddler's hand. "I don't mind."

Truly he didn't, for it kept him close to Ruth and her

family. The sisters did resemble one another, but each had somewhat different features. Most people would consider Beatrice the beauty of the family, but Sam preferred Ruth's paler blue eyes and fairer complexion. Her features were also finer, more delicate. Her skin looked soft as silk.

Jen, on the other hand, was dark and tall. The family resemblance could be found in her facial features, though her eyes bordered on hazel, as if all the colors on the palette had been thrown together. Minnie was the shortest, her hair a muddy-blond, almost brown, but her eyes matched those of her oldest sister.

"New in town?" The minister's question pulled Sam from his assessment of the sisters.

Beatrice took her son, allowing Sam the opportunity to shake Pastor Gabe's hand.

"Just arrived on Friday." Sam was surprised by the minister's strong grip.

"Thought I saw you the other day," the minister said. "You're working on the new store, right? Peter Simmons mentioned you had him do some carpentry for you."

Ruth's head turned at those words, her approval clear.

Sam, on the other hand, suspected the minister really wanted to know what type of store Sam was opening. He tried to relax his shoulders. The questions would get more and more probing by the day, and people would expect answers. He shouldn't have come to church today. He shouldn't have agreed to spend any time at all with the townsfolk. In the past he'd maintained his distance until after the grand opening. But it was too late now. He'd introduced himself to Ruth and her family, and there was no going back.

He concentrated on the minister and forced what he hoped was a casual smile. "Peter does fine work for someone his age. I was quite impressed."

The minister proved just as unshakable. "He certainly has God-given talent and the willingness to share. That's what we're all about here. Sharing."

The emphasis wasn't lost on Sam. Pastor Gabe expected open communication and honesty. Ruth expected the same. Both hung on Sam's response.

He used his smile to deflect the question. "Wouldn't expect anything different."

"Neither would I." The minister's grin told Sam he understood the bluff, but wasn't calling him on it this time. "Let me add my welcome to the others. Staying long?"

"Can't say yet." That was true. After the grand opening, he would probably go to another location. "I hope it'll be a while." He was surprised to find that was also true. In just two days, Pearlman's tidy homes and friendly folk had captivated him.

"If you need anything while you're here, just ask," Pastor Gabe said.

"Thank you, but I can't see what I'd need."

"The offer's open. I know pretty much everyone in town. We might be small, but we have big hearts."

That sounded like a great advertising slogan. Sam mentally tested it for his store but dismissed the idea. In a town the size of Pearlman, Hutton's was anything but small. When finished, it would be the largest retail establishment in town. Only the airplane-engine factory covered more square footage.

"I'll keep that in mind," he replied, glad to escape into the fresh air.

Beatrice followed. "Thank you again for your help."

"My pleasure," he said, though an hour tending the boy had exhausted him more than a full day of work.

Ruth, still holding Beatrice's little girl, joined them in the shade of a large maple. "We're having a picnic this afternoon. In the park. You should join us, Beattie. The children would love it. Maybe Blake would come, too." She glanced toward Sam. "Mr. Roth agreed to join us. You wouldn't mind, would you?"

"The more the merrier," Sam dutifully replied, though the presence of Beatrice's family would put a crimp in talking to Ruth.

"I—I don't think so." Beatrice's gaze flicked to the street. "We're busy."

That sounded like an excuse, but Ruth didn't press the point. "Maybe next time."

"Maybe." Beatrice hurried toward a sleek black Cadillac that had just pulled to a stop. She opened the rear door and lifted the children inside.

What a cad of a driver! A hired man ought to get out of the vehicle and assist the lady.

Sam started forward until he noticed that the dark-haired man behind the wheel sported a fashionable suit. The little girl called him "Daddy." That cad was Beatrice's husband. Sam recognized the distracted self-absorption of careless pleasure-seekers, whose quest for self-indulgence knew no limits because they'd been born privileged. Money bought them out of scrapes. Money insulated them from recrimination. Sam's wife had been one of that set, and, to some extent, so had he. But she had paid the price for her sins, while he lived to regret his every day.

The driver leaned across to open the passenger door. Beatrice grabbed her expensive beaded bag off the fender and climbed in. Her diamond ring flashed in the sun, and the truth finally sank in. Beatrice had married into money.

The Foxes would not lose their shop. Beatrice could bail them out.

Chapter Five

Ruth selected the plainest dress in her closet. The yellowish-beige calico print drained the color from her complexion. Sam would never notice her in this dress. His gaze would settle instead on Jen.

By the time Ruth descended the stairs, Jen had vanished, in spite of her promise to pack the picnic basket.

"Where did your sister go?" Ruth asked Minnie, who was plunking out a melody on the old piano.

"To the airfield." Minnie pounded on the middle C key, which stuck in humid weather. "Why can't we get this fixed?"

"For the same reason we didn't buy new dresses this year. Daddy's treatment."

Minnie's shoulders slumped. "I'm sorry for complaining. It's just that I get so tired of being poor."

Ruth hugged her baby sister from behind. "Sometimes I get blue, too. Just remember how rich we are in each other."

"I know, but sometimes I wish I could have something new."

Ruth suspected this had to do with Minnie's hope that Reggie would notice her. "I do, too. If I remember right,

I have some scraps of brocade that would make a nice little handbag."

"No, thank you." Minnie pulled up the stuck key and pushed it down again, where it remained. "This is impossible. I can't play a thing."

"Would it help if I sang the note for you?"

"No." Minnie closed the music book. "You get ready for the picnic. Wear something pretty. It's your big chance, after all." She managed half a smile.

The poor girl was definitely pining for Reggie. It would do no good to reveal that Ruth intended this afternoon to be Jen's big chance, but it wouldn't happen if her sister didn't get home soon. "Did Jen say when she'd be back?"

"By one-thirty."

That didn't leave enough time to prepare the food for the picnic. Ruth blew out a sigh of frustration. That was Jen. Always racing on to the next exciting thing and forgetting her responsibilities at home.

Ruth headed for the kitchen and spent the next hour fashioning a respectable picnic lunch from leftovers and Mother's canned peaches and pickled beets. She hoped Sam wasn't famished, or there wouldn't be enough to go around.

After packing everything into the basket, she got a niggling feeling that she was forgetting something. One by one she checked off the contents. Lemonade, sandwiches, silverware, napkins, cups...

"Can I at least buy some new sheet music?" Minnie called from the living room.

The mercantile might extend credit for food but not for luxuries. "We haven't the money."

Then she remembered what she'd forgotten. Sam's catalogs. She fetched them from her dresser and tucked them into the side of the basket. As a second thought, she cov-

ered them with a napkin. If Minnie saw these lavish catalogs, she would pester Ruth for a new dress.

She'd just finished laying the blanket on top of the
basket when Jen bounded through the kitchen door. Ruth
glanced at the clock. One-forty.

"You're late."

Jen wrinkled her nose. "You're wearing that dress?"

Ruth smoothed the beige calico skirt. "It's light and
comfortable."

"It's ugly and old-fashioned. Sam will never be attracted
to you in that."

That was the point. "Appearance shouldn't matter."

Jen rolled her eyes. "Most men aren't nearly that high-
minded. Put on something else. Even your gardening dress
is prettier than that."

Ruth hefted the basket off the table. "There's no time.
It'll take us twenty minutes to walk to the park. If we want
to get there before Sam, we have to leave now."

Jen groaned. "At least wear a pretty hat."

Ruth grabbed her straw garden hat with the wide brim.
"Minnie, let's go," she called out. "Jen, could you fetch two
fishing poles from the shed?"

"Why?"

"In case Mr. Roth would like to fish."

"But you don't—" Jen's eyes widened. "Ooooh. That's
the point." She grinned. "You're craftier than I thought."

"I am no such thing."

Jen's Cheshire-cat grin only broadened. "I'll fetch the
poles and meet you in the alley."

Moments later, Ruth led her sisters down Main Street.
The park was several blocks away, and with the heavy
basket, she had to walk slowly and take many breaks. No
breeze had come up yet, and the heat felt oppressive, so
she kept to the shaded side of the street.

Half the town had decided to go to the park. The tables in the pavilion were already taken, and a game of baseball commandeered much of the open area. Dogs ran after balls and barked excitedly. Children giggled and squealed in games of tag or ring-around-the-rosy. Ruth had promised Sam that he could find them near the pavilion, so she picked a spot in front of the building.

"It's in the sun," Minnie complained. "We'll die of heat."

"You'll be fine." Ruth set down the basket and pulled off the blanket.

Jen leaned the poles against a tall oak and helped her spread the blanket. In an hour or so, the sun's travels would bring the shade away from the pavilion and over them. As Ruth smoothed out the blanket, she watched for Sam. Rather than help, Minnie wandered off looking for Reggie. At first Ruth was irritated, but then she realized this could work to her advantage. Once Sam arrived, she'd excuse herself to find Minnie and suggest Jen take Sam fishing.

"He likes you," Jen said as they settled on the blanket.

Ruth pushed Sam's catalogs into the bottom of the picnic basket and took out the napkins rather than deal with her sister's pointed remark.

Jen didn't give up. "I saw the way he maneuvered into Beattie's pew so he could sit with you."

"He was just being helpful."

"What bachelor volunteers to watch a toddler? Honestly, you're so blind sometimes."

Ruth flinched. It wasn't so much that she was blind to Sam's attentions, but rather she preferred he direct them toward Jen. Her sister could dazzle a man like Sam, could endlessly entertain him with her crazy ideas and impulsive behavior. Ruth, on the other hand, would soon bore him.

She moved the jar of pickled beets into the shadow of the basket. "You might call it 'blind.' I call it 'realistic.'"

She lined up the plates and placed one knife, one fork and one spoon on each, taking care that the knife blade was turned inward.

"Realistic?" Jen snorted. "How dull."

Ruth choked back a sudden ache. Was she dull? Doomed to a safe life without excitement? Realism guarded against pain. In exchange it demanded the surrender of any chance at limitless joy.

"I'm not like you and Minnie." Ruth fetched stones to put on each corner of the blanket in case a breeze arose. "I'm a homebody. I prefer a simple life. I like daily routine. Our family is my life."

"Is that all?" Jen leaned close. "You must want romance. Everyone does."

Ruth couldn't admit the ache deep in her heart. "I've accepted my place. The dress shop and the family are enough for me."

Jen handed her a stone. "You're settling."

"Maybe I want to settle." She looked straight into her sister's eyes. "Don't worry about me. Find a man you adore, one who loves you with all his heart, and marry him."

Jen's eyes twinkled. "Speaking of adoring men, yours is almost here."

Something between panic and delight jolted Ruth. At the sight of him, she instinctively reached up to check her hair and in the process knocked off her wide-brimmed straw hat. My, Sam was handsome! She couldn't take her eyes off him. He strode toward her with the casual ease of a man who knew his place in the world. In his hands he carried a small carton tied with string that could have come from only the bakery. And he was within earshot. How much of her conversation had he overheard?

Her nerves fluttered as she smoothed her ragged old dress. Maybe she should have worn something better.

Sam smiled at her and held out the carton. "For you."

"You didn't need to bring anything." Though her knees quaked, she managed to get out the words.

He handed her the carton. "Of course I did."

His smile sent warmth clear to her toes, but when he bent and retrieved her hat, she nearly stopped breathing.

"I believe you lost this." He held out the hat.

"Yes. Thank you." Not one intelligent word remained in her head. She took the hat with her free hand. Now what? Should she set down the cake? Put on her hat? Or invite him to sit?

Pastor Gabe's wife had noticed Sam's arrival and was whispering something to her sister-in-law, who'd joined them with her husband for what looked to be a family picnic. The Grattans watched from a table in the pavilion. No doubt they expected a man like Sam to gravitate toward them, not one of the town's poorer citizens.

Though the corner of Sam's mouth lifted in a half smile, his gaze took in her dowdy dress. Jen was right. Sam, who loved color, could find nothing appealing in an old beige dress and straw hat. That was precisely why she'd worn it, so why the regret?

"Would you like to walk before dinner?" Sam held out his hand to her, not Jen.

Ruth wasn't sure she could walk one step. He stood near, so close that his bergamot scent curled around her in a welcoming embrace. Logic dictated he could not possibly be interested in a dull wallflower with glasses, yet he'd asked her to join him.

Though her pulse raced, her practical side urged her to refuse. This course would lead to only humiliation and heartbreak. Yet as he took the carton from her hand and gave it to Jen, she wanted to believe it was possible for a gallant swan to love an ugly old goose in real life as well as the storybooks.

"I'd love to see the river, and I can think of no one better to show me." Sam held out his arm. "Your sister won't mind watching over the picnic for a few minutes."

Though Jen usually balked at anyone assuming she would do something, this time she grinned and waved them on. "Go. I have things under control here."

Ruth's heart fluttered wildly. Sam wanted to walk with her, just her, along the river. She glanced at Eloise Grattan and her mother. They'd be so envious, perhaps even incredulous. The most handsome man to set foot in Pearlman wanted to stroll on the river path with Ruth Fox. In full public view.

The path sloped downward through the woods. Directly ahead, a wooden platform had been constructed to provide a view of the river and the pond upstream. Already several rowboats dotted the expanse. He led her onto the overlook. A family crowded the opposite side, the little girl pointing excitedly to a great blue heron stalking through the shallows downriver. Sam paused in the shade of a tall maple. From there, they could admire the pond, where sunlight sparkled off the water like a thousand diamonds.

"It's beautiful, isn't it?" she said softly. The colors of the river—from sapphire to emerald—never failed to inspire gratitude for God's creation.

Sam settled along the railing beside her. "It is. Almost as pretty as you."

The compliment heated her cheeks. "I meant the river."

"I know." He placed his hand beside hers on the railing.

So close. Almost touching. She could barely breathe.

"What is its name?" Sam asked.

"What? Oh. The river. It's called the Green River, and that's Green Lake, even though it's more like a pond."

"The Green River. After the color of the water."

"One of the colors." She squinted into the sunlight. "It's clear brown in the shallows and white at the rapids."

"And on the far side of the pond, it's ultramarine blue." He pointed to the northeast, where several boats lingered in the bright sunlight.

"That's the best fishing hole."

"I noticed you brought fishing poles. Do you fish?"

Ruth gulped. This was her chance to tout Jen's ability with rod and reel. Her sister could fly-fish with the boys and outcatch most of them. Ruth should implement her plan, but she couldn't let go of this moment with Sam.

"I haven't fished since I was a little girl. Daddy used to bring me and Jen here."

She must have sighed because he chuckled softly. "Good memories?"

"The best. Though I was a terrible fisherman. My line always got tangled, and the fish would swallow the hook. I never felt them bite. Jen, though, can catch anything." It hurt to promote her sister, but she mustn't think of herself. She must consider what was best. "Do you like to fish?"

He shook his head. "Haven't done it since boyhood."

What a relief. He wouldn't want to fish with Jen. "Did your father take you and your brother fishing?"

He looked toward the pond. "We lived near a river. Harry and I would go down there often, but he was the better fisherman." He turned back with that broad smile. "A bit like you and Jen."

"Except you probably didn't kill the fish in the process of catching them. Daddy would scold me, and I felt terrible." A sudden pang of regret caught the words in her throat. She swallowed hard and leaned on the railing for support. "I stopped going along. I—I wish I hadn't. But you can't turn back time."

"No, you can't." He sounded almost wistful, memories playing across his face for just an instant before he shut them down. "But we could give it a try. What do you say we take those poles of yours and throw in a line?"

Fish with Sam? She couldn't cast a fly. Hadn't attempted it since she was ten or twelve. If she tried now, the hook would end up caught in a tree or—even worse—in his clothing. That was not the kind of catching Jen had in mind with her marriage idea.

"No." She shook her head. "No, Jen's the better fisherman."

If he were disappointed, it didn't show. He shifted his weight, and his hand grazed hers, sending a pleasant warmth up her arm. This was a man who would take care of those he loved. He would protect and hold them close. The way he'd stepped in to help Beattie revealed his generous, compassionate nature.

"It's not about the catching," he said. "It's about enjoying time with someone, like you did with your father." His smile could light a cathedral, but it couldn't dispel the pang of regret that hit her at the mention of her father.

She bowed her head. Daddy might never come home. He might never fish again. She had wasted precious years.

Sam laid his hand on hers. "You love your father dearly, don't you?"

She drew in a shaky breath. How could she explain? All her life she'd known her father suffered from a weak heart, but his condition had grown worse in the past year. Many days he'd stayed on the sofa or in bed. He hadn't gone to the shop since October. Mother had brought the ledgers home then, so he could keep the accounts, but everyone knew it was only a matter of time before he couldn't do even that. The sanitarium was his last hope. She blinked back tears.

"I'm sorry," Sam said. "I didn't mean to upset you."

Before she realized what had happened, he'd taken her in his arms. The thrum of his heart steadied her, and the warmth of his arms felt oh-so secure. For a moment, she closed her eyes and drank in his strength as she struggled to regain emotional control. How good it felt to be held. She wanted to linger there, but people would soon notice.

She pulled away and forced a smile. "I'm all right. I know he's getting the best care possible at the sanitarium. We're optimistic the regimen will strengthen his heart."

"Heart?" His brow pinched in concern.

"My father had rheumatic fever when he was young, and it weakened his heart."

"I see." He sounded sympathetic but withdrew to the railing and stared across the pond.

A chill swept through Ruth. The momentary closeness had been lost. Sam wanted no part of a family poised on the brink of loss.

"I'm sorry," she murmured. "You don't want to hear my troubles."

"You don't have to apologize." But his jaw remained set, and he wouldn't look at her.

Desperation made her panic. She hadn't meant to turn him away. "Normally I wouldn't talk about such personal things. You must think me overly emotional."

"Your father sounds like a good family man."

"The best."

"Did he teach you to sew?"

"He taught me how to follow a dress pattern, how to sew straight seams, how to keep the books. He taught me everything." She struggled against the memories that threatened to bring tears. "He encouraged me, even when my results were awful." Despite the pain, a laugh bubbled to her lips. "I made him a little stuffed elephant each year.

The first one was terrible. Only Daddy could tell that it was an elephant. He said it was perfect."

"That's what a father should do." Sam sounded almost wistful.

"Your father must have taught you a lot, like how to sell things."

He looked perplexed for a moment. "Ah. Sales. Yes. He did teach me the business, but not like your father taught you. I attended college."

"Oh." The differences between them loomed large again. Rich, handsome and a college man. Just like Reggie Landers. How could she ever interest someone like Sam? She couldn't, and she'd best accept that now before the inevitable heartache. No more personal chatter, no sharing and no sympathetic hugs. She'd stick to business.

"I brought the catalogs with me." She cleared her throat. "After lunch, I'll show you which dresses Mrs. Vanderloo chose. I will repay you, but it might take a while."

He said nothing for long minutes, nor would he look at her. The silence loomed like a wall of dense fog. When he finally spoke, indignation cracked his voice. "Dresses? In the middle of our conversation you're thinking about those dresses?"

She shivered. "You did ask me to give you the catalogs."

"Yes, give me the catalogs but not repay me. I won't take one penny from you."

Ruth could not accept charity. He didn't yet know that Mrs. Vanderloo had chosen the most expensive gowns in the catalogs. One cost a shocking ninety dollars. Ninety! For just one dress. And Ruth had promised her three, one more than Sam had offered to buy.

She wrung her hands. "I-it turned out a little differently than planned. She insisted I give her a third dress. I must pay for that one at the very least."

She waited for the explosion of anger.

Nothing.

She hazarded a peek.

His jaw worked, and his expression had frozen, but he didn't shout. Instead he nodded slowly. "I see." Then he walked to the far side of the platform, his back to her.

What had happened? One moment Sam was comforting Ruth. The next she'd turned as cold as her icy eyes. Business! He didn't want to discuss business. He wanted to know more about her, her family and her childhood. He wanted to hold her until her sorrow lifted. He wanted to tell her everything would be all right. He wanted to help. Or maybe it was just guilt. Maybe he'd overstepped propriety, and she'd rightly stepped away.

He stared across the pond, not seeing the fishermen or couples in rowboats. He didn't care about catalogs or Mrs. Vanderloo's dresses or how many Ruth had promised the conniving woman. He liked Ruth. She was nothing like Lillian. Polar opposites, and not just because of social standing. Ruth was honest and compassionate. She cared about others. She cherished her family. The antithesis of Lillian. Ruth backed away when he got too close.

He yanked off his hat and raked a hand through his hair. What had he been thinking? Sam Rothenburg had come to Pearlman to open a department store, not get involved with a woman who would despise him for doing just that.

Therein lay the problem.

Unlike his father, he couldn't crush the competition, not when he could look in her pale blue eyes and see the obstacles she faced. He hated to see good people struggle. Ruth couldn't possibly afford to buy even one of the replacement dresses. No matter which ones Mrs. Vanderloo had chosen, all would be too costly, for Sam had given Ruth catalogs from the most expensive stores in New York. He could kick himself for that blunder, but then, he'd never intended for her to repay him.

He heard her footsteps draw near.

"I didn't mean to chase you away." Her voice was soft, hesitant, the kind of voice he longed to come home to each night.

He shook that thought out of his head.

"I'm sorry, but I needed a moment." Until he'd arrived in Pearlman, Sam never apologized, yet around Ruth he seemed to do nothing but apologize. If a business relationship was all she wanted, then he must respect her wishes.

He faced her. "Why don't you show me which gowns Mrs. Vanderloo chose?"

"All right." She looked past him. "The catalogs are in the picnic basket."

He offered his arm, but something on the far side of the pond caught her attention. She stepped to the rail, her brow furrowed.

"What's wrong?" he asked.

"Nothing." She jerked away from the railing and smiled quickly. Too quickly.

Her pinched expression belied her words. She'd seen something or someone that troubled her deeply. Yet when he followed her gaze, he saw nothing out of the ordinary. Whatever it was, she must not want to explain, for she hurried back toward the park without him.

Chapter Six

Ruth couldn't keep her mind on conversation during the picnic. After what she'd spotted across the pond, she wanted to circle to the other side and give Blake Kensington a dressing-down. But she had asked Sam to join them and couldn't very well disappear in the middle of lunch. So she nodded occasionally to something Jen or Sam said and kept a lookout for Blake's return.

Sam apparently shared Daddy's interest in politics. He rattled on about President Harding's West Coast trip. Her gaze drifted back to the north end of the park. Anyone hiking to the far side of Green Lake would return by that path.

Jen elbowed her.

"What?" Ruth snapped to attention.

Sam repeated the question about President Harding's intentions for the trip.

"Oh, I don't know. I'm not terribly interested in politics."

Jen, who loved to debate Daddy, took over. "My father thinks he's trying to escape scandal. I think he wants people to see him as the next Teddy Roosevelt. Ridiculous. Real adventurers risk their lives trying new things like flying." She then droned on about the airfield and the airplane-motor factory until poor Sam's eyes glazed over.

Ruth should rescue him, but she couldn't concentrate on anything but Beatrice's marriage. Hadn't her sister intimated there were problems? Didn't she look exhausted and worried lately? Ruth couldn't stomach food. Instead she folded and refolded her napkin while she watched for her brother-in-law. The longer lunch dragged on without a sighting, the less certain she became. Maybe the man only looked like Blake. Maybe her brother-in-law had a good explanation for going to a secluded part of the woods with another woman.

Another woman! There was no excuse.

Ruth clenched her fists as the image of Blake putting his arm around the waist of the dark-haired woman burned into her brain. The man had the same build and coloring as Blake. It must be him. If she spotted him entering the park from the northern path, she'd have proof.

"Who are you looking for?" Jen's question broke through the worry fogging Ruth's mind. "Minnie is talking to Anna Landers."

"I know." Ruth couldn't very well pretend she'd been looking for Minnie when her baby sister sat not twenty feet away. "I was just looking around. Not for anyone in particular."

"You are, too. Your head will snap off if you swivel around one more time."

"Really, Jen," Ruth scolded. "Where I look is none of your business."

Her sister leaned close and whispered, "You should pay attention when Sam's talking to you." The expression on his face confirmed that he had indeed been trying to catch her attention. "He must have asked you about some stupid dress catalog a hundred times."

"Oh, dear. I'm sorry." She pulled the catalogs from the bottom of the basket. "I should have given these to you when we first returned." An hour earlier, she'd been dismayed by his reaction to the news that she'd promised Mrs. Vanderloo three dresses, but that worry had disappeared the moment she saw Blake with another woman. She handed over the catalogs. "I marked each gown with an *X*."

Jen's jaw dropped. "You're buying dresses from a catalog?"

"It's not what you think," Ruth said.

"Mr. Roth is buying you dresses?"

"Jen!" Ruth could not believe her sister would say such a thing in front of Sam.

Sam laughed. "I wish I was. Instead, I'm replacing the gowns that got ruined when I barged into your sister."

"Ooooh." Jen gave Ruth a smug look. "I understand completely."

Ruth cringed at her sister's tone. No doubt she figured her matchmaking was well under way. As soon as Sam left, Ruth would put an end to that speculation, but for now she could only confirm Sam's explanation. "Mr. Roth did make that generous offer."

Jen's grin broadened. "I can guess why."

"I'm sure you can't." Ruth glared at her sister before shifting her attention to Sam. "I'm sorry about the cost. I asked her to stay within reason, but she insisted on choosing the priciest gowns."

"She would," Jen muttered before sticking her nose in the air to mimic the uppity woman. "Nothing is too good for a Vanderloo."

Jen's imitation of Mrs. Vanderloo's voice was so accurate that Ruth would have laughed if they hadn't been in public. "That's not nice!"

"Why—" Jen fluttered her hands just like the socialite "—we're practically related to the Vanderbilts."

"Hush," Ruth hissed, before checking to make sure none of the Vanderloos was seated nearby. "What if she ends up being your mother-in-law?"

That stopped the mimicry. In fact, Jen looked as if she'd swallowed one of Mrs. Vanderloo's famously large hats.

Ruth turned back to Sam and found him mildly amused. "Jen is quite the actress."

"So I see. I hope I don't fall into her repertoire."

"Never," Jen insisted. "You are thoroughly unmockable."

Ruth felt a pang of regret. The romance she'd sought to encourage was under way. She should promote Jen's best qualities, as they'd agreed, but she couldn't get the words out.

Minnie chose that moment to drop onto the blanket. Her eyes looked swollen and her lower lip quivered. Ruth could guess why. Minnie must not have seen Reggie all day. Instead, she'd spent the past hour talking to Reggie's sister-in-law.

Ruth gently touched her baby sister's arm. "Are you all right?"

"Of course." Minnie scowled and edged away. "It's a perfect day. Just per-fect. Can't anyone give me a little peace?"

Something had happened, but Ruth would never learn what in front of Sam. She'd have to ask Minnie later.

"It's been a long day." Ruth began packing up the remains of the picnic. "And I have an early day tomorrow." She screwed the lid on the empty beet jar.

"Me, too." Sam stood abruptly, catalogs in hand. "Ladies." He touched a finger to his hat. "Thank you for the excellent luncheon and even better companionship."

"Thank you for the cake. It was nice to meet you, Sam." Jen extended her hand, which he shook. "Hope to see you again soon. I know Ruthie does. Isn't her hair pretty today?"

Goodness! Ruth could slap her sister. If this was the type of assistance Jen planned to offer, then her marriage idea was bound to fail. Any man, especially one as experienced as Sam, would run fast and far.

But instead of running, Sam laughed. "Yes, it is. And I look forward to seeing you again, too, Miss Jen." He reserved his smile for her and merely nodded at Ruth and Minnie.

Ruth should be pleased. That was what she'd wanted. Instead, dejection settled over her as she packed up the remainder of their picnic.

Sam walked away with the catalogs tucked into his jacket pocket and a tune on his lips. The casual ease of his stride and the jaunty angle of his hat caught and held Ruth as firmly as a spider's web snared a fly.

"He likes you," Jen repeated for what had to be the hundredth time.

Ruth gritted her teeth. "I think his affections lie elsewhere."

Jen plopped down next to her. "Have a little faith."

It would take more than faith. Ruth stacked the plates and shoved them into the basket. They were a sorry lot, moping over liaisons that could never happen. Maybe that was for the best. She scanned north one last time. She had either missed Blake or mistook him for someone else. She prayed it was the latter.

Out of the corner of her eye she saw Sam striding up the rise onto Elm Street. Every step he took pounded the realization a little deeper. All her life she'd heard the same thing. No man could ever fall for plain old Ruth Fox.

Especially not a man like Sam.

* * *

It hadn't taken Sam long to figure out that Ruth was trying to match him with Jen. Why she would do that after she'd lingered in his arms earlier that afternoon was the mystery. Not so mysterious was Jen's even more obvious attempt to promote Ruth. Through the years, Sam had learned to spot far subtler matchmaking attempts.

Ruth's and Jen's clumsy efforts brought a smile to his lips.

In fact, he rather didn't mind being the object of their attention. Usually he steered well clear of any woman who harbored designs on him. After Lillian, whose artful manipulation had thoroughly deceived him, he stayed away from unmarried women. Marriage? Never. Though young ladies clamored for his attention, he wouldn't so much as dance with one. At first people understood. The grieving widower and all. Too soon the mothers and daughters came at him from every side, encouraged by his own parents. Mother thought he needed someone. Father wanted a grandson to carry on the Rothenburg name. Sam had obliged by meeting one or two but always made it clear he would not remarry. None could tempt him.

Until Ruth.

As Sam climbed the steps of the boardinghouse, he regretted dropping his guard. He should never have allowed Ruth into his heart, should never have shared the smallest detail of his life, should never have listened to her family's troubles. Somehow that woman had ensnared him more securely than all the machinations of the most artful grand dame.

The wide porch was empty at this hour, for the sun beat hot against all but the farthest corner, where a fat tabby occupied the only shaded chair and flicked her tail in warning lest Sam consider removing her.

"It's yours," he promised as he picked up a copy of the weekend newspaper that had been left behind by another of the boarders.

After settling into a caned chair, he skimmed the front page. The top story detailed a new contract at the airplane-engine factory. The rest dealt with people he didn't know. He flipped the page to find an editorial speculating on his store. The article hinted at several possibilities, from automobile showroom to feed store. Sam chuckled. Nowhere did it mention a department store.

He sat back in satisfaction, easing his aching back and legs. Arms behind his head, he decided a nap was in order until he spotted Miss Harris striding quickly toward the boardinghouse, patting her hat and dark hair into place. She also boarded here, along with the floor manager and the architect.

"Good afternoon," he said since she didn't appear to notice him. "I see you're giving your feet a break today."

"Oh. Mr. Rothenburg." She paused on the step and looked around before joining him. "If I'd known I'd have to hike through the wilderness, I would have worn boots." She shooed away the cat and sat down.

Sam managed to hide a grin. Nothing around Pearlman qualified as wilderness, not like the Canadian wilds that Father had taken Harry and him to as youths. Enamored by how Teddy Roosevelt had built his strength through physical trial, Father had once dragged Sam and Harry on a tenting "expedition" in early May. A late-season snowstorm collapsed their tent, and they nearly froze. That had been the last testing in the wild. Father conducted future tests from the comfort of his home.

Miss Harris leaned her head back with a sigh.

"Trying day?" he asked.

"Productive day."

"Is that so?"

"I got the answer. It seems impossible, considering they own half the town, but they don't know."

Sam breathed in with relief. In a week and a half, everyone would know that a Hutton's Department Store was coming to town. All this ridiculous subterfuge would end, and life could return to normal. He'd leave, and the excitement would settle down. Pearlman would step boldly into the future. Gone the sleepy town, replaced by commerce and progress.

Across the road lay the airfield, quiet on this Sunday. Far to the right stood the large airplane-engine factory. Across the way and to the left stood the flight school. Gnats clouded the late-afternoon shadows. Swallows swooped through the air with more grace than any man-made flying machine. Again Sam's thoughts turned to Ruth and how he could convince her not to pay for any of Mrs. Vanderloo's dresses.

Maybe after the truth came out, she'd remember that kindness and forgive him.

Ruth stared at the stack of unpaid bills on Daddy's desk. She had to do something. Jen's idea had been a ridiculous fantasy. Marry a wealthy man? What had possessed Ruth to agree to such a scheme? Such were the dreams of schoolgirls, not grown women. Marriage depended on the improbable joining of a man's and a woman's will and purpose. It could not be accomplished in short order or on command.

Have a little faith, Jen had said.

Well, Ruth had prayed and prayed for a husband for years, and what did it get her? Nothing. Clearly God had other plans for her, and she'd done her best to accept them. She would take care of the family and run the business. But she would never have a family of her own, and no crazy plan was going to change that.

The family's growing debt concerned her more at the moment. Work was the best solution. She needed a job that would allow her to run the dress shop during the day and earn wages at night. That meant working in a factory. Perhaps Simmons Aero-motor was hiring. The newspaper lay on the sofa. Ruth picked it up and began to flip to the back, when she saw an editorial speculating on the type of business that would open in the old carriage factory. Sam's business.

She sank onto the sofa and read the ideas. Most were preposterous, but one stood out. A furniture store. Furniture was upholstered. She could sew, and the largest factories were only an hour away in Grand Rapids.

What had Sam said? That the business would open in a couple of weeks? Maybe that was enough time. Maybe Daddy could hang on long enough for her to find a job that would earn the kind of money he needed for treatment.

A light rapping at the door broke her thoughts.

Ruth glanced at the clock. Nearly seven o'clock. Perhaps one of her sisters' friends was calling.

She heard the front door open.

"Ruth?" It was Beatrice, and, judging from the lack of noise, she hadn't brought the children.

"In the living room." Even as she said the words, Ruth remembered what she'd seen at Green Lake. Her pulse accelerated. Did Beatrice know? Had something terrible happened? She rushed to the front door.

Her sister was carefully removing her dainty straw hat, encircled with silk flowers. Not one strand of Beatrice's blond hair fell out of place. Her fashionable lace-and-linen dress didn't display a single wrinkle. Beatrice hung her beaded bag on one of the pegs, and Ruth was ashamed of their humble home. How different from the lavish house Beattie now shared with her husband and children. Three stories. Mahogany furniture. Silver tea service. Five sets of china. Five! Mother had barely half a set left after all the pieces they'd broken.

Beattie embraced Ruth with genuine warmth. "Where are Genevieve and Wilhelmina?" Only Beatrice would use their younger sisters' much-detested full names.

"They went to the cinema. Apparently a Rudolph Valentino film is in town. And the children?"

"At their grandparents' house." Beattie sighed, and only then did Ruth see the faint worry lines creasing her brow. "I'm glad we have a chance to talk alone."

Oh, dear. Beatrice did know about her husband's dalliance. To hide her dismay, Ruth tugged her sister into the living room. "Let's sit. I'll make tea." Anything to delay the awful truth.

"No, thank you." Beatrice settled on the edge of the sagging sofa, hands folded on her lap, as composed as if she were about to inquire after Ruth's health. How could she stay so calm when Ruth's stomach was tied in knots? "Shall we catch up?"

Catch up? Thoughts tumbled like rubber balls in Ruth's mind as she set the newspaper aside and sat beside her sister. Such an innocuous question. Maybe Beattie didn't know about her husband's trip to the far side of Green Lake.

Ruth drew in a shaky breath. "About what?"

Beattie's laugh tinkled softly, like a silver spoon on fine porcelain. "A certain man, perhaps? Tall, dark-haired and exceedingly handsome. Willing to watch a squirming toddler just to sit next to you?"

With a start, Ruth realized her sister hadn't come here to

talk about Blake or her marriage. This visit was intended to promote Sam.

"Don't believe everything that Jen and Minnie tell you," Ruth said. "Mr. Roth is new in town, and I invited him to join us at church. Mother and Daddy would have done the same."

"Yes, they would have." Yet Beattie's smile made it perfectly clear she didn't accept that explanation. "And to the park also?"

Ruth drew in her breath sharply. Beatrice had been at the park this afternoon? Maybe her eyes *had* deceived her. Maybe it *was* Beatrice with Blake, and Ruth had spotted a dark hat, not dark hair. "Oh. Yes. The park."

Beatrice didn't seem to notice Ruth's discomfort. "What a handsome man, and a real gentleman. I could tell he's fond of you."

"As a friend, perhaps." After all, he'd promised to see Jen again, not her.

"Perhaps. Or maybe more than friendship if you give it time." Beattie clasped Ruth's hand. "Don't chase this one away."

"I don't—" Ruth began, but it wasn't true. She did push men away. It was easier than suffering the inevitable disappointment. Though the regretful incident ten years ago topped the list, Ruth had heard and overheard enough to know that men did not find her desirable.

"It's worth the risk," Beatrice said.

"Maybe." The rumors about Blake that swirled around town nagged at Ruth, but she could not tell her sister what she'd seen. She could only warn her. "Sometimes a man can hurt you badly."

Beattie smiled softly. "Great joy risks great pain."

"I don't think I could bear it."

"Of course you could." Beatrice hugged her close. "You're

the strongest person I know. Always taking care of Mother and Daddy and the dress shop. I don't know how you hold up under everything."

Ruth's throat constricted. "It's not the same. Mother and Daddy will always love me. But how do I know a man will?"

"You just know. Deep inside. Maybe it's your heart. Maybe it's God telling you that he's right for you. All I know is that when you find the man you'll love for the rest of your life, you know it. Maybe not right away. I didn't like Blake one bit when we were younger, but in time I knew he was the one for me."

Ruth held her breath and willed away the painful memories. Spilling them would do no good.

"Give it time," Beattie said. "Give Mr. Roth a chance."

"There is no time." At least here Ruth could speak with confidence. "He's only in town a couple weeks."

"Then we must hurry. The Grange dance is next Friday night. You'll need something to wear. I wouldn't rely on our sisters' good intentions, and there's not enough time to start from scratch. Perhaps you could alter one of my gowns."

Ruth bitterly recalled promising to attend. "I could never fit into one of your gowns. Why, I'd have to let out two full sizes. There's not enough seam allowance for that."

"Perhaps one of my maternity gowns could be altered."

"Never!"

Beatrice laughed. "You're right. They would be a bit dowdy. Perhaps we can create something new. You could do something based on one of your sketches."

"Jen talked to you, didn't she? She thinks I can make a gown out of scraps. Well, I can't."

"Perhaps there's another option." Beatrice crossed the room to where Mrs. Vanderloo's ruined dresses hung from the open kitchen door. "Whose are these?" Beattie ran a hand over the mint-green lace dress. "Beautiful fabric."

"Except for the stains. Both gowns are completely ruined."

"Maybe not." Beatrice touched a finger to her lips, deep in thought. "The gowns are in the old style, with all that excess fabric. And at least two sizes too large for you. With your talent, you could find a way to work around that stain on the green dress and create a lovely drop-waist gown that would fit you perfectly."

Ruth cringed. Mrs. Vanderloo would go into a conniption if she saw Ruth wearing her old tea gown. "I can't. It's Mrs. Vanderloo's. I dropped both of them when Mr. Roth ran into me."

"Can you get the stain out?"

"I've tried, but it's permanent. We're going to replace both gowns with new ones."

Beatrice's eyes widened. "Then she doesn't want them back?"

"She said she never wanted to see them again."

Beatrice lifted the skirt of the green gown. "Perfect."

"No, it's not. If I showed up at the dance wearing her old dress, she'd accuse me of stealing."

"Then change it into something entirely new. Dye the fabric. Add a sash or a different colored underskirt. You're so talented, Ruth. You could turn this into anything at all." She ran her fingers over the ivory georgette. "Why, you could make this one into a wedding dress."

"Wedding?" Ruth choked on the word.

"Jen told me her idea."

"It's ridiculous."

"Is it?" Beattie held the ivory gown against her body. "This would fit all three of you, but you best of all."

The dressmaker in Ruth immediately pictured a gown

for Jen and just as quickly tossed that image aside. Jen and georgette did not go together. She was more canvas jackets and leather boots. Hardly wedding-dress material.

"I think it's charming that our sisters want to help you find a beau," Beattie said as she returned the dress to the hook. "You deserve it, Ruth. No one would make a better wife and mother. You'd probably do a better job than me."

"Never. You're a wonderful mother."

Beatrice turned away to dab her eyes. "Forgive me, but sometimes I'm beside myself with the children. If only Blake would help more. But then, he's so busy with the store." She mustered a shaky smile. "Look at me blubbering away about my insignificant problems when I wanted to encourage you."

Ruth hugged her sister. "No one loves those babes more than you."

"I—I wonder sometimes. Tillie and little Branford are such a handful. Blake says the noise drives him crazy. He wants quiet and order after a hard day's work."

Ruth squeezed her sister's hand. What could she say? "I don't think any home can be quiet and orderly when there are little ones around."

"I know." Beattie drew in a ragged breath. "And I know it will pass, but…" She paused for so long that Ruth thought she wouldn't finish. "Things aren't the same between us since Branford was born."

The admission lanced through Ruth. Was that Blake at Green Lake? She wasn't certain enough to tell Beatrice. "I'm sure it'll get better when the children grow a little older."

Though her sister nodded, both knew that no one could ensure such a promise.

"I'll pray for you," Ruth added.

Beattie attempted a smile. "Thank you. And I'll pray for you and Mr. Roth."

Ruth started to tell her sister that a relationship with Sam was hopeless, but Beatrice seemed to cling to that promise of romance as if it would somehow cure the problems in her own. For that reason, Ruth kept quiet.

Beattie grasped Ruth's hands with desperate hope. "Promise me you'll make the dress for the dance."

"All right." Ruth would not disappoint her, but she had no intention of dancing with Sam Roth or any other man.

Chapter Seven

Shortly before nine o'clock on Monday morning, Ruth approached the bank, letter in hand. Instinct told her that the interview wouldn't be pleasant. No payments had been made on the note all year. Yet the bank manager, Mr. Shea, knew Ruth's father and mother were gone. He wouldn't call her there for a scolding. He would wait until Daddy returned home. This must be some trivial matter.

She arrived before the bank opened and waited with Reggie Landers for the clerk to unlock the doors.

Reggie, leaning against the side of the bank as if he'd been there for hours, touched a finger to his straw boater. "Good morning, Miss...?"

It did not bode well for Minnie's hopes if he couldn't remember Ruth's last name. "Fox. Miss Fox."

"Fox. Yes." He struck a jaunty pose, much as Sam would do, and clicked his fingers. "I've heard that name before. Don't tell me. It was at a party."

"Perhaps." Ruth couldn't break Minnie's heart by reminding Reggie that he'd likely seen Minnie working at one of the grand parties.

"I remember. The Valentine's Ball. That's it. But it wasn't you that I saw."

"True. I have never attended." Nor received an invitation. She tried desperately to remember if Beattie had gone this year. It was the sort of affair Blake wouldn't miss. "Perhaps you saw my sister."

"That's it. The girl manning the punch bowl. She works for Sally's mother."

Reggie could not have any feelings for Minnie. He barely knew who she was. Poor Minnie!

"Tough to get good help these days." He pulled out a pocket watch and flipped open the cover. "One minute past nine. Even the bank can't keep accurate hours."

As if on cue, Ruth heard the scrape of a key in the lock and Miss Evans pushed the door open. Seeing as the church bells just now chimed the nine-o'clock hour, Ruth begged to differ with Reggie's pocket watch.

"Miss Fox." Miss Evans held the door for her. "Mr. Shea will see you in his office. Mr. Landers, please follow me. I have your disbursement ready."

Ruth plodded toward the bank manager's heavy oak door. It stood ajar, signaling he was ready for her.

"Miss Fox." Mr. Dermott Shea stood when she entered, his middle-aged frame just as heavy as that oak door and his ponderous walnut desk. "Please have a seat." He motioned to the chair across the massive desktop and waited for her to sit before he retook his seat.

Before him sat a folder, which he opened and then proceeded to glance through as if he had no idea of its contents.

After what seemed like minutes, Ruth prompted him. "You did ask to meet this morning."

"Yes, yes." He fiddled with his spectacles, pushing them up the bridge of his nose. "When I sent the letter, I hoped your mother would have returned by now. I had heard she only planned to visit a couple days."

"That was her original intent, but in her last letter she indicated she was staying another two weeks."

"I see." He cleared his throat. "Well, then, it can't be helped."

"What can't be helped?"

He took off his spectacles and folded them atop the closed folder. "You do have a means to contact your parents?"

She nodded slowly as her stomach knotted.

"There is a matter of business that they must address before the end of the month."

"But that's only—" she counted out the days "—nine days including today, and my father cannot travel."

Mr. Shea stroked the corners of his mouth. "I feared that would be the case. Can he be reached by telephone?"

"Not directly. The sanitarium has a telephone, of course, but the doctors have stressed that my father is not to hear anything that might unsettle him."

"I see." Shea drummed his fingers on the folder. "Perhaps your mother can make the decision. Could you contact her this morning?"

Ruth had no idea how she would pay for a long-distance telephone call, even if she could reach Mother. She had to call the hospital and leave a message. Then Mother would have to spend more to call her back. "If this is a matter of finance, Mother left me in charge of both the personal and business accounts. You may speak to me." She straightened her spine and did her best to look authoritative.

The banker paused a good long while. "You will relay this information to your parents?"

Ruth could barely breathe. "What information, sir?"

Again he opened the folder and riffled the papers, this time with his spectacles off. "Our records indicate no payments have been made this year on the property loan. Indeed, we cannot find record of any last year, either."

That knot in her stomach twisted tighter. She hadn't checked last year's records.

"For the dress shop?" she asked, though she knew the answer.

Though somber, Mr. Shea exhibited compassion. "If you can find proof of payments, we will check our books."

But Ruth knew there would be no proof. She bowed her head. "With my father's medical bills—" The words caught in her throat. She hated to admit weakness, and poverty was a weakness. Didn't God promise reward for those who loved Him? And didn't she love Him? Didn't she attend church and pray and read her Bible?

"I understand." Mr. Shea leaned toward her, all earnestness. "Truly, I do, but the bank doesn't hold the note on the dress-shop property."

Ruth stared. "But I thought…"

Mr. Shea looked uncomfortable. "It's an unusual situation involving one of the bank's board members, who wished to retain ownership of the property until the loan is paid but didn't want to handle the paperwork."

"Does the bank do this often?"

"No." Mr. Shea fiddled with the papers in front of him. "And if he hadn't been on the bank's board of directors, I doubt such an arrangement would have been approved. But it was done years ago and was to your father's benefit, since the property owner charged a far lower rate of interest than the bank could offer."

"Then the owner is generous." A tiny bubble of hope took shape. "Perhaps if he knew our situation, he would give us more time. Father needs additional treatment." She bit her lip, as if that could draw back the private information she'd just spilled. "It's costly."

Mr. Shea looked sympathetic. "I'm very sorry. Truly, I am, but I understand the property owner has received a solid offer from a buyer. A cash offer. He's anxious to sell."

"Can he do that? I thought my father had a contract."

"Unfortunately, the agreement stipulates that the property reverts to the seller if payments are delinquent by—" he checked the paperwork "—six months or more. It's been a year and a half, Miss Fox. The owner has already been quite generous."

Ruth felt faint. "Then you're saying we've already lost the dress shop." The words fell like lead. What would they do? The dress shop was her life. She couldn't do anything else.

"The property owner is willing to sign over the deed to your father if the balance—principle and interest—is paid."

Ruth choked. "The full amount?"

"I'm afraid so."

"But that's impossible. The balance must be over a thousand dollars."

Mr. Shea pushed a piece of paper across the desk. The figure he pointed to with his pen made her gasp.

"But we'll never be able to pay that much," she cried. "Not now. Perhaps if I talked to the owner and explained our circumstances, he'd give us more time."

"I doubt that would help. He is already aware of your father's circumstances."

The delicate wording didn't take away the sting. "This other offer, is it better than what we're paying?"

The banker leaned back. "I'm not privy to that information."

It had to be. Moreover, with the outstanding debt, the owner must fear Daddy would never be able to pay the entire loan. If Daddy died…

She swallowed hard. "I must try to convince him. Please? The dress shop is our family's only means of income. Without it, my father would have to leave the sanitarium." She clutched the handle of her handbag so tightly that the metal bit into her palms.

Mr. Shea hesitated a long time before finally looking her in the eye. "I had hoped to discuss this with your mother, but it appears there won't be time for that. Are you in a position to get your parents' approval?"

"I am."

"Then I believe I can offer you some hope. If you can bring your payments current by the end of the month, the bank will pay off the seller and assume the note at the current rate of interest."

Ruth's hope flickered to life. They owed far more than she could scrape together, but the house mortgage must be nearly paid off. If she could convince her parents to borrow against the house... But why hadn't they done that already? Or had they? Was that how they planned to pay for the additional treatments? If so, that left no means to pay up the delinquent loan.

"I'm sorry, Miss Fox, but that is the best we can offer." Mr. Shea truly did look sorry.

Ruth stiffened her back. She would not give up without a fight. "Thank you, and thank the bank board. I would still like to speak with the property owner. Perhaps he can give us more time to come up with the money."

Mr. Shea stared at the paperwork again, this time tapping the end of the fountain pen against his desk blotter. After a long pause, he blew out his breath. "I wouldn't ordinarily reveal this information, but your parents likely know that Holst Vanderloo holds the note on that property."

The bubble of hope burst. The Vanderloos would never

grant an extension. Not now. Not after she'd ruined Mrs. Vanderloo's gowns.

Ruth's head spun. They had to come up with an exorbitant sum by the end of the month, and there was no money in the accounts. She should call the sanitarium, but if Daddy learned of this, he would leave. She couldn't let him sacrifice his health. Ruth had to come up with a moneymaking scheme quickly, or she would lose the dress shop.

On Tuesday, Sam walked around the repaired display case while Peter Simmons looked on with a mixture of pride and worry. "It looks good."

In fact, the case looked great, and Peter had somehow managed to fix it in a few short days. If Sam hadn't known where it had broken, he would never see the repair. Both the color and the grain of the new wood blended seamlessly with the old.

Sam ran a hand over the repair. "How did you manage to match the wood so well?"

Peter grinned. "Pretty good, huh?"

Sam could respect a craftsman who wanted to keep his methods to himself. "Best I've seen."

The lad stood even taller under the well-deserved compliment.

Sam pulled out his wallet and doled out payment, adding a little for the excellent work. "Where did you learn to craft wood like this?"

A cloud passed over Peter's face. "Back at the orphanage. Mr. Galbini—he was one of the guys that came in to help out sometimes—taught me how to do things."

Orphanage? Sam couldn't recall if anyone had mentioned that Peter was an orphan. It did explain why the boy bore no resemblance to Mrs. Simmons.

"Well, he did a fine job teaching you." Sam tucked the wallet back in his jacket. "I'll send the crew over to pick it up."

Peter stared at the money in his hand. When he looked up, he had a funny look on his face. "Ya gave me too much, sir."

"Consider it a bonus for a job well done." Sam clapped the lad on the back. "And on short notice. I appreciate you setting aside your other work."

Peter looked so hopeful that it nearly broke Sam's heart. "Then I can keep it all?"

"Every dollar."

Peter's joy helped make up for the confusion of yesterday and the puzzlement of this morning. One minute he thought Ruth liked him. The next she'd turned away. He'd purposely shown extra deference to Jen to test Ruth's feelings, but Ruth didn't react. The image of her calm, unreadable face was burned into his memory. Then this morning he'd called out a greeting as she crossed the street to her shop, but Ruth hadn't so much as lifted her head. The disappointment had settled into the pit of his stomach like an overly rich meal, unrelieved until Peter's joy reminded him that happiness could be found in other places than a woman's approval.

"Thank you, sir." Peter held the payment reverently. "It's a lot more'n I expected."

"What will you do with the windfall?"

"Give a tithe to the church and most of the rest to my ma, but I'm thinking I might spend a little to take a gal to the dance on Friday."

"A dance, eh? That sounds like a fine idea. Where will it be held?"

"Down at the Grange Hall." Peter pointed to the southeast, a direction Sam hadn't explored yet.

"Well, you have a fine time with your girl."

"If she'll go with me." Peter did not look hopeful, and Sam ached for the lad.

The boy was beanpole-thin and still all angles. His plain brown hair stuck out, and his orphanage background would not endear him to most girls his age. Sam recalled all too well the way girls gravitated toward the handsome and the rich. Peter had the more enduring qualities that would one day make him a fine husband, but he might have to wait a couple of years for the girls to outgrow their idealistic expectations. That would be tough. To an eighteen-year-old, a couple of years might as well be a million. Peter needed encouragement now.

"Treat her like she's the most important person in the world," Sam suggested, "and she'll go with you."

Peter's brow furrowed. "How do I do that?"

Sam stifled a chuckle. "Give her a pretty flower."

"A flower?" Peter looked as if Sam had suggested he hand over the British crown jewels.

"A rose would do. Even a wild lily, as long as you tell her she's as beautiful as the bloom."

Poor Peter looked skeptical.

Sam tried another idea. "Memorize a poem and recite it to her." That one might be a stretch. The suggestions rolled off his tongue easily enough, but as he said them, he knew that wasn't always enough. He'd done all that with Lillian, thinking he was pursuing her only to discover after they wed that the exact opposite was true. But Peter didn't need to hear about Sam's sore luck with women. "Anything you do is bound to work as long as it comes from your heart."

The lad's eyes sparked with hope. "I sure hope you're right. Minnie's got her heart set on this college fella."

Sam's skin prickled. "Minnie?"

"Yeah, Minnie Fox."

Sam had been giving advice to win over the sister of the woman he hadn't succeeded in attracting. "So you like Ruth's little sister."

Peter stiffened. "Not so little. She's eighteen like me."

Sam smothered a smile at the lad's seriousness. "I apologize. I simply meant that she's younger than Ruth." Ruth of the honeyed hair. Ruth, whose pride wouldn't allow her to accept help. Untouchable Ruth. But then he recalled her trembling in his arms. In that moment, she'd shown vulnerability, and he'd wanted so badly to turn her sorrow into laughter.

"You should go to the dance," Peter urged.

Sam suspected the lad wanted moral support, but a dance would only invite problems. "I'm a stranger here. Besides, I don't have a girl to invite."

Peter shrugged. "There's plenty o' unattached gals that'll dance with a fella."

Spinsters, no doubt. Heart sinking, he realized that applied to Ruth. He couldn't let her sit to the side while the other girls danced. Maybe he should go. But a dance was just the sort of social event that would invite questions. He should work late at the store and avoid contact with any of the locals. "I'll think about it."

"It's the biggest dance of the summer," Peter said. "After Founder's Day, that is, but you missed that. Everyone will be there."

"Everyone?"

"Pretty near. Minnie says even her sisters are gonna go."

Ruth. Sam imagined whirling her around the dance floor in a pretty new gown. Ice-blue, for her eyes. Her long hair flowing over her shoulders. Her cheeks flushed from the exertion. Nothing like Lillian. Not a hint of deceit or manipulation. Ruth typified goodness and honesty.

"Maybe I will," he murmured.

Maybe he would take one more chance.

* * *

Jen burst into the dress shop at the very moment Ruth closed the shears on the front panel of the ruined lace gown. Dressmaking always calmed her nerves, and a sleepless night had left her drained and on edge. Yesterday had been disheartening. First the bank debacle. Then her inability to locate a high-paying night job. At this point, Jen's plan was their only hope of saving the dress shop, and that showed little promise of success.

"Do you know what I heard?" Jen panted.

"It can wait until you catch your breath." Ruth examined the errant cut. Thankfully, she'd sliced into the stain. "You look like you ran here from the airfield."

"I came from the drugstore. Do you know what Mrs. Lawrence said?"

"I don't care to hear gossip." Jen was prone to fanning small flames into raging bonfires, and this sounded like just such an occurrence. Moreover, Mrs. Lawrence, who harbored a speakeasy behind the drugstore, was not the most accurate source of news.

"It's not gossip. It's fact." Jen took a few more breaths. "You won't believe what Mrs. Vanderloo is saying about the dress shop."

Ruth didn't want to hear this. No doubt any unkind words stemmed from her husband's ownership of the property, but it still irked her that the woman had demanded the three most expensive gowns in Sam's catalogs. "We shouldn't pass on rumors."

"It's not a rumor. She's saying that we're incompetent. That you ruined her dresses and showed up late with her gowns."

The word *incompetent* stabbed into Ruth more painfully than a needle, but the facts of her statement were unfortunately true. Jen's crazy plan had so distracted Ruth that she'd finished late. But no, she couldn't blame Jen. The fault was entirely hers, and that meant accepting Mrs. Vanderloo's angry criticism.

So Ruth continued to cut the panel. "Everyone is entitled to her opinion."

"You don't care that she's spreading lies?" Jen looked aghast.

"I did ruin her dresses." The irony that she was cutting one of them to pieces at that very moment stilled her hand. "And I was late."

"That doesn't make you incompetent. You're the best dressmaker I know."

Jen's rallying to her defense warmed Ruth's heart. "Thank you, but it doesn't change the facts."

"The fact is that it was an accident. I saw it. You were backing out of the store when Mr. Roth came storming down the boardwalk. He had his head down and didn't see you. If it's anyone's fault, it's his."

"Tell me you didn't say that to Mrs. Lawrence."

"Of course I did. Someone has to set the record straight."

Oh, dear. Now Sam would be furious with Jen. Ruth's hope to match them was falling apart. Only one thing could salvage the situation. She must tell Mrs. Lawrence about Sam's generous offer.

She rose. "Will you watch the shop for a bit? There's something I need to do."

"But I have to go to the airfield. I promised to get things ready for the new students."

Ruth was always amazed that anyone wanted to fly those rickety-looking contraptions, but the flight school drew a continuous flow of students from April through November. "Can't it wait? I'll only be a few minutes." To emphasize the point, Ruth fetched her handbag and hat from the back room.

When she returned, Jen had a smug smile on her face. "Fifteen minutes. I'll give you fifteen minutes."

Ruth had the distinct impression that her sister planned some mischief, but Jen didn't say another word.

"All right," Ruth agreed. "Fifteen minutes."

She pushed out the door, only to find herself once again face-to-face with Sam Roth.

"Miss Fox."

Was she correct that the color had drained from his face the moment he saw her? He must have heard what Jen said to Mrs. Lawrence. "I can explain."

"Explain what?"

"Oh, um…" Oh, dear. He hadn't heard that Jen had blamed him for the problems with Mrs. Vanderloo. She felt that irritating blush heat her cheeks. "I need to explain something."

"I gather that."

She fidgeted with the clasp of her handbag. How exactly could she put this so he wouldn't get angry with Jen? "My sisters are fiercely protective of the family."

"Understandable."

She watched Mr. Devlin skid his Model T to a halt in front of the newspaper offices across the street. He hopped out and raced into the office as if he had breaking news to rush to the presses. Oh, dear, was foreclosure fit news to print? Would she wake in the morning to see her family name in the headlines of the *Pearlman Prognosticator?*

"Miss Fox? Miss Fox?" The way Sam repeated her name, he must have said it several times.

"I'm sorry. I…well, I'm a bit distracted."

"Perhaps we'd better step into the shade." He motioned to the shadows along the buildings.

"No. I'm all right." She pulled her thoughts to the less pressing matter at hand. Sam would understand. He would forgive. Unlike the Vanderloos. She forced a smile. "Apparently Jen heard that one of my clients said I was incompetent—" she choked on the word "—because I'd ruined her dresses, and Jen...well, Jen said that it wasn't my fault. I'm sure she didn't mean to put all the blame on you." She held her breath, waiting for him to explode in anger.

Instead, he laughed. "Is that all?"

She blinked at his reaction. "But it's not fair."

"It's true." Oh, his smile could warm the coldest winter day. "I did cause the problem."

"But Jen didn't know you offered to pay for the dresses, because...because—" She ducked her head rather than face him.

"Because you still think you need to buy them." He tipped her chin. "Look at me, Ruth Fox. You don't need to spend a penny. I want to do this. Please allow me this gift."

A thousand emotions boiled within her. The feel of his hand as he cupped her chin. The concern in his eyes. The compassion. The generosity. Not only did he forgive Jen, but he also wanted to pay for the dresses. Ruth had never met anyone so willing to help a stranger. He couldn't possibly know how desperate their financial situation was and how much this gift meant to them. Maybe once Mrs. Vanderloo saw the dresses, she'd be appeased, and her husband would either grant them a little more time or call off the property sale entirely.

"How can I ever thank you?" she choked out.

"You just did."

She drew in her breath at the warmth of his brown eyes. Cocoa-brown, comforting as a cake just out of the oven. "Thank you," she whispered.

Though he had removed his hand from her chin, she still felt the connection as strongly as if they'd been stitched together by invisible thread.

"You might also agree to save me a dance on Friday," he added.

The air left Ruth's lungs in a whoosh. This Friday's dance was supposed to be Jen's opportunity. Not hers. Jen could win over a man. Ruth only drove them away. Dance with Sam? In front of the entire town? She might be able to create a passable gown, but she couldn't dance. Not one clumsy step.

Still, around Sam she could almost believe anything was possible.

"Just one," he said. Oh, that smile promised such joy.

Dare she? Beatrice said that great risk brought great joy. She bit her lip and nodded.

Sam grinned. "Good. We'll whirl across the floor like professionals."

Oh, dear. She should tell him she couldn't dance, but he was already walking away. Maybe she'd get sick before Friday.

Chapter Eight

With the display case back in place the following afternoon and the first merchandise due to arrive at the end of the week, Sam felt confident the store would open on time. At the moment, the odor of fresh paint and varnish permeated the air, but large electrical fans circulated the fumes out the upper windows and brought the fresh air in. By the grand opening the store would smell fresh and new.

From his vantage point on the mezzanine, he could see the whole floor take shape. Women's clothing up front. Menswear farther back. Children's clothing to the left. Accessories in the center. Household items in the rear. The shelves and racks and display cases were in place, except toward the back, where workmen were still plastering the walls.

Sam tapped his fingertips on the railing. The plastering should have been finished before he arrived, but nothing could be done about it now. The men did work quickly once set on a task, but the plaster had to dry before it could be painted. He figured the last of the painting wouldn't be done before Monday.

To stay on schedule, he'd have to unpack some of the merchandise before the last of the painting. Risky, but he saw no alternative. Once the clothing went on display, the huge space would come to life. Color and texture. Glittering metal against sumptuous softness.

As the workers finished up for the day, Sam closed his eyes and imagined Ruth dressed in one of the stunning new gowns he'd ordered. Pale blue chiffon would bring out her eyes. A rhinestone necklace would sparkle like drops of dew on a morning lily. He'd lead her onto the dance floor, and within a few steps the shyness would melt away. Then everyone would see her God-given beauty.

"Mr. Rothenburg?" Miss Harris called out from behind him. "A long-distance call from your father just came in."

Sam groaned. The old man was checking up on him again. Sam was tempted to tell Miss Harris to inform Father that he was busy, but he didn't want to put her through the man's wrath.

"I'll be right there." Sam took one last survey of his store and returned to the office.

Miss Harris shot him a sympathetic look and pulled her handbag from the desk drawer. "I can wait until you're done."

Like everyone else, she'd put in a long day.

"No need to stay." Sam preferred to keep this telephone call private anyway.

She looked relieved and hurried out before he changed his mind.

Sam took a deep breath before facing yet another demanding conversation. Maybe Ruth had a point in going without a phone in the dress shop. She didn't have to deal with long-distance management. Father wanted the store ready yesterday. Someone must have told him the plastering was running late. He ran through the likely snitches. Miss Harris, perhaps, but she'd been loyal to him during this whole start-up. The floor manager was Father's man, but so were the work crews. Anyone might have reported the progress delays.

He took his time settling into the chair before picking up the receiver. "Father. To what do I owe the pleasure?"

"What's taking you so long?"

Sam took a deep breath and shrugged off the implied insult. "The store is on schedule for an August third opening."

"That's not what I meant. I expected a report on the property next door by the end of the day Monday. It's Wednesday. Afternoon."

Sam gritted his teeth as he reordered his thoughts. Saying one word about the dress shop felt like betrayal. If Ruth knew his father wanted to purchase the property, she'd think Sam had befriended her only to gain the upper hand in a real-estate transaction. That wasn't true. He'd never intended to steal away her store. Its demise might be an unwelcome result of Hutton's opening next door, but he wasn't to blame. Or was he?

"Well?" Father demanded. "Did you do anything, or do I have to send Harry out there to finish the job?"

Anger flared deep inside. Father had always pitted him against Harry. Sam's younger brother was more like Father in temperament—decisive, unemotional, ruthless. Sam took after his mother, a fact that Father never hesitated to point out.

"I have things under control." Sam kept his words measured so he wouldn't betray the emotion behind them.

"Your brother should have been born first," Father snapped. "He would have assessed the property the same day and negotiated directly with the owner. Instead, I had to step in and discover the bank is holding up the transaction. No doubt they want a cut, and for what? Standing in the way of progress, that's what. Who ever heard of such a convoluted way to do business?"

"I don't understand what you're talking about. The bank holds the note, don't they?"

Nothing came across the line in reply, and Sam hoped they'd lost the connection.

Father growled, "Apparently, you haven't done a thing. If you had, you'd know about the bank arrangement."

"This might come as news to you, but I'm trying to get a store open on time."

Father ignored Sam's excuse. "The bank is acting as agent for the owner, for a cut of the interest. If the buyer defaults—and he's already in default—the property reverts to the owner."

Sam felt sick. If what Father said was true, then Ruth's family had already lost the dress shop. Only they didn't know it.

"Then there's nothing to be done," Sam murmured as he envisioned Ruth learning the terrible news, closing the shop and watching Father raze the building. He gripped the telephone receiver so tightly that his fingers ached.

"There's plenty to be done," Father snapped. "That incompetent banker gave the buyer until the end of the month to pay up." Over the line, Sam heard his father slam down his fist. "Ridiculous, small-town way to do business, if you ask me."

Relief washed over Sam. Fox Dress Shop could still be saved, if the Foxes could come up with the money. But that was the problem. If they'd had the money, the payments wouldn't be delinquent. Why hadn't the oldest sister stepped in? That diamond ring and string of pearls around her neck would go a long way toward paying off the loan. The one thing Sam had observed about the Fox sisters was their closeness. When one fell into trouble, the others leaped to support her. If Beatrice hadn't acted, then she must not know. Perhaps none of them knew. Their parents were away, their father in the hospital. Ruth might be completely oblivious to the looming disaster.

"What do you expect me to do?" he asked his father even as he settled on a completely different course of action.

"Find out who the owner is. The bank won't tell me, but the owner's name is bound to be on the deed. Get his name to me right away. Do you hear me?"

"Yes, but…" Sam struggled to come up with something that would both deflate his father's interest in the property and buy him time to warn the Foxes. "It's a small lot, hardly worth the trouble."

"It's a dress shop next door. Competition must be eliminated."

Father's thirst for commercial domination had never sounded so wrong. Sam swallowed the bile rising in his throat.

"It's a tiny shop in a small town. They're no competition."

"You getting soft on me, boy?" Static crackled on the line, but Sam still understood every word. "This is business."

"Business." Sam echoed the hollow excuse for reprehensible behavior. Why had he never considered the consequences that Hutton's brought to a neighborhood or town? If Father progressed on this course, and every indicator said he would, then Ruth's family would suffer. According to what Father said, the only way the Foxes could keep the shop was to bring the delinquent payments current. Judging by their paltry number of customers, business was stagnant. The family couldn't save their shop without help. The moment this call ended, Sam would find that help.

"I want the owner's name tomorrow," Father insisted, finally drawing to a close. "Today, if possible. I expect you to get it right this time, or I'll send someone who can."

Without another word, the line clicked dead.

"I don't know what to do," Ruth admitted to Beatrice.

After closing the shop for the day, she'd joined her older sister and the children at the park. On this hot evening, they'd gratefully claimed a shaded bench. After throwing bits of stale bread to the ducks and chasing pigeons, the children had finally settled down. Tillie set up a tiny tea set, and little Branford fell asleep. The boy's long lashes brushed his hot cheeks as he slept with arms thrown wide, completely trusting his mother's care.

Ruth sighed. "If only I could know that kind of peace, but I can hardly sleep an hour or two before waking and worrying about what's happening."

"What is happening?" Beatrice's fine voile skirts spread out in a pastel pink cloud as she leaned to her right to clasp Ruth's hand. "Have you received news about Daddy?"

"No, that's not it."

"Then what has you so distressed? Surely it's not that nice Mr. Roth."

"No. Not him." Ruth hesitated. Beattie had enough troubles of her own, but Ruth could think of no other way to get the money to pay off the loan. "I had a meeting with Mr. Shea Monday morning."

Worry flickered across Beattie's face. "At the bank?"

Ruth nodded. "They sent a letter to the house requesting a meeting." She took a deep breath before plunging ahead. "Apparently the man who holds the note on the dress shop received an offer to purchase the property."

"I don't understand." Beatrice's brow creased. "Isn't the mortgage with the bank?"

"Apparently the bank is only facilitating the loan. If we can't find the money to bring the payments current, we could lose the dress shop." She didn't want to explain the ins and outs of the situation when the bottom line would do. Thanks to the bank's generous offer, they had to make only the back payments.

Beatrice looked down at her hands. "You want me to help."

"I'm sorry. I can't think of anyone else who could loan us the money." Ruth bit her lip.

"But I thought Daddy had money set aside."

"All gone."

"How?" Beatrice's eyes grew wide.

"The medical treatments. Fewer customers." Ruth couldn't bear to mention her mother's mismanagement of the accounts. At this point it made little difference. "I'm afraid we're broke."

Beatrice stared at Ruth a long moment before shakily looking away. A hand rose to her throat. "Poor Daddy."

That was the worst of it. "I'm afraid he might have to leave the sanitarium."

"Thus Jen's plan."

"Thus Jen's plan. It's pie in the sky, but that shows how desperate we are. If we lose the dress shop, I don't know what we'll do."

"Oh, Ruth." Beatrice's eyes glistened with unshed tears. "Have you told Mother and Daddy?"

Ruth shook her head. "Daddy isn't supposed to have any stress."

Beatrice sighed. "This news would certainly be stressful."

"I don't know what to do. I've gotten to the point that I'm actually considering Jen's idea, but how could it possibly succeed? Marry into wealth? Impossible."

"Not quite impossible." Beatrice clasped Ruth's hands. "Mr. Roth is quite taken with you."

Ruth yanked her hands away. "I wish everyone would stop assuming he is interested in me. Jen would suit him better. She's lively and vivacious."

"But he likes *you*. I could see it in his eyes, in the way he watched you and looked after you."

Impossible. Men simply were not attracted to her. Never had been. Never would be. Especially men like Sam. "But I wear glasses."

Beattie laughed. "What difference does that make? Any man worth having will see beyond the surface to your inner beauty."

Ruth cringed at the familiar platitude. Experience had taught her otherwise. The pretty girls got beaus. The pretty girls drew attention. Plain girls sat on the sideline. She jutted out her chin. "I've accepted my place in life. God gave me skill with the needle so I could help my family."

"Is that what you truly believe?"

Ruth could not admit that she longed for a husband and family of her own. "I'm content."

"Oh, Ruth. You deserve so much more than being content. You deserve love."

"I have my family's love, and that's enough for me."

"But a husband...and children." Beatrice gazed at Tillie, who was arranging the cups and saucers in a perfect, precious circle. "You can't imagine the joy."

And the pain. That was the part Beatrice was leaving out. Ruth knew Blake Kensington, had known him as long as Beatrice. For a moment she almost let slip her deepest secret, how Blake had cruelly used her to get to Beatrice, but revealing that would only open raw wounds.

So she squeezed Beattie's hand. "They're wonderful children."

At that, Tillie looked to her mother. "Aw right?"

Beatrice smiled. "You've set it up perfectly." She knelt on the blanket and lifted a jar of lemonade from their basket. She then poured some of the cool liquid into the pretty little porcelain teapot. "Tillie, dear, will you serve the tea for us?"

Tillie's eyes shone at her mother's trust. Her clumsy hands could barely hold on to the teapot, but with determination she began to pour.

"You're so good with Tillie and Branford," Ruth said softly so she wouldn't distract the serious business of pouring "tea."

"You are, too." Beattie patted her hand. "You have a loving heart. Any man would be fortunate to have you for his bride."

"Bride?" Ruth choked on the unfulfilled wish. From the time she was Tillie's age, Ruth had dreamed of walking down the aisle to her beloved's side.

Beattie's laugh tinkled on the hot air like a cool breeze. "I believe Jen and Minnie might be right about Mr. Roth's affections, but there's only one way to find out." Beatrice leaned close to whisper. "You need to spend some time together. Friday's dance will give you an ideal opportunity to ascertain his feelings."

His feelings? Ruth's stomach roiled at the thought of dancing with him in front of everyone. "What am I going to do? He asked me to save him a dance."

Beattie's eyes lit up. "How wonderful."

"Not so wonderful. I don't know how to dance."

"You don't? But...I thought everyone learned in school."

A decade later, Ruth was still embarrassed by her failure. She could still hear the laughter. *Ribbit. Ribbit.* All elbows and knees and nerves. She'd stumbled time after time until the instructor gave up, saying it wouldn't matter anyway since Ruth would never be asked to dance. "I couldn't learn."

"Done, Mama." Tillie looked at them with obvious pride.

Lemonade soaked the blanket and pooled in the saucers. Instead of scolding, Beattie commended her daughter.

"It looks so pretty," Ruth added as she scooted forward to join the party.

Beatrice caught her arm. "Don't fret. I'll teach you to dance."

Ruth appreciated her sister's confidence, but she didn't know how Beattie would succeed where others had failed.

Right after Father ended the call, Sam left to find the one person who could help Ruth's family. He got Beatrice Kensington's address from the clerk at the mercantile. Their house was several blocks away, at the foot of what Ruth called "the hill" and others dubbed "Kensington Estates." The area didn't have a sign demarking it from the rest of Pearlman, but the distinction was evident from the shift to stately homes and manicured yards.

The fresh air and brisk walk reinvigorated Sam, but the idea that he might be able to thwart Father's property deal put a tune on his lips. He nodded at the pastor as they passed. Just off Elm Street stood a large Victorian house with an inviting porch. The wrought-iron gate slipped open easily, and the yard, bursting with blooms, promised a sunny reception.

Instead, the maid who answered the door informed him, "The missus took the children to the park."

Sam thanked her and headed to the site of Sunday's picnic, where he'd comforted Ruth, only to have her push him aside in an obvious attempt to promote Jen. Then the woman did an about-face and promised him a dance on

Friday. He would never understand what went through the female mind. Thankfully, he wouldn't have to deal with her today.

Or so he thought.

The moment he entered the park, he spotted the fashionable Mrs. Beatrice Kensington seated on a blanket in the shade of a tall oak. Her little girl held up a miniature teacup, but the energetic boy appeared to have exhausted himself into a nap. Unfortunately, a fourth figure rounded out the group, and even from a distance he could tell it was Ruth.

How would he broach the subject in front of Ruth? It was going to be difficult enough to convince Beatrice. If necessary, he'd decided to reveal his father's involvement, but he couldn't tell Ruth that. She would put an abrupt and permanent end to their growing friendship. Yet he must speak to Beatrice Kensington today.

He would wait them out. Perhaps Ruth would leave first. Then he could address Mrs. Kensington without the presence of her sister.

Spotting a discarded newspaper on a bench, he dropped to the seat and unfolded the paper. He then slid to the other end of the bench, where a lilac bush, its blooms long spent, offered a bit of a screen. The Fox sisters sat less than twenty yards away. The little girl's squeals of delight reached his ears. He lifted the newspaper and pretended interest in an article on President Harding's anticipated arrival in Vancouver. Occasionally he peeked at the Fox party. They showed no indication of leaving.

Something thudded against his shoe.

"Sorry, mister."

Sam lowered the newspaper to see a lad of perhaps twelve. The towheaded boy waved an errant baseball. Sam noted the children on the diamond waiting for the lad to bring back the foul ball.

"Your team winning?" he asked.

The youngster burst into a gap-toothed grin. "Ten to nothin'."

"Keep up the good work."

"Yessir!" The lad sped off with the ball.

Sam watched the lad return to his chums, and a surprising ache rose inside. He hadn't thought about children for years. Lillian had miscarried early in their marriage and barred the door to her bedroom afterward. Then she'd died. He'd been resigned to never having a son, but the boy's grin revived a long-lost hope. A son to play ball with. He sneaked a glance at Ruth.

The tea party was still under way. The breeze had shifted, however, and now carried the group's voices his way. Beatrice's soprano came through more clearly than Ruth's softer alto, but from one side of the conversation—interspersed with little Tillie's cries of delight—he could make out the general tenor of their talk.

"Next you serve the tea cakes."

No doubt Beatrice was instructing her daughter.

After a lengthy pause accented by murmured approval, Tillie shrieked with delight.

"Hush now. Don't wake your brother."

Good thinking, there. Little Branford would put a smashing end to their little tea party.

The voices dropped lower, and Sam inched a little closer to the end of the bench. Noting a party of four ambling up from the river, he raised the newspaper. Unfortunately, their laughter drowned out Beatrice and Ruth. One of the women looked familiar. He'd seen that dark bobbed hair and coquettish manner before. Sam racked his memory until he figured out that she was the woman who had foisted herself on him the first afternoon in town. That woman would not hesitate to bring him to everyone's attention.

He pulled the paper closer and waited for them to pass. And waited. Surely they would walk this way eventually, but they hadn't passed yet.

He hazarded a glance. They'd crossed to the pavilion. A nattily dressed man held the annoying brunette. She cradled her head on his shoulder. He slung an arm around her shoulders. A memory flashed through Sam's mind. His best friend and his wife in an intimate embrace.

Sam crumpled the edge of the paper.

"I don't know what else to do." Ruth's plea interrupted his agonized memories.

If he could hear her, she must be close. He sneaked a glimpse. Sure enough, Ruth had pulled her sister to the other side of his lilac bush, close to the children but out of earshot.

Sam shrank behind the newspaper. He shouldn't listen to this conversation. He should announce his presence or walk away, but either action would reveal that he had been sitting there all this time.

"Could you please ask?" Ruth said.

Sam could almost hear Ruth clutch her sister's arm.

Beatrice's voice had grown soft. "Of course I'll ask, but you know I can't promise anything."

Sam wondered if they were discussing the outstanding debt.

"I know," Ruth said, "but I can't think of any other way. I'm losing hope."

Beatrice sucked in her breath. "You have to have hope. God promised to see us through hard times."

"He did, but He didn't say there wouldn't be hard times. Do you think Blake will loan us the money?"

They were discussing the debt.

A long pause ensued before Beatrice sighed. "I don't know."

Only it sounded more like *no*.

Chapter Nine

Thursday night, after Jen and Minnie had fallen asleep, Ruth crept downstairs to the living room and lit an oil lamp. The warm glow gilded the pages of the ledger but didn't change the result. No matter how many times she recalculated, the answer was always the same. They were broke.

Beatrice hadn't yet asked her husband for help, and Ruth worried that the request might further damage her sister's marriage. Yesterday, she'd told Beatrice to forget she'd ever asked, but that left her with nowhere else to turn.

No solution worked. Only the impossible remained—Jen's idea. That did not promise good results, for the task fell to the least likely sister to win a man's heart. Ruth wasn't romantic-minded like Minnie or beautiful like Beatrice. She didn't captivate a man's adventurous side like Jen. No, she was plain old Ruth. Dressmaker. Homebody.

The dance was tomorrow night, and she wasn't ready. Despite Beattie's efforts to teach her the basic steps of a waltz, Ruth still tripped over her own feet. Her gown had been cobbled together from Mrs. Vanderloo's ruined gown and scraps of fabric. Once there, what charming words could she come up with to win over Sam's heart? Ruth didn't have

Jen's wit or Beattie's graciousness. Under duress, her mind went blank.

"Lord, how is this possible?" she whispered into the still night air.

The dark room hung heavy with the day's heat, and the shadows that danced beyond the lamp's range mocked her. *Impossible. Hopeless. Worthless.*

She struggled against the flood of doubt. How could she succeed? Yet Daddy's well-being sat squarely on her shoulders.

"What do I do?" she whispered into the darkness.

Read the Word. Mother's answer to any of life's problems popped into Ruth's mind.

Ruth ran her hand over the dark leather cover of the family Bible, cracked and darkened around the edges. The gilded letters had worn off long ago, leaving only the embossing. Ruth drew strength from the generations that had turned to God's Word for answers.

She opened to the Gospel of Luke, her favorite. At first she read from the beginning, but soon began to skim through the pages until her vision blurred.

She leaned her head against the back of the chair and closed her eyes.

She was tired, so tired. Her eyes ached. Her brain ached. Every muscle in her body cried for sleep.

Read the Word.

Her eyes flew open. Mother's words rang in her ears, as vivid as if she'd heard them spoken.

The oil lamp still glowed. The words no longer swam, but nothing stood out, either.

She flipped the page. Then the next. And the next.

She read about the prodigal. And the master who entrusted his fortune to three servants. But none of that helped.

She turned page after page through Luke and into the Gospel of John.

Again the words blurred. Again she rested her head against the back of the chair and closed her eyes.

Tired. So tired. Just a little rest. A few minutes.

Read the Word.

Ruth jolted awake. No one had said that, yet the words felt jarringly real. So much so that they'd driven every bit of tiredness from her bones.

This time when she looked down, her gaze landed on one verse.

Abide in Me, and I in you. As the branch cannot bear fruit of itself, except it abide in the vine; no more can ye, except ye abide in Me.

She'd heard this passage about the vine and branches many a time, but how did it answer her problem? A vineyard was not a dress shop, nor did this chapter say anything about managing a vineyard except to prune unproductive branches.

She groaned in frustration. This exercise hadn't helped one bit. In the end, the only course left to her was the most impossible. And the most difficult.

"Lord, help me win Sam's heart."

It was her only hope.

Late the following afternoon, Sam tapped the end of a fountain pen on his desk blotter and stared at the telephone. His research had led to an unsettling conclusion. Vanderloo owned the dress-shop property, and Sam could do nothing to help Ruth. All that remained was the call to his father that would seal Ruth's fate. He'd avoided doing so until now, doubtless incurring Father's wrath, but he'd reasoned that if he waited until the end of the business week, he would have the weekend to come up with a solution.

The time to place that call had arrived.

In the silence of the empty store, his thoughts bounced wildly between impossible scenarios. Beatrice could still come through. He might persuade his father to drop the matter. Vanderloo might not slam the door in his face next time. Each stood less than 1 percent chance of success.

Most likely Father would buy the property and force the Foxes out of the dress shop. What happened next played over and over in Sam's mind. Ruth's father would leave the hospital. The family would descend into poverty. Mr. Fox would die, sending Ruth and her sisters into mourning.

All because of Sam's insistence they open a Hutton's in Pearlman. An unexpected detour a year ago en route to Grand Rapids had brought him here. The quaint town reminded him of his most treasured childhood memory. Their family had been stranded in a small Pennsylvania town at Christmastime due to a snowstorm. With the trains not moving and telephone lines down, they'd had no choice but to celebrate the holiday there. Father had strolled the streets with them. It was the only time Sam could recall his father showing genuine joy. He'd even bought Sam a gift.

Sam lifted the old kaleidoscope and aimed it at the window, where the descending sun filtered through the leaves of the maple next door. Through the eyepiece he watched the colors and shapes shift with every turn of the tumbler. As a boy, he'd been fascinated with the piece. Its working had seemed wondrous. One day Father explained how mirrors and bits of colored glass created the patterns. On that day Sam lost faith in the unseen, but science could not mend a broken heart.

He raked a hand through his hair. He'd run out of time and options. The call must be made.

He lifted the receiver and reached the local operator,

who placed the long-distance call. After several rings, Mother answered.

Her gentle voice always lifted his spirits.

After the usual inquiries about her health and happiness, he had to relinquish the pleasure for pain. "Is Father home?"

"Not yet. It's so good to hear your voice, Samuel." Mother always used their full names.

Sam relished his mother's affection, but as much as he would rather talk to Mother, his father expected a response. "Do you expect him soon?"

"You know your father." Her wistful sigh reminded Sam of the countless days she'd waited late into the evening for her husband's return. At his entrance, she would rush to greet him, only to be brushed aside with some excuse as he stormed to his study. Mother had never complained and never showed any hurt feelings. If Sam remarried, he'd do better by his wife.

He drew a breath. "I could use your help."

"Me?" Her shock could be heard over the static-filled line.

"With Father." Then Sam explained the situation with Ruth's family and that Father wanted to buy their dress shop.

"I see," she said slowly. "You must like this Miss Fox a great deal."

Like Ruth? Mother's words thundered over the line. He did like her. He enjoyed every moment in her company, but this wasn't about his esteem for Ruth. For Mother to think that it was meant he'd blathered on too much about Ruth's fine qualities.

"That's not the point," he said, driving the conversation away from dangerous emotional territory and back to the matter at hand. "The property is inconsequential to

Father, but vital to the Fox family. It's simple charity." But even as he said the words, he knew they weren't true. His involvement had passed the bounds of charity days ago. "Can you speak to Father about it?"

Mother sighed deeply. "He wouldn't listen to me."

Sam heard the pain and isolation behind her words. "I can't believe that." But he knew the truth of it. Father didn't listen to him, either.

"Oh, it's all right. I learned long ago that your father only hears what he wants to hear."

"It wasn't always that way. Remember our Christmas in that little town in Pennsylvania? Father laughed back then. I remember him holding me up to look in the shop windows."

"People change, Samuel."

Lillian's face flashed through Sam's mind. People did change, for the worse. "I have stunning proof of that."

"Please don't hold on to bitterness over what happened with Lillian."

"I'm not bitter," he snapped, "and I don't want to talk about her. It's over and done."

"I'm glad to hear that. Only by letting go and forgiving Lillian can you begin to love another, like your Miss Fox."

Love Ruth? Sam's gut knotted. He wasn't ready for that sort of commitment. "I'm too busy with the company to think about the future."

Mother sighed. "You sound so much like your father."

She could not have said anything that cut more deeply. "I'm nothing like Father."

"I know, dear. Do remember that you can count on God to get you through whatever may come. His love is steadfast. Place your faith in the Lord, and you'll never be disappointed."

Sam appreciated his mother's ability to draw peace from

her faith, but he couldn't place all his trust in an unseen God. "I need to change Father's mind, and I hoped you could make him understand how much the Foxes need that dress shop."

"You can do that yourself. He told me this morning that he plans to leave for that little town of yours on Monday."

Sam sat back heavily. That meant Father would arrive on the last day of the month, no doubt to sign the property deal the following day. If Sam was going to help Ruth's family, he must come up with a solution in the next three days.

"Please give Miss Fox my best," Mother said. "I hope to meet her one day."

Introducing Ruth to his parents meant courtship. Sam gripped the telephone receiver tightly, as if he could close off this topic by squeezing shut the line. He was not ready for courtship or marriage. He'd vowed never to enter that arena again, but Mother's words opened his eyes to the obvious.

Marriage was the one sure way to save Ruth's family.

Even before Ruth arrived at the Grange Hall, her stomach had knotted. She couldn't get a bite of supper down. Her hands shook. Her knees quaked as she climbed the steps into the hall. The wooden floor shook under the pounding of many feet. The band played a lively tune.

She couldn't do this.

Attract Sam Roth? What had she been thinking? She had placed all her hope on the hopeless. For despite her sisters' fussing over her hair and gown, she still looked like an old goose in a princess's gown.

"I'm going home."

"No, you're not." Jen corralled her. "You're dancing

with your Mr. Roth." She and Minnie dragged Ruth toward the line of eagerly waiting girls.

Thankfully, Ruth couldn't see the others clearly. Jen had talked her into leaving her glasses at home. The blur of dresses swirling across the floor made her head spin. These girls wouldn't make a misstep. They wouldn't endure awkward pauses in the conversation.

"This is a bad idea." One dance lesson was not enough.

Ruth shrank when Mrs. Vanderloo swooped near on the arm of her husband. Even though Ruth had dyed the ruined gown and restyled it completely, she feared the woman would recognize it.

"Go out there." Jen pushed her toward the line of girls hoping to claim a dance partner. "No one will ask you to dance when you're standing back here with the wallflowers."

"But—" Ruth almost explained that she was comfortable with the wallflowers, that she *was* a wallflower, but Jen and Minnie had spent precious money crafting her an elegant turban to match the dress. Its rhinestones drew too much attention, in Ruth's opinion, but her sisters had been so excited. Beattie had even loaned Ruth her crystal necklace. For a moment, Ruth had almost believed the reflection in the mirror. The elegant woman looking back at her could live in Kensington Estates, but that was only a looking-glass fantasy.

Here at the hall, reality set in. No fancy gown or glittering turban could hide the fact that plain old Ruth Fox had come to the dance to catch a man.

"I'll join you," Minnie said, tugging her toward the line of girls waiting for a dance partner.

"Me, too." Jen grabbed her other hand.

Ruth's stomach lurched. "I need air."

Ruth's sisters either ignored her or didn't hear, and Ruth

could not break their iron grip. Her stomach spun faster than a sewing-machine pulley.

"I can't see," she hissed.

"We'll tell you who's coming," Jen said. "There's Peter Simmons, and he's carrying a yellow rose. Minnie, get ready. He's headed for you."

"No, he's not." Minnie hissed back at Jen.

Ruth could feel her youngest sister's tension and could sympathize.

The lanky young man stopped in front of Minnie and shoved the flower at her. "Wanna dance?"

Minnie trembled. "I'm busy." She looked left and right. "I'm waiting for someone. I'll check the door to the hall." Without another word, she fled.

Ruth felt rather than saw Peter's dejection. The unclaimed yellow bloom fell to the floor, and then he excused himself and left.

"It's so tragic," Jen sighed. "He likes her but she can't think of anyone but Reggie."

"Peter's the better guy." It didn't feel quite right calling him a "man" just yet.

"At least with Minnie standing scout at the door we'll know when your Mr. Roth arrives. Don't worry. It'll work out perfectly."

Ruth did not see how. She had come here to win a man's affection and get him to offer marriage. It was wrong, terribly wrong. A gentleman should take the lead, like Peter did with Minnie, not vice versa.

She would gladly give up the entire night in order to run home to hide in her bedroom. But if she didn't do this, Daddy would have to leave the sanitarium. She must attempt to win over Sam, no matter how painful. She took a deep breath and stepped forward.

Her knees wobbled, but she somehow managed to arrive

at the line of waiting girls. She must be the oldest of the lot. Even Eloise Grattan was too sensible to place herself on display like this. At least she couldn't see the sneers that undoubtedly followed her.

"Here's a spot," Jen said, squeezing them both into the narrowest gap. "Hello, Jane."

Though Ruth couldn't make out her features in the dim light, the girl's response identified her as Jane Grozney, whose older sister, Paulette, had married at seventeen and had her first baby a year later. Jane had been in Minnie's class and, according to her sister, was eager for a husband. How could she ever compete with girls Minnie's age?

Ruth hugged her aching midsection.

"Stop looking so nervous," Jen ordered. "And put your arms down. You're wrinkling your dress."

"As if you ever cared about wrinkles." Teasing her sister doused some of the nerves.

"Here comes Gil Vanderloo."

Oh, dear. He probably intended to snub her or say something nasty. Ruth edged back, but Jen yanked her forward.

"Hi, Gil. How's college?" Jen asked brightly.

Ruth pinched her sister's arm to get her to stop. The last thing she wanted was to talk to any Vanderloo.

"Would you care to dance?" His nasal tone insinuated superiority.

Ruth drew in her breath. She couldn't tell whom he'd asked to dance. If it was Jen, perhaps she should encourage her. After all, Jen had suggested Gil as her first choice.

"Go ahead," she whispered to her sister.

But instead, Jane Grozney warbled a throaty "Me?" and left with Gil.

"I'm sorry," Ruth said.

Jen laughed. "He's too short anyway. And painfully dull."

Ruth could imagine Jen's wrinkled nose even though she couldn't see it.

"Oh!" Jen chirped, her grip on Ruth's arm tightening. "There he is. Oh, Ruth. I wish you could see Sam. He's so handsome in his black tuxedo. Oh, my. His vest must be silk, and he has a white rose in his lapel. Every single girl is looking at him."

That did not make Ruth feel better.

Jen squeezed tighter. "He's headed this way. Stand up straight. Your turban's a little crooked. And the clasp on your necklace worked its way to the front."

Jen fussed over her until Ruth pushed her away. "Stop it. He probably wants to talk to you anyway. He only asked me for one dance."

Ruth expected her sister to protest, but Jen's attention was focused straight ahead at the mass of moving humanity that looked to Ruth like nothing more than a swirl of color and motion.

"Mr. Roth," Jen said as a tall, dark figure halted before them.

"Miss Jen. Miss Fox." He drew in his breath ever so slightly. "I've never seen anyone so lovely. That shade of blue makes your eyes shine like sapphires."

Ruth felt the blood rush to her cheeks. Jen's eyes were hazel, and she wasn't wearing blue. He wasn't looking at Ruth's sister. He was complimenting her.

"I trust you saved a dance for me," he said.

Ruth nodded. She couldn't tell him that no one else had asked her to dance. She couldn't say a thing.

"Good. I hear the band starting a new tune. Ah, the 'Tennessee Waltz.' Shall we?"

Ruth's pulse accelerated, and she forgot every step that Beatrice had drilled into her head. Every instinct told her to flee, but Jen shoved her forward. If Sam extended his arm, Ruth couldn't discern it in the dim light.

"You did promise," he urged.

"She's just shy," Jen announced to Ruth's mortification, "and hasn't danced much."

"Don't be afraid," he said softly. "Just follow my lead."

His lead? She was supposed to follow? Ruth gulped. Beatrice had mentioned the man leading, but the instant Ruth heard it wasn't her responsibility, she'd stopped listening. She never dreamed it meant she had to do something.

Jen must have figured out the problem because she whispered, "Lift your hand."

"I'll be with you for every step." He took her hand and placed it on his arm.

Ruth's nerves fled under Sam's confident strength. His compliments comforted her. If only they didn't have to dance, but he guided her onto the nearly empty floor. Only one other couple remained from the previous dance. She stood in the open, where everyone could see her fail.

Ruth clutched his arm tighter.

"You'll have to let go." He chuckled and gently pried her hand from his arm.

After facing her, he took her right hand in his left while his other hand wrapped around her waist. His touch generated the most delicious sensation. Not the kind of excitement that Minnie talked about all the time, but the feeling of being secure and cherished. Had he felt it, too? The tender connection held them together with the fragility of a silk thread, but even silk could bear much weight if many strands were woven together. With Sam's assistance, perhaps she could do this.

Her heart thumped and her head spun as the room narrowed to just the two of them. This close, she could see him, and what she saw took her breath away. He gazed at her with such tenderness that she melted. Those cocoa eyes drew her in. The gentle smile made her forget that she was a poor spinster. Sam Roth treated her like a queen.

From far away the strains of the waltz urged them to move. The air had grown thick, and the music faded. She sensed the movement of his body to her right, but her feet stuck to the floor. By the time he'd taken one long step, she was hopelessly behind. She shuffled rapidly and counted faster, but he was ahead of her again. This time she took a bigger step and landed square on his foot.

He groaned.

She cringed. "I'm sorry."

Then she stepped on his other foot. Mortified, she shot backward out of his grasp and careened into another dancer. The impact sent Ruth off-balance. She flailed her arms, but could not recover. Everything slowed.

No. No. No. This could not happen. Not in front of everyone.

Yet it was happening. Sam slid out of view as she went down.

Chapter Ten

Sam caught Ruth and pulled her close. She felt so right in his arms. So vulnerable. So lovely. Her porcelain complexion. Her perfectly curved lips. So thoroughly kissable.

Her eyes widened, and her mouth drew into a perfect circle.

Had she read his thoughts? The middle of a dance floor was no place to claim a first kiss, not with a woman like Ruth.

Still, he couldn't rip his gaze away. The stunning dress of silver-blue lace atop midnight-blue satin only highlighted the flush of her cheeks. He'd never seen anyone so beautiful. Her eyes were especially brilliant tonight. He could not ignore their pull. Nor could he deny that in the course of one short week, his feelings for her had surpassed mere friendship. Any man would help a woman who'd stumbled. He wanted to prevent her from ever stumbling again. He wanted to wipe away every tear and worried look. He wanted to make her smile. That made the decision he'd arrived at after talking to his father more palatable. But not here, in front of everyone. This must be a private moment. He must convince her to join him outside.

"Ruth." Her name shone with the luster of the finest pearl, and he could get no further.

Her lips softened at the mention of her name, and without thinking, he cradled her head. Such soft skin. Such luminous eyes. He brushed his thumb down her temple. That was when he realized why her eyes looked so different tonight. And why she'd stumbled.

"You forgot your glasses." He withdrew his hand from what had been far too intimate a gesture. "No wonder you tripped."

Her smile crumpled, and liquid pooled in those lovely eyes. Her lips, so inviting mere seconds ago, now quivered. She ducked her head, but not before he saw the flush of embarrassment on her cheeks.

She liked him.

Now *he* felt a little shaky. During his debate over what to do, he'd never considered that she might already harbor feelings for him. That fact threw his perfectly logical plan out of kilter. A practical marriage was one thing. Marriage for love was quite another. He'd married Lillian for love and look how that turned out. Peter was in love with Minnie, who'd scorned the lad's attempt to win her heart. Sam had found Peter outside, dejected, and no amount of encouragement could convince the boy to go back into the hall.

Sam could understand. The room closed in on him. He couldn't breathe. He had to get out of the hall. Now.

But Ruth awaited his next move.

He fought back the desire to flee. Ruth deserved to be treated with respect, not abandoned on the dance floor.

"I need to go outside for some air." He motioned toward the door, unsure she could hear over the music.

"Me, too."

He wasn't sure he wanted her following, but her shy

smile whisked away the doubts. Ruth was not Lillian. She did not manipulate men. She kept no secrets.

He offered her his arm. When she placed her pale hand on his black sleeve, he marveled at the delicate fingers. Though his heart pounded and he longed to pull her close, he kept her at a respectful distance as they threaded through the crowd. Some of the older ladies watched with unconcealed interest. Whispered comments were exchanged behind fans and gloved hands. Clearly he had violated Pearlman's strict standards of propriety. He hoped Ruth's poor vision prevented her from noticing.

Between eager girls, proud mothers and curious businessmen, Sam got stopped dozens of times before reaching the door. Perspiration dampened his brow. The air thickened. He was sick of fending off questions. Somewhere en route, Ruth had slipped her hand from his arm. When at last Sam reached the exit, he raced down the steps, eager to escape into the open. He could breathe again, could settle himself and do what must be done. He paced back and forth, drawing in the cool evening air. Sam made several passes before he realized that Ruth stood on the stoop.

"You followed."

She nodded and ducked her head.

Something was wrong. "Did you forget something inside?"

She shook her head, lip quivering. "I—I…" She reached to her right, hand waving, seeking…

She couldn't see.

Sam chided himself for selfishly storming out of the hall. "Some gentleman I am, dashing off like that."

He climbed the steps and took her arm. She gratefully slumped against him, and he edged her toward the railing. Once she'd grasped it, he eased her down the steps. Crossing the uneven ground in front of the hall proved just as treacherous as the steps. More than once she stumbled. Each time he tightened his grip on her arm, and she managed to recover her balance.

Only when they'd moved beyond earshot of any listeners did he speak. "Promise me you'll never forget your glasses again."

She turned away and wrung her hands. "I—I didn't forget them." Her shoulders shook.

Oh, no. She was crying. This was not going well. "You need them to see." He swiped at his mouth, wondering what made a woman do something so foolish. Vanity? Or was she trying to impress him? "Listen to me. I couldn't care less whether or not a woman wears glasses."

In the light of the full moon, he saw her shake her head. "Yes, you do."

He lightly cupped those quivering shoulders. "No, I don't. You're beautiful with or without them."

She wrenched away. "Don't say such things. I know it's not true."

"Yes, it is." He positioned himself in front of her so she couldn't walk away. "Have I ever lied to you?"

She shook her head but again turned away.

He was not about to let her hide from him. Not when it was this important. "My late wife was what society called beautiful."

Ruth gasped softly and lifted her face. "You're widowed?"

"She died almost eight years ago."

"I'm sorry. How did it happen?"

He felt the question quiver on the cool air, like the moths fluttering around the lit windows. For eight years he'd tried to bury the pain of that night. He'd told no one of Lillian's betrayal, not even his mother. Everyone assumed she had accepted a ride home with Ned because Sam had left the party early. They assumed her death caused his agony. Of the three who had known the truth, only Sam was still alive. He could lock away the truth forever, but as he looked at Ruth, he had to admit the toll that secret had taken.

The decision was simple. Confide in Ruth, reopening the wound, and gain her trust. Or hold on to that secret and lose her confidence.

He took a deep breath. "She died in a motorcar crash." The flat words couldn't fully mask the hurt of that night. "It was raining. They were traveling too fast. The coroner said she died instantly. A broken neck."

Not so for Ned. He'd lingered long enough to beg for forgiveness, but Sam couldn't give it. He couldn't accept his best friend's betrayal, and he couldn't forgive the man, even on his deathbed.

"I'm so sorry," Ruth whispered, bringing him back to the present. "I had no idea."

He tried to shrug away the past. "It was a long time ago."

"Time doesn't always heal." She lightly touched his sleeve, her eyes liquid in the light of the full moon. "Especially when you lose someone you love."

He ought to explain how the love he'd once had for Lillian had ended the moment she announced she wanted a divorce. No Rothenburg ever entertained the prospect of divorce, no matter how bitter the marriage. He'd refused. She'd laughed at him, said she was leaving anyway. He'd stormed out. Then she and Ned had made that fateful drive.

"I'm so sorry." Ruth clasped his hand, drawing him back to the lovely woman before him. Her gentle manner somehow eased the painful memories.

"It's over and done." For the first time in eight years, he could almost believe that. Nothing would change the past.

Mother was right about that. All Sam could do was make a better future, and that started with Ruth Fox. "I didn't mention Lillian to gain your sympathy. I wanted to make a point. Society considered her beautiful, but that kind of beauty is superficial."

Her brow puckered. "That's not why you were attracted to her?"

"Of course not." The idea was ludicrous. Or was it? He had reveled in everyone's congratulations for snagging the prettiest girl. He'd ignored Lillian's selfish vanity, prodded on by sophomoric pride over claiming the prize. Only after the ceremony did he see the cracks in her character.

"I was young and foolish," he admitted, "and I paid for that."

Ruth gazed at him with compassion.

"Listen to me." He held her shoulders so she couldn't slip away from the only truly important thing he'd said tonight. "True beauty is much more than a pretty face." He brushed a thumb across her cheek. "Though you certainly have that. True beauty shines from deep within."

Once again she ducked her face.

He wasn't going to let her escape that easily. "You are beautiful from the inside out, Ruth Fox. And from the outside in." He felt her tremble. "Start believing it, because it's true." He searched for some way to make her see herself accurately. "Love shines through you. Your love of family. Your love of sewing. Your faith." He almost choked on the last, for he hadn't been diligent in that respect. But Ruth was. Ruth surely was.

She still wouldn't look at him. All he could see was the white of her teeth nibbling her lower lip, as if afraid to admit that he might be right. "I—I do like to sew."

Sam could have groaned. She'd chosen the least important virtue, but it was a start. "Did you make that beautiful gown you're wearing?"

Her face lifted, revealing a surprisingly impish smile. "I made it from the ruined dresses."

"Mrs. Vand—"

"Hush!" She pressed a gloved finger to his lips. "She'll hear you." But Ruth looked pleased that he'd noticed.

An idea formed in his head. "I'm not the only one who admired the dress. When I first arrived, I stood in the back looking for you. I couldn't help overhearing many of the women commenting on your gown. They wondered how you'd managed to buy New York fashion. Some speculated you borrowed one of your older sister's dresses. Mrs. V— your client—was of the latter opinion."

She giggled before pressing a hand to her mouth. It might have covered the curve of her lips but not the delight dancing in her eyes. "She did?"

He nodded. "You should use that to your advantage."

"In what way?"

The idea came into focus, a way to help her out of trouble without taking the drastic step of marriage.

"You said you made this dress from the ruined gowns. I imagine many women have out-of-date gowns with perfectly serviceable fabric. They could be remade into new, fashionable gowns." Even as he said the words, he realized the negative impact this would have on his store's sales and consequently on Father's opinion of his abilities. But Ruth needed this. Her family needed this. And a little drop in the sale of ball gowns might be offset by increased sales in other items if he advertised properly.

Ruth hesitated. "I suppose I could do that."

"Of course you could. Tell the ladies that it wouldn't cost nearly as much as purchasing a new gown, yet they will have a dress in the latest fashion."

Her eyes widened as she grasped the full meaning. "And it wouldn't cost me as much because I wouldn't have to order expensive fabric. Why, this could open up new business for the dress shop. Maybe even—" She halted, her brow drawn. "But it would take two or more gowns to make one. The design would be difficult and time-consuming. I'd have to sketch it for the customer and get her approval." Bit by bit she worked through the details. "But if I made it like I made this dress, it would work. Dye the fabric, perhaps add a new sash or bow, and it would be a completely new gown." With every word she grew more and more excited.

"Oh, Sam!" She clasped her hands together. "Do you know what you've done? You've saved my family." Then she threw her arms around his neck and kissed him on the cheek.

The impulsive gesture startled Sam at first, but after a moment he had to admit that Ruth felt better in his arms than any woman ever had. And when she tilted back her head to look at him, all smiles, he abandoned every intention of honoring Pearlman's strict standards. Her eyes glowed. Her lips beckoned.

Sam seized the opportunity and kissed Ruth.

Energized by Sam's idea—or perhaps his kiss—Ruth sketched a design for a blouse that she could make from the rest of the ruined ivory georgette tea gown. Saturdays were always slow at the shop, so no one interrupted, not even her sisters, who were still sleeping when she left the house at seven-thirty.

Ruth drew from her memory of the outfits in Sam's catalogs to create a "middy" blouse. Its boyish cut suited someone like Jen. By adding a long, squared-off roll collar, turned-back cuffs with pearl buttons and a wide sash at the hip, it echoed a middy without the naval flair. Lace appliqués in front enhanced its femininity while offering additional modesty.

That thought sent a flush of heat through her. Sam had kissed her. Kissed her! Her hand shook so much that she had to set down the pencil and flex her fingers to calm herself. She would think the kiss nothing more than an impulse if not for his words. He'd called her "beautiful." Her. Ruth Fox.

She bit her lip to stop a swell of conflicting emotions. Ten years ago, Blake had called her "pretty," and that had turned out to be a lie. He'd used her to get to Beatrice. Sam had no cause to lie to her, but he was wealthy and handsome like Blake. On the other hand, Sam had proved reliable. He kept his word. He'd watched little Branford for Beattie. He'd gallantly rescued her at the dance. And he'd given her the idea that would save the dress shop. She could trust Sam Roth.

"Thank You, Lord." She lifted her voice in gratitude for answered prayer before returning to the task at hand. She could use the blouse to demonstrate that stylish new garments could be created from old.

While Ruth hunted for scraps of lace, her thoughts drifted. Sam liked her! So much so that he'd kissed her. No man had ever kissed her before, not romantically. Right here and now, she could dance that waltz without stumbling. One-two-three, one-two-three. She glided around the dress shop with the ivory georgette dress as a partner.

He liked her.

He thought her beautiful.

He'd practically said that she was lovelier than his late wife, a society belle.

And he'd given her the answer to her prayers. If she could prove that this new venture would bring in a lot of extra business, she might convince the bank to buy the property and give Daddy a mortgage. All she needed was a stack of orders. Those would have to come from the wealthy, like the Vanderloos and Kensingtons. And Roths.

She sighed as she recalled Sam's kiss.

He liked her.

Maybe he even loved her. What would those women think if they knew he'd kissed plain old Ruth Fox? They would be horrified. Shocked. They might consider it a mere dalliance on his part, but she knew it was much more than that. Sam had struggled to tell her about his late wife. She saw his pain. That wasn't flirtation. A man exposed his soul only when he trusted a woman. And Sam Roth had thrown off every cloak of protection so she could see who he truly was. Only a man in love would do such a thing.

Her thoughts tumbled from business to romance and back again all morning. She cut the first panel two sizes too big and had to redo it. She stitched a seam with the fabric facing the wrong direction and had to rip it out and start over. If she kept this up, she'd lose more money than she'd make with Sam's idea.

The bell over the door signaled an arrival.

"Good morning." Beatrice hurried inside and tugged off her gloves. "It's too hot for these."

"The day is off to a warm start." Ruth had not expected to see her sister at this early hour. "The necklace you loaned me is at the house."

Beatrice waved that off. "I'll get it later. I came here to see you. How did the dance go?"

Ruth would not mention the embarrassing stumble. What did it matter now anyway? "Fine."

"You danced?"

Ruth nodded. She knew what her sister really wanted to know. "With Sam."

Beattie sighed. "Was it wonderful?"

"I couldn't begin to describe it." Ruth felt her cheeks heat.

"What happened?"

Beatrice had always been closest to Ruth. They shared everything. Ruth couldn't keep back a smile. "I think he likes me."

"Of course he does. As well he should. You're a wonderful catch." Beatrice sighed again, heavily this time. "I'm glad because it makes my news a little less painful."

Ruth could guess what Beatrice had to share. "You asked Blake?"

Beatrice's bleak expression told Ruth that her sister had not succeeded. "He refused. I did try."

It was a bitter blow, but Ruth wouldn't let anything ruin her day. "You did your best."

"But I want to help. I offered to sell some of the china, but…"

"Blake refused." Ruth finished what her sister could not bear to say.

"I can talk to my father-in-law."

Ruth shook her head. The senior Kensington had to know of their financial troubles, for he was president of the bank. "I think there might be another way." Ruth then told her sister about Sam's idea.

"Mr. Roth suggested this?" Beatrice looked surprised. "He's proving almost too wonderful to believe. The idea does have promise, though. I have some gowns that could use updating. Maybe Blake would agree to that."

"I'm not looking for your money. I need a way to reach the women on the hill."

Beatrice's eyes lit up. "Of course. Monday's Women's Club meeting would be the perfect place to announce this new service. I will bring you as my guest."

Ruth breathed a sigh of relief. "Thank you." Everything was turning out for the best.

Beatrice grew serious again. "But we have another matter to discuss. Did you talk to Minnie this morning?"

"Minnie?" Ruth stared at her sister. "No. She was still sleeping when I left this morning. What happened?"

"This is her day to clean the parsonage."

Ruth had been too distracted by thoughts of Sam to recall that Minnie was supposed to work this morning. "I forgot to wake her. Did Felicity call you?"

Beatrice nodded. "Don't fret. I woke up Minnie and sent her on her way, but I think something serious happened last night. Did you happen to notice when Minnie left the dance?"

Ruth didn't want to admit that she both could not see and was outside with Sam most of the evening. "I thought she was with Jen."

"Apparently not. Sally Neidecker saw Minnie down by the river with Reggie Landers."

"What?" A thousand thoughts shot through Ruth's head, none of them positive. "Why would she go there with him? He didn't even know who she was earlier this week. It doesn't make any sense. Sally must be mistaken."

Beatrice lifted her eyebrows. "Then why were Minnie's eyes red? I told her what I heard, but she wouldn't explain."

"Then it must be true." Ruth crumpled the ivory georgette. No dressmaking scheme would get them out of financial trouble if the wealthy women in town associated the family with scandal. "How could she do such a thing?"

"Now, we aren't sure she did. Let's assume it was all innocent until we learn otherwise. Minnie is a good-hearted girl."

"Who is easily misled, especially by someone she's been sweet on since she first saw him. I've heard about Reggie Landers's wild ways, that he frequents the speakeasy."

Beatrice's expression tightened. "I'm not saying he's

the perfect gentleman. He certainly wouldn't be my first choice. He is clearly Minnie's, though, and we need to respect that."

"Even if he misleads her?"

Beatrice sighed. "First we need to discover what happened. If Minnie won't talk, see if Jen knows anything. She wasn't at the house when I got there."

"She's probably at the airfield. I'll talk to both of them. We have to clear this up before there's been any damage."

"I'm afraid it's too late for that." Beatrice picked up her handbag. "Apparently Mrs. Neidecker has already fired Minnie."

Chapter Eleven

Jen stood at the stove heating leftover soup when Ruth arrived home from the shop. She tugged off her hat and gloves, glad to be rid of anything that made her hotter. The house was stifling.

"Is Minnie back from the parsonage?" Ruth asked as she opened the kitchen windows, hoping for some hint of air to flow through the room.

"Not yet." Jen wiped her brow on her sleeve.

"Use a handkerchief," Ruth chided. Did her sister have no manners?

Naturally, Jen ignored her, so Ruth got to the point.

"I heard Minnie left the dance with Reggie Landers."

"Who told you that?" Jen's mouth twisted in distaste. "Sally Neidecker?"

Ruth wondered just how much Jen did know. "Why don't you tell me what happened."

"For one thing, they didn't leave together."

"And?"

Jen shrugged. "How am I supposed to know, except that Minnie came home alone."

"You let Minnie leave the dance without you? I asked

you to look after her. Now I find she met a man, alone, and you did nothing to prevent it."

"Minnie's eighteen now. She can make her own decisions."

"What if she makes the wrong one?" Ruth could barely control her indignation. "She has such unrealistic ideas about men. Someone like Reggie Landers is bound to break her heart or…or worse."

"Reggie wouldn't take advantage of her."

"How do you know that?" Ruth had no trouble imagining the handsome troublemaker doing just that. Then what? Who would insist he do right by Minnie? What if he refused?

"Because he's a decent guy at heart."

"A decent guy would not meet a young woman alone in the dark." Ruth shoved aside the fact that she had done the very same thing. She was older, wiser. Minnie knew nothing about men. "You must have heard the stories about him."

"I thought we weren't supposed to listen to gossip."

Ruth gritted her teeth. "I've seen him go to the speakeasy."

"Half the men in town frequent it. It doesn't make a person bad."

Ruth's jaw dropped in disbelief. "How can you say such a thing? It's illegal and immoral."

"I thought we weren't supposed to judge others."

What had gotten into Jen? "Are you telling me that you don't think drinking and gambling are bad? Those vices destroy families. That is not the kind of life God called us to live."

Jen waved the soup ladle at her. "It doesn't mean we should condemn everyone who falters. Jesus came for the sinners, not the righteous."

"I realize that, but it doesn't mean we should sit idly by and watch an innocent fall prey to those very sinners."

Jen rolled her eyes. "Stop treating Minnie like a baby."

"I happen to care about my sister."

"And I don't?"

"Apparently not. If you did, you would have watched her and kept her safe. Mother would never have let us spend time alone with a bachelor in the dark of night."

"Well, you're not Mother." Jen tossed aside the ladle and stormed to the kitchen door, pausing just long enough to add, "Don't you lecture me, Ruthie." Then she left, slamming the screen door behind her.

Ruth sank into the kitchen chair. How had everything gone so wrong? The day had started wonderfully, with warm memories of Sam's kiss. He had given her a possible answer to their financial woes. All had fallen into place. Then Blake had refused to lend them money, and Minnie had made a terrible mistake that cost her her high-paying job.

Ruth closed her eyes and rubbed her aching temples. What was she to do? Her sisters had run amok. The dress shop was floundering, and they were out of money. The crush of worry brought tears to her eyes.

"Are you all right?" Minnie's voice was so soft that Ruth almost didn't hear her.

She opened her eyes to see Minnie standing at the screen door. "Just a few worries, is all."

"Oh." Minnie released the door and crossed the room to sink into the chair beside Ruth. "I suppose you heard about Mrs. Neidecker firing me."

Ruth nodded. "But I'm more worried about you. Is that why you were crying last night?" She'd learned with Jen that accusations got her nowhere. If she hoped to help Minnie, she'd have to offer love, not rebuke.

"No." Minnie hung her head and traced the wood grain on the old kitchen table. "Maybe a little."

Ruth chose her words carefully. "There will be other opportunities—for work as well as for love. You're young and pretty. You have plenty of time."

"Like you?"

In the past, Ruth would have cringed at the reminder of her spinsterhood, but last night she had learned to hope.

"Yes, like me." Ruth squeezed Minnie's hand. "I think Sam likes me."

Minnie could muster only a weak attempt at a smile, which confirmed Ruth's suspicions that the tears had come from a matter of the heart. She decided to try the direct approach.

"Did something happen between you and Reggie?" She brushed a strand of hair from Minnie's forehead as the girl's shoulders sagged.

"How did you know?"

Such a mournful tone!

"I guessed." Since Minnie wasn't offering any more information, Ruth sucked up the courage to ask, "Did he hurt you?"

"No!" Minnie's eyes blazed. "Reggie wouldn't hurt a soul. He's not horrible like some people say. He's the kindest man I know. Except Daddy, of course. And maybe your Mr. Roth, but I don't know him much. Reggie would never hurt me."

Ruth bit her tongue to stop from pointing out that he must have said something hurtful or Minnie wouldn't have been crying. "I'm glad to hear that."

"He's terribly kind." Minnie sniffled and then wiped her nose with the back of her hand.

Ruth handed her a clean handkerchief.

Minnie balled it in her fist. "He just isn't interested."

Ruth recalled the conversation with Reggie at the bank. He hadn't even remembered who Minnie was. Poor girl! "I'm so sorry."

Minnie's lower lip quivered. "He acted like he didn't know me, like he'd never seen me before. But he always called me a 'peach' when he saw me at the Neideckers' house. Why would he give me a nickname if he didn't like me?" She pressed the wadded-up handkerchief to her eyes.

Ruth could think of one distinct possibility. Brothers teased sisters. Reggie treated Minnie like a little sister.

"If I'd known," Minnie sobbed, "I wouldn't have made a fool of myself." Her breath hitched. "And then I wouldn't have lost my job. I shouldn't have gone after him. I should have danced with Peter. At least then I'd have *someone*. Oh, why did I do it?"

Lacking words, Ruth hugged her little sister close. She knew the pain of hoping for a special boy to notice you. Maybe he was rich or prominent. Maybe he said something to raise the hopes of a poor girl. He didn't mean anything by it. He might even think he was being kind, but she took it as interest. Was that what Ruth had done all those years ago? Had Blake spoken casually, perhaps even from kindness, as if to a little sister, and she mistook his words for romance?

She squeezed her eyes shut and rubbed Minnie's back. It didn't matter. The cause and the outcome were the same. "Because you were in love."

As Ruth had been. Thankfully, she had never said a word to Beatrice.

"Why doesn't he love me?" Minnie sobbed.

"I don't know. No woman ever knows." Ruth choked down the bitter pill that she'd let years of remorse destroy numerous chances for romance. "But you must have faith that God will bring the right man into your life at the right time."

"Like your Mr. Roth?" Minnie pulled back to look at Ruth. "Do you think there's someone like him for me?"

Ruth tucked a strand of hair behind Minnie's ear. Her heart soared with such hope that she could not hold back a smile. Sam liked her. Sam had kissed her. In spite of Ruth's fears, God had granted her another chance.

"I'm sure there is."

Sam's mother had drilled into him that Sunday was the Sabbath, a day of rest. His father, on the other hand, ignored biblical commands and worked clear through the day. Sam attended morning worship, but he couldn't stop thinking about how much still needed to be done at the store. He could not sit around reading, eating and conversing when his father would arrive in two days to pass judgment.

So, when Ruth asked Sam to join them for Sunday dinner, he declined.

She'd looked disappointed, even a little surprised, but had accepted his decision without debate. "Perhaps next Sunday, then."

"I would like that."

Except there might not be a next Sunday. If the grand opening didn't succeed beyond expectations, Father would send Sam back to New York. Even if the store did succeed, he'd still be sent to another location. That was his job at Hutton's. He breezed into a town, worked with the store manager to improve profits or set up a new program and went on to the next location.

Only this time was different. This was his store, his chance to prove he deserved to inherit the company presidency. That justified working on Sunday, but he wouldn't force his workers to do so. They'd put in extra hours all week, and the store was ready to be stocked. Boxes of merchandise waited in the storeroom. Pricing and shelving the goods would take every hour between now and Friday's grand opening.

"I'll help," Miss Harris volunteered as he packed a couple of waxed-paper-wrapped sandwiches into his valise. She removed the lid from the large jar at the end of the boardinghouse's kitchen counter. "Let's take a few cookies. Mrs. T. made snickerdoodles yesterday."

He gratefully accepted a couple of the cinnamon-coated sugar cookies. "You don't have to give up your Sunday."

"What else would I do? This town isn't exactly filled with entertainment options."

Sam rather liked that about Pearlman. "They have a cinema."

Miss Harris wrinkled her nose. "I saw that film a year ago." She popped a chunk of cookie in her mouth. "Might as well earn a little extra money."

If only Sam could hire Ruth and her sisters. Unfortunately, a month's wages wouldn't pay off their debt.

"Well, then, let's go." He grabbed the valise. "I appreciate the help."

He held the door for Miss Harris and, once they reached the street, offered her his arm. As usual, the woman wore shoes that made it difficult for her to walk without losing her balance.

She hung on his arm. "On Friday, this will be over. Do you know where you're going next?"

He shook his head. Father never told him in advance where his next assignment would be. Usually Sam didn't care, but this time he wanted to stay. He wanted to make the Pearlman Hutton's his own. He wanted to spend time with Ruth. "I hope I get to stay."

Miss Harris laughed. "Here? The vice president of operations in this tiny town?"

It did sound impossible, but there had to be a way. When answers couldn't be found, Mother placed her faith in God, but this didn't seem the kind of matter that God would care about. Why should He waste time helping Sam stay in Pearlman when other matters were more important? Wars, hunger, poverty. The Fox Dress Shop. Friday night's idea had eased his guilt for the moment, but dawn had erased that. A few orders wouldn't bring in the cash the dress shop needed. He must find another answer. He'd start with the bank.

"I'll do it Monday," he muttered.

"Do what?"

Sam had forgotten he was walking with Miss Harris. "Nothing. Just a matter I need to attend to Monday morning."

"Well, no use worrying about it today." She squeezed his hand and leaned close. "I understand the drugstore has ice-cream sodas. Shall we get one after we finish at the store?"

"If we finish early enough." The thought of a cool soda sure sounded good on such a warm and muggy day, but Miss Harris's clinginess was beginning to irritate him. He wondered if she wore those precarious shoes on purpose. She sure was hanging on tightly. Bringing her to the soda fountain would only encourage her and start rumors that would find their way back to Ruth.

"We'll finish in plenty of time." Miss Harris leaned her head on his shoulder. "Even if I have to work twice as fast."

Uncomfortable with the direction this was heading, Sam stepped to his left to put a little distance between them. He'd done that several times before, and each time she followed. This time was no different. No matter what he did, he couldn't shake her without causing a scene, and he couldn't afford to irritate any employee a few days before the grand opening.

What had given her the idea he cared for her beyond that of an employer? Yes, he'd helped her hobble back to the store when her feet hurt. Yes, he'd agreed to her plan to find out if anyone in town had figured out that he was opening a Hutton's Department Store. Yes, he'd complimented her on her stellar work. She must have taken that kindness as personal interest, which it most certainly was not. Her pointed attention was making him very uncomfortable. If anyone saw them...

"Excuse me, Miss Harris." He removed her hand from his arm and made a show of looking for the key to the store.

"Sam?" Ruth's voice shot straight to his gut.

"Ruth. Miss Fox." He whirled around to see her stepping off the back stoop of a small house directly behind the dress shop. Why hadn't he considered where she lived? It only made sense they'd live nearby, and with the employee entrance to his store on the same alley as her back door, it was a wonder they hadn't crossed paths before.

Ruth looked from him to Miss Harris. "You said you were busy today."

"I am. We are." He hoped he didn't look as guilty as he felt. "We have work to get done. Miss Fox, this is Miss Harris. She's the office secretary."

The women greeted each other coldly, and then Ruth zeroed in on the first part of his excuse.

"You're working on a Sunday?" Her frown told him exactly how she felt about that.

"It can't be helped. Too much to be done before the grand opening."

"Oh. I see." But she clearly did not. "When is that?"

"Soon." He shot a look at Miss Harris telling her to be

quiet. The banner was ready, but, in Ruth's eyes, a Friday opening would not excuse him from working on the Sabbath. "You see, my father is due to arrive midweek. He will expect things to be in order."

"Of course." Ruth's taut expression belied her words. She didn't understand at all.

"I'm sorry," he offered, knowing it was too weak. "I would rather have had a home-cooked meal at your house."

At that, Miss Harris's gaze narrowed. Great. Now he'd infuriated two women. Ruth was too kind and gentle to chide him, but Miss Harris wouldn't hold back once they entered the store. He had no choice but to face her wrath, for, as his mother would say, he'd cooked the stew and now he had to eat it.

He held up the door key apologetically. "We should get to work."

"Fine." Ruth's expression froze into an unreadable mask.

He would have to make a lot of amends later.

Ruth tried to forget the way that woman hung on Sam's arm. She'd even laid her head against his shoulder. In public! Miss Harris, the office secretary. As if that excused her from suspicion. No, all that position gave Miss Harris was constant access to Sam. Though Ruth knew her feelings bordered on jealousy and she ought to believe Sam, as the hours passed, she found more reasons to mistrust him.

Workplace romances had led directly to marriage in recent years. Hadn't Anna Simmons worked for Brandon Landers before they wed? And Darcy Shea worked on Jack Hunter's plane. They had married, too. Miss Harris posed a serious threat. More than serious, for the woman was a pretty, petite brunette. She didn't wear glasses. She sported the latest fashion and wore shoes that cost more than Ruth made in a month. Worse, Sam looked like a boy caught sneaking cookies from the jar.

In comparison to Miss Harris, what could Ruth offer? Debt, an ailing father and sisters who were more often in trouble than out of it. No man of sound mind would take on that burden when he could have a pretty woman who clearly adored him.

By dusk, Ruth had convinced herself that Sam had kissed her only out of pity. A man in love did not turn down dinner with his beloved in order to work with another woman. On a Sunday. Alone together. She could picture them working side by side. His hand would brush hers. Miss Harris would lift her lovely face to him, begging for a kiss.

Ruth pressed her hands to her cheeks. *Stop this!* But the thoughts wouldn't stop. If anything, they sped past faster and faster, like a moving-picture show run at too rapid a speed.

She paced the living room. Maybe Ruth had been wrong about Sam Roth. She should never have trusted him. She should have stuck to her plan to help the family. They needed her. In fact, Minnie was still moping around the house—out of both a job and the object of her affections. Ruth would try to cheer her. Busy hands might take both their minds off disappointing relationships.

"I could use your help at the dress shop," Ruth said. Minnie was fairly good with needle and thread. "I hope to bring in new business by speaking at the Women's Club tomorrow. Someone will need to watch the shop."

Minnie nodded, head still hung low, and shuffled off to her bedroom.

Ruth sighed. On top of Minnie's woes, the loan had to be paid before Wednesday. She needed dozens of orders at the Women's Club meeting to have a chance of convincing the bank to help her.

Between bouts of anger and self-pity, she composed a short speech for the meeting, but every time she rehearsed it, she recalled that Sam had given her the idea. Then tears threatened, and a terrible ache would start.

"Are you all right?" Jen asked the moment she walked in. She plopped onto the sofa and propped her elbows on her knees, chin in her hands. "You're moping around here like Minnie. Missing Sam?"

Ruth shook her head. She didn't want to talk about him. "I'm just rehearsing a speech for the Women's Club meeting tomorrow."

"Must be some speech if it's making you weepy."

Ruth couldn't suppress a smile at Jen's tart response. Her sister could cheer up the most melancholy soul. "You have a way with people. Have you ever considered becoming a nurse?"

"I'd rather do something important like fly airplanes or find a cure for rheumatic fever, but there's no money for either."

Dear, practical Jen. "Maybe there will be one day."

"Oh?" Jen's eyes widened. "Did Sam ask you to marry him?"

"No!" Ruth was startled by the rush of feeling that question brought. "Certainly not." She clutched at the ache in her midsection. "Nor do I expect it. He made it quite clear that he will be leaving Pearlman soon. Once his business opens, he'll go elsewhere."

"I don't believe that for a minute, but even if it is true, you have to fight for him. He loves you. I know it."

"I'm not so sure."

"Well, you'd better start acting like you're sure. You need to let him know how you feel. Have you told him?"

Ruth stared at her sister. "How do you know so much about men? I can't remember the last time a man asked you to an event."

Jen shrugged. "They tell me things."

"Really?"

"The man has to make the first move, but at some point the woman has to let him know she's interested."

Ruth's thoughts drifted back to Friday night's dance. Had she let Sam know how she felt? She'd hugged him, yes, and impulsively kissed him on the cheek, but any friend could do that. Yet, that was when he'd kissed her. She hadn't pulled away, but had she truly kissed back? She'd been surprised at first and uncertain how to respond. Once she let him take the lead, the emotion of the moment had swept her away. She remembered little else of that night. Had she let him know that she was falling for him? Probably not. Maybe that was the problem. Maybe if she'd told him how she felt, he would have accepted her dinner invitation rather than go off with that pretty woman.

"I could have done better," she admitted.

"Well, you have until Friday to take care of that."

"Friday?"

"Didn't you see the banner?" Jen looked appalled. "It's hanging on the front of his store. Grand opening Friday."

Five days. Five short days. At least half of that would be spent trying to save the dress shop. And Sam would be so busy at the store that he'd work late hours. With Miss Harris. Her stomach twisted. By her calculation, they wouldn't meet again until church on Sunday.

That would be too late.

Chapter Twelve

Though Sam considered buying flowers for Ruth, he doubted mere blooms would spur her forgiveness. Saving the family dress shop stood a better chance of turning her heart.

At the opening of business on Monday morning, Sam approached the banker, Mr. Dermott Shea, to find a solution to the mess that the Foxes found themselves in.

"How much is due?" Sam asked.

The banker steepled his fingers. "Let me get this straight. You are Samuel J. Rothenburg's son."

Sam stared in disbelief. Shea knew? Sam struggled to comprehend why Father would have given the bank his name. A fool could connect the dots and realize that a Hutton's Department Store was opening in Pearlman.

The muggy room hummed with the undercurrent of knowledge. If Shea told anyone… But wait. Shea must have known that information for days, and neither Sam nor Miss Harris had heard any speculation come near the truth. That could mean only one thing. The banker had revealed nothing. Sam could trust his discretion.

Sam struck a casual pose, as if Shea's revelation meant nothing. "Yes. I'm his oldest son. I realize this might be difficult to believe, but my father and I don't always share the same opinion on matters. Father doesn't know the situation that the Fox family faces. I see no immediate need for the piece of property. Our current location is more than sufficient. Perhaps something can be worked out."

Shea relaxed slightly, though he still looked wary. Sam couldn't blame the man. His father was not known for kindness. Ruthlessness, yes. Compassion, no. But Sam wasn't cut from the same cloth. For the first time in years, he was proud to admit he had some of his mother's temperament in him.

Playing the casual charmer would not work with a man of Shea's caliber. Sam leaned forward slightly and looked the man in the eye. "I see no reason why both businesses can't succeed."

The banker maintained unnerving calm. "Even if this sale doesn't go through, the property's owner still wants the payments brought to date."

Sam expected as much. "That's why I'm asking how much is due."

"That is confidential information."

"Even to someone interested in paying off the sum?"

Shea stared at him. "Now, why would you do that?"

"My reasons are none of your concern. My ability to pay is. I can have my bank wire the funds to you this afternoon."

The banker's eyebrows rose. "That's a generous offer, especially since it counters that of your father. However, as you stated, your reasoning is none of my concern." He opened one of the folders on the broad walnut desk. "I can't reveal the details, but I can show you a payment schedule." He pulled out a sheet of paper and folded over the top before placing it in front of Sam. The payment schedule included several rows of payments, which abruptly stopped well over a year ago. The total due was staggering. It would completely drain Sam's savings, leaving him with nothing should Father disown him over this.

Sam put his finger on the total. "Is this the final figure?"

"Plus a two-percent penalty."

"On each payment or the total due?"

Shea's jaw tensed. "The bank will cover the penalty if the payments are brought current."

Even without the penalty, who could afford that sum? Certainly not Ruth's family. If they had the money, they would have paid it already. He'd hoped Beatrice Kensington would come to their rescue, but she hadn't. Why not her husband's family? After all, the bank bore the Kensington name.

"The eldest daughter married into local money, I understand."

Shea retrieved the payment schedule, placed it in the folder and slapped the folder shut. "I've already disclosed more than I should have, Mr. Rothenburg. If you have further questions, I suggest you speak with the principals involved."

Sam gritted his teeth. This was going nowhere. He'd come to the bank to find a solution. He wouldn't leave unsuccessful. "Would Mr.—" Sam caught himself before revealing that he knew Vanderloo owned the property. "Would the property owner consider partial payment of the amount due?"

Shea's eyebrows drew together. "How much?"

"Say, half." That would leave Sam with enough in his personal account to survive several months if Father fired him.

"I doubt that would be enough, even though your father's offer is below market value. The owner is anxious to sell."

So Father was trying to get the property cheap. That didn't surprise Sam, but it gave him another idea. "Suppose I offer full value for the property." He could make enough off rent from the revamped dress shop to cover loan payments.

"You want to buy the property?" Shea looked understandably stunned.

"I'll contribute the same half of the amount currently due as a down payment if the bank will lend me the balance."

Shea tapped his fingertips on the folder. Seconds passed. Sam's chair squeaked as he settled back to wait out the verdict. If Shea meant to intimidate him into offering the full cost, it wouldn't work. Sam was a patient man. For Ruth, he'd craft this deal. He could imagine her joy when she learned her family wouldn't lose the dress shop. It would be worth every penny.

"I can't speak for either the owner or the bank board," the banker said.

"You can ask."

"I can," Shea conceded.

Sam rose. "Shall we shake on that? I am relying on your discretion to keep this transaction anonymous. No one must know that I'm involved."

Shea's eyebrows rose at that. He started to say something, then shook his head and extended his hand. "All right, Mr. Rothenburg. I'll ask the owner first and get back to you. If he approves, we will approach the bank board."

"Good, but I need the answer soon. Preferably today." Before Father arrived.

Shea's lips thinned. "I understand."

Sam believed the man truly did. He shook the banker's hand and hoped his offer would be enough to stop the sale.

* * *

This month, the Women's Club met at Felicity Kensington Meeks's house. The parsonage, though elegant by parsonage standards, showed the wear and tear of an eleven-year-old boy and an infant girl. Felicity greeted Ruth warmly and suggested she and Beatrice sit next to Mariah Meeks Simmons in the tight ring of chairs encircling the formal parlor.

"You don't need to stand when you speak," Felicity added. "We're a cozy group."

Indeed they were. In addition to their close proximity in the cramped room, the dozen women chattered so loudly in so many different conversations that Ruth's ears rang.

She gratefully sank into the chair beside her sister and accepted a cup of tea and a shortbread cookie from Mariah.

"Try to relax," Mariah said with a smile. "They might look fierce, but piranhas only live in jungle waters."

Ruth giggled, half at Mariah's description and half from nerves. Her family's future hinged on this meeting and a roomful of women predisposed to look down on her. If not for Beatrice, she would never have been invited to this exclusive club.

The teacup jiggled on its saucer, and Ruth cautiously rested it on her lap. She ought to have refused the tea. Her hands shook too much, and she couldn't drink a drop anyway.

Across the room, Mrs. Vanderloo stared at Ruth while Eugenia Kensington criticized the flowers and shrubs around city hall, which apparently did not live up to her high standards. Sophie Grattan and her cohorts held court to Mrs. Kensington's left while Mrs. Evans and those residing on the hill clustered to Mrs. Vanderloo's right. Ruth noted that Anna Simmons, wed to Brandon Landers earlier that year and thus eligible to join the club, was not in attendance.

That left Ruth as the only woman aside from Beatrice who wasn't born to wealth, and every woman in the room knew it.

"You'll do fine," Beatrice reassured her. "I'm right here, and my mother-in-law will support you, too. No one would dare speak against a Kensington."

Ruth drew in a shaky breath. She'd never been good at speaking in front of others. In school, her mind went blank whenever she had to stand in front of the class to recite or debate. If not for her written work, she would have failed. That was just for a grade. This could decide her family's future. What if her thoughts fled when she was supposed to speak? Beatrice couldn't leap to her rescue. Ruth hadn't fully explained the new dressmaking idea to her. But they both knew how important this was. If Ruth hoped to save the dress shop, she must convince these women to bring their business to her.

Mariah returned to her chair after serving tea to the last arrival. That was apparently the signal for Eugenia Kensington to begin the meeting. The diminutive yet powerful woman stood, and the room instantly quieted.

"Good morning, ladies." Mrs. Kensington swiveled to look each woman in the eye.

For some, that might have been encouragement, but Ruth got only more nervous. While Mrs. Kensington talked about club business, Ruth fingered the clasp on her handbag. Inside that bag was the outline of her talk. If she could get it out without spilling the teacup perched on her knees, she could rehearse what she was supposed to say. The sentences that had rung so clear this morning now blew away on the breeze billowing the curtains.

With great care, she eased the clasp open enough to

slide her fingers into the bag. The teacup jiggled, and Ruth froze. No one had noticed. She allowed a single breath and resumed her search. She carried very little in her bag. No compact or comb. A couple of hatpins. A handkerchief. A few coins. And the speech. The tips of her fingers brushed against the paper. Aha! Without a sound, she slid it out.

"Miss Fox?"

"Oh!" Ruth started, and the teacup tilted. Horrified, she watched as liquid slopped over the edge onto the saucer. The whole thing started sliding off her knees. Ruth dropped the speech and somehow managed to catch the cup before it spilled all over Mariah.

Mrs. Kensington frowned.

"Why don't I take this off your hands?" Mariah took the cup from Ruth. "It appears I gave you a mismatched cup and saucer."

The set looked perfectly matched to Ruth, but the ladies all smiled at Mariah's breezy explanation. The orphanage director had touched many of these women's lives, and they granted her great leniency. Unlike the rest of the privileged class, Mariah dressed plainly and practically. She spoke her mind with refreshing candor coupled with humor. Though Ruth didn't cross paths with her often, she liked the woman immensely—even more so at this moment.

Mariah turned to Ruth. "I understand your dress shop is going to be offering a new service."

By looking at Mariah, Ruth found the nerve to speak. "Yes, we are."

Mariah nodded encouragement, and the words flooded back into Ruth's head.

She dared look around the room like Mrs. Kensington had. "You all know how expensive new gowns can be."

Many of the women nodded, but Mrs. Vanderloo frowned.

Never mind. Ruth couldn't expect her business anyway. She'd focus on the others.

"Your closets probably have several perfectly serviceable gowns that are simply out-of-date." With each word, Ruth's confidence grew. "Some of you may have seen the gown I wore to Friday's dance at the Grange Hall."

Again, the women nodded, and Ruth recalled that Sam had overheard some women wondering how she could afford such a gown.

"I didn't buy it."

That brought a murmur from the ladies.

"Nor did I borrow it."

The murmurs stopped, and puzzlement took over.

"I made it." Ruth let that sink in for a second. "From old dresses and scraps." She hoped Mrs. Vanderloo didn't figure out that it was *her* old dresses that had served as the foundation.

"You did?" Felicity exclaimed. "I would never have known. It looked like it came straight from New York."

Ruth reveled in the praise. If Felicity liked her gown, others would buy into the idea. "Yet it cost me much less than a new gown."

That brought a chorus of interest.

Ruth sealed the deal. "I can do that for you, too. Bring your old dresses to the dress shop, and I'll sketch some designs. You choose whichever one you like, and I'll make it for a fraction of the cost of a new gown. Why, when you consider the cost of shipping from New York, you'll save a fortune."

Mariah nodded. "It makes perfect economic and practical sense. God intended us to be good stewards of the resources on this earth. Why throw away perfectly good dresses when they can be put to use? Moreover, we'll be supporting a local business and helping out one of our own. I, for one, will stop by the shop tomorrow."

Her bold acceptance of Ruth's plan led nearly all the women in the room to pledge their support. With each promised order, Ruth's spirits rose. This would work. It would truly work, and she owed it all to Sam.

Then Mrs. Vanderloo stood. "I hate to stick a pin in your idea, Miss Fox, but there's no need to spend money on old dresses when we can get a new one at a very inexpensive price right here in Pearlman."

"Indeed we can," Mrs. Kensington echoed, her chin held high.

"This won't take business away from the mercantile," Ruth hastened to explain to Beatrice's fearsome mother-in-law. "I will specialize in tea and ball gowns."

"Well, then. I suppose it's all right," Mrs. Kensington said.

Mrs. Vanderloo shook her head. "I'm not talking about everyday dresses, either, though I'm not surprised the Foxes are making a last-ditch attempt to save their little dress shop."

Ruth choked back a very unseemly wish that she'd dropped her teacup on Mrs. Vanderloo's lap.

The woman looked at Ruth with absolute triumph. "You won't have much business once the Hutton's Department Store opens next door."

"Hutton's?" She'd heard the name, of course. Hutton's Department Stores were located in large cities, like Detroit and Chicago and New York. "In Pearlman?"

The other women expressed equal astonishment.

"Impossible," Mrs. Kensington insisted. "Branford would have told me. As city councilman, he is privy to everything that goes on in town."

"He didn't know this," Mrs. Vanderloo said over the crescendo of female voices, most in disbelief and protest.

Mariah put their thoughts most succinctly. "Pearlman is too small to support a store the size of a Hutton's Department Store."

"Is it?" Mrs. Vanderloo looked terribly smug. "Then tell me why the vice president of the company has been in town the past two weeks working on the old carriage factory."

It didn't take ten seconds for Ruth to put the pieces together. Mrs. Vanderloo could mean only one person. Sam. But what had she said about him? "Vice president of Hutton's?"

"Didn't you recognize the Rothenburg name?" Mrs. Vanderloo smirked. "Or didn't he tell you?"

"But—" Ruth began before cutting herself off. Sam Roth. Sam Rothenburg.

The room began to spin as the speculation escalated and the meeting came to a divisive end.

"It can't be," she said weakly.

The women were too busy exclaiming and chattering to hear or notice Ruth's distress. Only Beatrice and Mariah stayed by her side.

Beatrice hugged her around the shoulders. "Let's go home now."

"But it can't be. He wouldn't...would he?"

Mariah looked her straight in the eye. "We'll get to the bottom of this. I suspect there's a perfectly logical explanation. Most likely Mrs. Vanderloo misheard a bit of gossip."

Ruth hoped Mariah was right, but she couldn't be certain. After all, Sam hadn't told her his name right away. Jen had teased her over that point. At the time, Ruth thought she'd forgotten to ask, but maybe he hadn't told her because he didn't want to tell her. And when Jen pried it out of him, he'd given a last name of Roth. Then he'd befriended her.

Why? Why deceive and mislead her into thinking he cared for her? Why kiss her? To woo the competition? To misdirect her attention while he built his empire under her nose?

No wonder he'd insisted on paying for Mrs. Vanderloo's replacement dresses. They probably didn't cost him a thing. She bitterly recalled how quickly he'd come up with the catalogs. Oh, not from Hutton's, of course, but what bachelor kept clothing catalogs on hand? What a fool she was! She'd been so blind, so willing to believe only those details that fit her plan. Never once did she consider the truth right in front of her.

Ruth stood adrift in the middle of the room as the speculation swirled around her. Its current carried her downriver, and the roar of the rapids grew louder and louder.

Sam had lied to her.

That fact ripped the oars from her hands. She was helpless, unable to stop the coming disaster.

Beatrice picked up Ruth's handbag. "We're going home now. Come with me, Ruth." She wrapped her arm around Ruth's waist and gently tugged her forward. "Come, dearest."

The women's looks of pity greeted Ruth like familiar old friends. For a brief, glorious moment, Ruth had thought she could soar, but she'd claimed too much, climbed too high, and now her family would suffer the fall.

Felicity and Mariah cleared the way as Beatrice guided her out of the parlor.

"I'm sure she's wrong," Felicity said. But her expression was grim.

If true, the opening of a Hutton's would strike a blow to the Kensingtons, for a department store would steal away a goodly amount of the mercantile's business. But the impact they felt would not compare to what would happen to the dress shop. Mrs. Vanderloo was right about that. A

department store would take all their business. They'd lose
the shop. Daddy would have to leave the sanitarium. Her
worst fears would come to pass.

And she'd tried so hard. It wasn't fair. It wasn't right.
Why didn't God listen to her? Why ignore her prayers
now when they most needed help? She'd started to believe
God had sent Sam into her life to rescue her family. How
wrong she'd been.

Ruth dug her fingernails into the palms of her hands.
Once again, a man had used her for his own advantage.
She…she…

The awful words wanted to bubble to the surface, but
a woman of faith should never even think such things. So
she bit her tongue. But the thought still lingered.

She hated Sam Rothenburg.

Chapter Thirteen

Ruth stayed up late that night reading her Bible, but she couldn't focus on the words. Instead, memories battled emotion, and any message the Word might have given her went unseen.

When the lamp burned low and her sisters retired for the night, Ruth extinguished the flame to save precious oil. The darkness brought no relief. If anything, the memories became clearer.

Eight years old, sitting on a hard oak chair in the doctor's office during the heat of summer. He set the heavy spectacles on her nose and wrapped the bows around her ears. They pressed down until her head ached, but the marvels opened to her made the pain recede. She could see every medicine bottle on the shelves. The shifting mass of trees turned into individual leaves in every imaginable hue of green. She'd drunk in the world like a parched desert wanderer.

Then, after church the very next Sunday, deaf Mrs. Whitley, long since passed from this world, had pulled Mother aside to commiserate in what she no doubt thought was a whisper. "Poor little Ruthie won't stand a chance of getting a beau. Best get her used to disappointment."

That night and every night for months, Ruth had added a fervent plea to her bedtime prayers. "Please, God. Heal my eyes. Make me see again."

But He hadn't.

When school began in September, so did the taunts. *Frog eyes. Ribbit-ribbit. Goofy Ruthie.*

Mrs. Whitley had been right. Boys either tormented or ignored her. Ruth learned to accept disappointment and bury her hopes deep inside until the day that the boy she'd secretly adored for years sought her out. Blake Kensington, the richest and most handsome boy in town, came to her!

First he told her that she was pretty. He promised to buy her basket at the Founder's Day picnic. Buying her basket meant he would sit with her and signaled that he was her beau. Her basket came up for bid first. She waited with eager anticipation, but Blake didn't even bid. In the end, Daddy bought it. Devastated, Ruth worked up the nerve to ask Blake why he hadn't bid. He'd laughed at her and asked where she'd gotten such a foolish idea. He would never be interested in *Frog Eyes*. Then she overheard his mother tell another lady that only one Fox could possibly be good enough for her precious son: Beatrice. Minutes later, Blake bought Beatrice's basket.

Even at that young age, Ruth understood she'd been used. By threatening to court a lesser girl, Blake had secured his mother's approval of Beatrice. Ruth had retreated, humiliated and unable to tell anyone. Beattie was so happy that Ruth couldn't spoil her sister's joy, not that day and not through their courtship and marriage.

Now Sam Rothenburg had done the same. Only this time, Ruth didn't have to hide her hurt to spare a sister. Nor did she have to accept one minute in Sam's company.

"Things will look better in the morning," Beatrice had told Ruth after the meeting.

Ruth hadn't believed her at the time, but morning's gray dawn did bring renewed determination. Sam Rothenburg meant nothing compared to her family, and they needed her. She alone could save the dress shop. In the wee hours, she'd gathered her resolve. The department store wouldn't open for a few days. Business might decline after it opened, but not right away. She listed the orders the ladies had promised. Ten dresses. Two had even promised to bring her all their alterations. Altogether, it might be enough to convince the bank to take over the property loan from Mr. Vanderloo.

It made perfect sense to her. After all, the man simply wanted the full price of the property. It shouldn't matter who paid him.

So Ruth donned her best dress, had Minnie watch the shop and headed for the bank at nine o'clock in the morning, the list of orders tucked in her handbag. Clouds scudded across the sky, and a chill wind tugged at her hat. This last day of July felt more like autumn than midsummer. Birds chattered noisily, as if planning their migratory routes. People bustled down the sidewalk, heads bowed against the wind and jackets buttoned. A lone cheerful whistle broke the melancholy atmosphere.

Who could delight in such a gale?

She looked up and saw Sam round the corner of the store.

"Ruth!" He smiled broadly.

She turned away. The anger she'd tried so hard to dispel returned with a vengeance.

"I was on my way to see you," he called out.

Why? To gloat? Or to deceive her yet again? She couldn't talk to him. She couldn't even look at him.

She needed to cross the street, but two motorcars were coming from her right and a truck from her left. It was too dangerous to cross, but even more dangerous to stay put and endure more of what Sam had to dish out, so she hurried down the wooden sidewalk. Perhaps she could get far enough ahead that she could cross behind the truck before Sam caught her.

"Miss Fox! Ruth! Wait a minute!" he called out.

Her pulse accelerated along with her steps. Faster. Faster.

But his long legs outstripped her. Soon he'd be within reach.

The truck was passing now. Just a few more steps, and she could dart across the street. *Please, Lord. Don't make me face him now. I'm not ready.*

Sam touched her shoulder.

She shrugged him off and stepped into the street.

A horn blared. Brakes squealed. She turned her head in time to see a car bearing down on her. She screamed. It swerved. Then someone yanked her back onto the boardwalk. Only after her heartbeat slowed did she realize that the arm wrapped around her waist belonged to Sam.

"You could have been killed." His voice shook.

She was only aware that he still held her. "Please let go."

He released her. "Where are you going in such a rush?"

She rubbed her arms but could not look at him. "I suppose I should thank you for saving my life." But she did not feel thankful.

"Didn't you hear me? Didn't you see the car? You acted like you were running away."

I was. But she couldn't say that. She darted a glance at the street. Still busy. "I'm in a hurry."

"I can see that, but nothing is worth risking your life."

My heart is.

He circled around her.

She turned her head the other way.

He tried to tip up her chin.

She pulled away.

"What is going on?" he asked.

Oh, that she had the courage to tell him exactly what she thought, but the words of Pastor Gabe's sermon came to mind. *Love is patient and kind.* She felt neither patient nor kind. Instead, her emotions boiled and threatened to erupt in regretful words.

Since he demanded an answer, she stuck to fact. "I need to go to the bank."

"At least let me escort you across the street."

"My eyesight might be poor, but I am not blind."

He drew in his breath sharply. "I didn't mean to suggest you were."

She had to keep her face averted, lest she see his expression and lose her resolve. "Then please, allow me to attend to my business."

"I'm sorry if I somehow offended you. Please tell me what I've done."

He'd given her opportunity to speak openly. She could spit out every angry word that had crossed her mind since yesterday's meeting. Instead, a verse from James's Epistle came to mind. *Let every man be swift to hear, slow to speak, slow to wrath.*

Hear? She didn't want to hear more false explanations and excuses. He'd lied to her. She could never believe him again.

"At least look me in the eye, Ruth, and tell me what I've done. I promise to make it up to you."

What good were the promises of a liar? But she would never be rid of him if she didn't say something. The truth would do.

Seeing as the street had cleared of traffic, she summoned the courage to snap the silk thread that had once bound them together. "Thank you for saving me from the oncoming automobile, but I'm in rather a hurry, Mr. *Rothenburg*."

Before he could answer, she darted across the street.

Ruth disappeared into the bank before Sam realized what she'd said. *Rothenburg.* She knew his name. Someone had told her. Miss Harris? If so, he'd have words with her. On the other hand, two other people in town knew the truth: the banker and Vanderloo. Father had used his full name when dealing with the property. Sam suspected Vanderloo or the man's wife. Regardless of who spilled the secret, if Ruth knew, so would the rest of the town.

Sam raked a hand through his hair. What could he do?

Ruth had gone straight to the bank. There she'd learn that the family wouldn't lose the dress shop, at least not while his offer was under consideration. That ought to salve her fury, but she wouldn't know that he was the one who'd stepped in.

If a man takes away thy coat, let him have thy cloak also.

Sam shook his head. Where had that come from? He'd memorized Scripture in childhood, but he hadn't opened a Bible or recalled a verse in years. Moreover, it made no sense. No one had taken his coat, and he didn't even own a cloak. He shook off the thought.

He couldn't change Ruth's feelings, nor could he stop the town from learning that a Hutton's would soon open. He could only prepare for Father, who had wired last night that he would arrive on the afternoon train. Sam had worked the crew late getting the store ready, but the ball gowns still hadn't arrived. Beautiful gowns drew in customers, so he put them in the window display. Without a single ball gown, the displays and the sales would suffer.

He'd been on his way to ask Ruth if she would loan him that lovely blue dress she'd worn to the dance until the merchandise arrived. It could benefit them both. He'd have a display, and she would get both the credit for creating the dress and the business it would spur, but after that icy reception he doubted she would lend him a thing.

"Mr. Roth! Mr. Roth," called out a young woman's voice.

He looked back and spotted Minnie Fox standing in the dress-shop doorway. She looked both ways, as if afraid someone would see her, and motioned for him to come there.

Why?

She nodded encouragingly and again motioned for him to come to the dress shop.

Why not? He had planned to go there before Ruth marched off in a huff. If Ruth wouldn't listen to him, maybe her sister would. Surely Minnie would understand why he'd used the shortened version of his name. His name! That was it. Minnie had called him "Mr. Roth." That meant Ruth hadn't told her sisters what she'd learned. Maybe he could salvage this day after all.

"You did what?" Ruth screeched, the surprising news she'd received at the bank forgotten at her sister's announcement.

Minnie cringed and withdrew behind the dress-shop worktable. "You don't have to yell at me. I thought you'd want your dress on display in the front window of a department store." She sighed. "A Hutton's Department Store. Right here in Pearlman."

Ruth stared at her youngest sister. "You have no idea what that means, do you?"

"What what means?"

"A department store next door."

Minnie looked a bit wary as she offered up the first thing that came to mind. "Pretty dresses?"

Ruth shook her head. No wonder the dress shop was failing. If her sisters didn't understand the importance of their work, why should anyone else?

"It means people won't come to us for new dresses. We won't even get alterations. A store the size of Hutton's probably has its own alterations department." She threw her handbag onto the worktable.

"Oh." Minnie blinked rapidly. "I'm sorry."

Ruth felt a twinge of guilt as she tugged off her gloves. Her sister truly didn't know better. The blame lay with Sam, who'd used her family for the last time.

"It's not your fault. You did what you thought best. You couldn't know that I didn't want my dress on display." She sighed at the thought of her work in the front window of any store, least of all a big department store. "The damage is already done."

Her dress would grace the Hutton's front window. If Mrs. Vanderloo hadn't figured out yet that Ruth had used her ruined dresses to make the gown, she would have plenty of time to come to that conclusion. When she did, the woman's wrath would know no bounds.

Even the loan reprieve that the bank had given her wouldn't help. Someone had made another offer on the property, delaying the proposed sale. Mr. Shea wouldn't say who or how long, but he did hint that the second offer might benefit her family.

She clung to that faint hope, for it might let Daddy stay at the sanitarium long enough to get the treatments he needed. If he got well, she could endure any suffering, even having Sam next door.

Well, maybe not dealing with Sam every day. Hopefully, he'd gotten the message that she didn't want to talk to him again. She supposed she'd have to see him to get her dress back, but that was all until he apologized.

"Did he say anything else?"

Minnie drew circles with her finger on the worktable. "Nothing much."

Ruth felt a twinge of guilt. She'd reacted too strongly. "I'm sorry I got upset. I was just surprised." She removed her hat. "It seems to be a day of surprises."

Minnie sneaked a wary glance at her. "He said he hoped to see you at the grand opening."

Ruth choked back an ill-tempered response. Her anger was with Sam, not Minnie. "I don't think I'll be attending. If you see him, you may tell him that."

"You'll see him before that, won't you?"

"I doubt it." Ruth wasn't going to explain their falling-out. "He'll be busy getting his store ready. I'll be busy with all the orders I took yesterday."

"You're not going to work through meals, are you? He said he was going to the Wednesday-night church supper."

Ruth made a quick decision. "I'm not going this week."

"But you always go, and Sam wants to see you. He said he likes you."

"He did?" For a moment, her resolve wavered. He *had* kissed her. But then, he'd also withheld his full name and talked Minnie into giving him Ruth's gown. "It doesn't matter if he likes me or not. I'm not going."

"Not going where?" Jen breezed into the shop.

"To Wednesday's church supper," Minnie answered. "Ruth's mad at Sam."

"I am not mad at Sam." That was a terrible lie, but she would not have anyone—even her sisters—know how much he'd hurt her. "I'm simply too busy to go to the supper."

Jen plopped onto a stool. "You have to eat."

"I can eat here. I have a lot of orders to fill before Friday."

"You do? You mean yesterday's speech worked?"

"Don't act so surprised," Ruth said. "A good idea will bring in customers, no matter how poorly it's presented."

At least she hoped so.

The bell over the door tinkled lightly.

"What good idea?"

All three sisters whipped around at the sound of the dearest and most unexpected of voices.

"Daddy!" they cried in unison and, without regard for anything or anyone else, raced across the room and flung their arms around their beloved father.

Chapter Fourteen

~

After leaving the dress shop, Sam rushed to get the store ready for his father's arrival. By the time the crew quit for the lunch hour, each department had begun to take shape. Cases were filled. Most shelves had some merchandise on them. Half the mannequins were in place. He'd masked the empty ball-gown department by moving the tea gowns to the front. Hopefully Father wouldn't notice the scanty offerings in ladies' attire.

One major hurdle remained, and it couldn't wait until after lunch.

Sam cornered Miss Harris before she left the building. "Will you help me get this display finished?"

"I don't see why you're in such a rush."

"You know that Father is due on the afternoon train."

Miss Harris pouted. "But it's my lunch hour. We'll have two whole hours after I return, and the boardinghouse only serves lunch between noon and one o'clock."

"Two hours might not be enough time. Please?" He turned on the charm. "If you stay, I'll buy you lunch at the restaurant down the street."

She returned a coy smile. "You'll come with me?"

He was playing with fire, but he needed the assistance

of the best window-display designer on staff. "All right. If we finish with enough time to spare."

Women's clothing needed a woman's touch, and Miss Harris was the only woman currently in his employ. He would rather have had Ruth's help. Earlier, he'd planned to ask her to assist—for wages—if she would agree to loan him her dress. He'd even planned to break the secrecy surrounding the store and reveal his full name. Sam had never done that before, but he'd gotten to know Ruth so well over the past week and a half that he felt certain she'd understand and keep the secret.

Unfortunately, someone had ruined that. Sam could only hope Ruth's anger would be tempered by the pending reprieve for the dress shop.

"Well?" Miss Harris tapped her toe in irritation. "I'm not giving up my lunch hour just to stand around doing nothing."

Sam fetched the carton containing Ruth's dress and asked Miss Harris to set up the mannequin while he hung the backdrop featuring a moonlit night. He'd chosen that design in tribute to the night of the dance, when she'd thrown her arms around him in a rare display of emotion, inspiring him to kiss her for the first time. He hoped it wouldn't be the last.

"You need a man in the display," Miss Harris said as she pinned the dress in place on the mannequin.

Sam had chosen the colors and props—a silver-leaved tree and stepping-stones to hint at a romantic stroll—but he'd never considered two figures. Women's clothing brought in customers. Men's did not, but the romance of a couple might work, if tastefully done.

"Put him in full dress," she added. "I suggest the black serge swallow-tailed coat and a top hat."

"Too formal." Sam moved the tree to make room for

a second mannequin. "I like the idea of a couple, but this should be a casual encounter, hinting that romance is yet to come." He stood back and surveyed their progress. The backdrop needed adjusting. He climbed the ladder. "Dress him in a tuxedo. A little less formal occasion. He's interested but not yet committed."

"Ahhh." Miss Harris's eyebrows lifted. "Like you and the little dressmaker?"

The jealous remark grated on Sam's nerves. "Ruth is a talented designer. She made that gown from scraps. I've never known anyone who could create such a beautiful gown with so few resources."

Miss Harris's expression tightened. "I didn't realize you were in love with her."

In love? Sam liked her, sure, but love? "Even if it was any of your business, which it's not, I'm not in the market for a wife."

"Oh." Miss Harris frowned as she finished the female mannequin. "I see. Will you fetch a male mannequin?"

Though the awkward moment had passed, Miss Harris's words echoed in Sam's mind. Was he in love with Ruth? Was that why he thought of her day and night? Was that why her anger this morning hurt so much? Was that why he'd offered to spend half his savings on her?

The thoughts so preoccupied him that he stepped blindly from the window display and nearly ran into the man standing there.

"Son." Samuel J. Rothenburg Sr. glared at him, a stump of a cigar in the corner of his mouth. "I see I haven't arrived a moment too soon." His permanent scowl terrified employees and competitors alike.

Sam stiffened. "Father. I expected you on the afternoon train."

"Exactly."

Sam gritted his teeth. Father suspected Sam had botched the job and intended to catch him unaware. This time Sam wouldn't back down.

"Hello, Sam." Harry stepped from behind Father with a smug grin. "I see you've been keeping yourself busy around town."

The sarcastic comment made Sam swallow hard. How much of his conversation with Miss Harris had his father and brother overheard?

"A dressmaker?" Father sneered. "Now your incompetence makes sense. Good thing I brought along Harry to straighten out this mess."

"How are you, Ruthie?" Daddy's eyes crinkled at the corners, though the spark was gone from their pale hazel depths.

Ruth swallowed a lump and embraced the thin, graying man leaning on a cane. "Daddy." She could feel his bones beneath the jacket. "We didn't expect you."

"I know, dearest," Mother said, "but your father wanted to see the shop and home."

She didn't add "one last time," but Ruth felt it nonetheless. Her father looked frailer than she remembered. A strong wind would knock him over. The bluish tinge to his lips couldn't be a good sign, and the worry creasing Mother's brow confirmed it. When Daddy leaned to touch the blouse Ruth had begun yesterday, Mother reached out to catch him.

Jen and Minnie didn't seem to notice. They chattered about everything that had happened since Daddy left, from new students at the airfield to Minnie's disappointment with Reggie Landers.

"You were right," Minnie admitted.

Daddy sighed. "I might have been wrong, child. Never

judge a man's motives." He tweaked her nose. "Though you're wise to look elsewhere. He doesn't sound ready to settle down."

Minnie soaked in each word. "I will, Daddy."

"That's my girl." He looked around the shop. "How I missed this place. And all of you." He managed a faint smile. "You've done well, Ruthie."

Not well enough. But there was no need to tell him about the property and financial woes now that they had a little extra time.

"You need to rest." Ruth moved to her father's side. "Save your strength."

"For what, child?" For a brief moment, his eyes twinkled like old. "Time rushes along heedless of our wishes and desires."

Ruth blinked back a tear. "Then what would you like to do?"

He patted her hand. "Hear about your new beau."

Ruth's jaw dropped before she clapped it shut and cast a glare at her sisters. "Who told you I had a beau?"

Both Jen and Minnie disavowed any part of spreading this knowledge, though they didn't hesitate to add details.

"He's the most handsome man ever," Minnie said, "for someone his age. But he's perfect for Ruth. You should have seen them together at the dance."

Mother's eyebrows lifted. "Ruth danced?"

Minnie looked stricken. "Well, she would have if that clumsy Linton Metz hadn't tripped her up."

It was Ruth's turn to stare. Linton Metz hadn't tripped her. Was that what people thought?

"But Mr. Roth saved the day," Jen added. "He scooped Ruth up before she fell. Every girl in the room wished she'd lost her balance."

Ruth couldn't believe the tales her sisters were weaving.

"Beattie said everyone considers him the most eligible man in Pearlman," Jen added.

Beattie. Of course. Beatrice was the one who'd written Mother. Of all the sisters, she was the only one who practiced regular letter writing. The next time Ruth saw her sister, she'd caution her not to get her parents' hopes up over nothing.

"Jen and Minnie are exaggerating," Ruth said. "Mr. Roth—" the name stuck in her throat "—and I are just acquaintances. Nothing more. He requested one dance, and I obliged. That doesn't constitute a beau."

"You also picnicked together," Minnie pointed out.

"Along with both of you," Ruth said.

"And he sits with us in church," Jen added.

"Which is simply neighborly." Ruth would not let this supposed romance get out of hand.

Daddy chuckled. "That's my Ruth, ever wary of happiness."

His words hit hard. Was that the way she was? Afraid to be happy?

"Th-that's not it." Still, she felt the heat in her cheeks. "I just wouldn't call him a beau. It's not that he's formally courting me." She glanced at her father, and a terrible thought popped into her head. "He didn't write you asking for permission, did he?"

Part of her wanted Daddy to say that Sam had indeed written to him, but the other part knew that even if he had, she could never accept his courtship. The man had misled her about terribly important matters.

Daddy shook his head and coughed. His shoulders shuddered beneath his thin jacket, and Ruth rushed to his side. Daddy needed rest, not additional stress. There was no reason to tell him about Sam's betrayal. Within the week, Sam Rothenburg would walk out of her life forever. Then she need never think of him again. Everything would return to normal.

Ruth took her father's arm. "Shall we look around? I want to tell you about my new idea." If Minnie hadn't given her dress to Sam, she could show him. Instead, she had to settle for describing the plan, laying out her sketches and showing him the list of orders she'd garnered at the Women's Club meeting. "We have Beattie to thank. If she hadn't invited me to the meeting, I would never have gotten these orders."

"Oh, Ruthie," he sighed, his shoulders sagging. "You shouldn't have."

That was the last thing she'd expected him to say. "It was no trouble. None at all." Ruth glanced at her mother, whose face was drawn and pale. "We can use the extra business. It'll help the shop."

Her father bowed his head. "You should have talked to me first."

"I know, but—" Ruth felt her future slipping away. What did Daddy plan to do? Why had he come home? She cleared the lump from her throat. "Don't worry. We can handle every order. I'll work into the evening, and Minnie is becoming a good seamstress. You won't have to do a thing."

She appealed to Mother, who looked out the window rather than lend her support.

What was going on? Panic squeezed the air from her lungs. "I thought you'd be pleased. I want to make you proud."

"We are always proud of you." Daddy's voice trembled, and he reached for a stool. "I'm simply tired from the travel. Perhaps I ought to take that nap your mother has been insisting on."

Mother snapped to attention, taking his free arm. "Yes, you should. You've already overtaxed yourself."

With that, they closed the shop for lunch and went home.

Sam lost his desk to his father. As president of the company, Father could sit in any chair he chose. He now presided over this meeting from Sam's chair, leaving Sam and Harry to fight over the other chair in the room.

Sam stood, arms crossed, ready to do battle. Let Harry sit. His younger brother pulled the chair to the side so he could see both Sam and their father. Supremely confident, Harry crossed one leg over the other and leaned back to enjoy the fight.

"The store is ready to open." Sam started ticking off the completed tasks.

If Father had heard him, he didn't reply. Instead, he perused the paperwork Sam had given him. After long, silent minutes, he closed the folder with a grunt. "I sent for six experienced saleswomen from Chicago for the opening. Send the Detroit crew back. I suggest you fire Harris." He glowered at Sam. "But that's your call. For the rest of the positions, you'll need to hire locally."

Sam picked up on the most shocking directive. "Fire Miss Harris?"

"Too involved. Best get rid of her."

"She's a good secretary."

"Who has her eye on your inheritance—if you manage to keep it."

Sam gritted his teeth. "Then we'll transfer her."

Father leaned forward. "Or you."

That was what Sam had expected from the start, but he'd come to like Pearlman and the people in it—one in particular. "Maybe I'll stay."

Father's gaze narrowed. "Let me remind you that I decide where you're needed."

Harry grinned. Sam paced across the room to the window. The room had shrunk to the size of a prison cell. Sam needed air. From here he could look down at Main Street with its quaint shops and bank. The bank. Ruth. She must know by now that her dress shop had gotten a brief reprieve.

"Did you get advertising copy into the local newspaper?" Father asked.

"Of course."

"And the advertisement that you're hiring sales staff?"

"Interviews begin Monday." But Sam's attention was drawn to the sidewalk below, where an unfamiliar older couple stepped out of the dress shop. Pearlman didn't have many newcomers. He pressed against the window, trying to make out their features. Just before walking away, the man looked up. The resemblance to Ruth was unmistakable. Sam hoped the man was an uncle, but he feared it was her father. The fact that Ruth and her sisters soon followed sealed his identity. The man should be in the hospital. Only one thing could force Mr. Fox home. Despite his best effort, Father had somehow managed to push the property purchase through.

"How many do you plan to hire?" Father demanded.

Sam pulled his attention away from the window and the Foxes in order to settle it upon the man who ruined everything good in Sam's life. Hadn't Father promoted Lillian as the perfect bride? Sam had swallowed Father's recommendation, intrigued by Lillian's beauty and popularity. When he discovered his wife's infidelity two years later, Father had laughed it off as common practice. Not for Sam. He wanted a true and faithful wife. Someone like Ruth.

"Didn't you hear me?" Father said. "I asked how many

saleswomen you intended to hire. Harry would have lined up staff days ago."

"Two per department," Sam said through clenched teeth. That jab about Harry made him want to punch something. Father insisted that no locals be hired until after the opening, yet now he claimed Sam should already have the sales staff lined up.

"Not enough," Father barked. "You'll need a dozen saleswomen—more if you can get them cheap. You can pay bottom dollar around here. And bring in a top-notch seamstress to run your alterations department. I suggest transferring Miss Tinderhook from Cleveland."

But Sam didn't hear past the word *seamstress*. The head of alterations made a decent wage, enough to provide for an ill father. Sam would hire Ruth in an instant, but she would have to give up the dress shop. The head of alterations worked long hours. Ruth couldn't do both.

"Now, let's talk about mixing business with pleasure." Father leaned forward, his bushy brows drawn into black displeasure.

"I don't think—"

"Exactly. You don't think." Father banged his fist on the desktop. "Keep your dalliances on the side and away from the store."

"There is nothing between Miss Harris and myself," Sam reiterated.

Father waved a hand. "I didn't say there was. I'm talking about that dressmaker. In a town this small, that gold digger is likely to think you're serious. Cut off the relationship now."

Sam fisted his hands. One more word against Ruth, and he'd break the commandment to honor his father. "What I do on personal time is none of your business."

"It is when it affects *my* business. Imagine my surprise

when Harry called last night to get the closing figure on the property purchase and discovered the sale is off. Apparently someone made a counteroffer."

Sam looked out the window until he gathered his composure. Father must not suspect him. "I already told you that the property isn't worth the effort."

Father did not blink. His cold stare drove weaker men into stuttering fools. Not Sam. Not this time. He would fight for Ruth.

"Fortunately, I was able to step in before the deal was closed," Father said. "After a little sweetening of my offer, the owner was more than happy to accept."

No! Sam fisted his hands. How could Father do this?

"Money's the answer, boy," Father cackled. "Never forget it."

Sam felt sick. Money meant nothing. People mattered. Lives depended on the income from that little shop. No wonder Ruth's father had come home and she'd been so upset. Sam could not let his father win. He hadn't been able to buy Ruth's dress shop a reprieve, but he could still give her family hope by offering her the head-of-alterations position. If he acted quickly.

"You don't need me, then." Sam donned his jacket and hat.

"Where are you going?" Father demanded as Sam walked out of the office. "We have work to do. Decisions have to be made."

Father's shouts could be heard all the way along the mezzanine, down the steps and onto the main floor. But once Sam stepped outside, the joyful chatter of Pearlman wiped away Father's threats. The knot in his gut eased, replaced by the certainty that he was doing the right thing.

Chapter Fifteen

"You should sleep, Daddy." Ruth tucked the quilt around his legs.

He promptly shoved it away. "It's a warm day, Ruthie. I don't need a blanket, and I don't need to sleep. A little rest and a bite of lunch will do wonders."

"I'll make you a sandwich."

"No, Ruth." He caught her hand. "Your mother will do that. I want to talk to you. That's why your mother kept your sisters in the kitchen."

Ruth stared at his hand. Blue veins showed through the translucent skin. She didn't want to hear what Daddy had to say. She'd done her best to keep the shop going, but he'd been disappointed by her efforts. Rather than hear why, she changed the subject. "How long will you be visiting?"

"A while." He patted the chair next to his. "Have a seat. I want to hear about everything that happened while I was gone."

Ruth perched on the edge of the chair and knit her fingers together. "We're doing fine."

"I can see that." He smiled faintly. "You are such a responsible young lady. Jen is as feisty as ever. But Minnie seems too melancholy over what happened with her young man. Is something else bothering her?"

Ruth certainly didn't want to mention Jen's marriage scheme or that Minnie had lost her best-paying job. "She's just disappointed. I'm sure she'll be fine in a week or two."

"I'll take your word on that." He leaned his head back. "I can always count on you to tell me the whole story."

Unlike Sam. Ruth choked down the bile.

He lifted his head. "Now, let's talk about the dress shop."

Ruth examined her closely trimmed fingernails. "I told you about my new idea and the orders. I think we can turn the business around and make a profit."

"No, child. It's over."

"What do you mean?" Ruth gripped the arms of the chair. "We'll make it."

He shook his head. "Mr. Vanderloo owns the property, and he's selling it."

"But I talked to Mr. Shea this morning, and he told me that someone else made a better offer and wants to keep us as tenants."

"You talked with the bank?" Her father's gaze narrowed.

"I—I didn't want to trouble you."

"Child, this is not your problem." He shook his head. "In any case, it's too late. We needed to bring the payments current by the end of the day or ownership reverts to Mr. Vanderloo. He can then do as he wishes."

"But the other offer—"

"Makes no difference. The result is the same. We can't afford to bring the payments current, and we can't afford to pay rent. It's over."

Ruth clutched her stomach. The whole world was coming unraveled. "We'll open the shop somewhere that doesn't cost as much." She must do something. This was her future, all she'd worked for over the years.

"No, child. There's no money to start again."

Ruth trembled. "We could work from here, from the house. The sewing machine would fit in the parlor."

"I'm sorry, child." His voice trailed off, softer with each word. "It's no use. A Hutton's Department Store is opening next door."

He knew. Ruth swallowed hard. "That doesn't matter. We'll make specialty dresses. Do alterations. Whatever it takes."

But he shook his head slowly, his face so wan that she feared he would collapse. "No, Ruthie. I haven't the strength."

"You don't have to do a thing." Ruth grabbed his hand. "I'll do it all. You concentrate on getting better. We need you." Tears blurred her vision. "We love you, Daddy." She hugged him and let the tears flow. "I love you." Everything was falling apart. Everything she'd ever known and loved was ending.

He patted her back. "I know, child. I love you all, too, but we don't choose our time to go. The Lord does."

Though Ruth knew that in her head, her heart still ached. Daddy wasn't getting better. He wouldn't have life-saving treatment. "I don't want you to die."

"We all must leave this world, child." He hushed her and rubbed her back as if she were a little girl frightened by a nightmare. "But through our faith in Jesus Christ, we know that we'll see each other again."

Ruth couldn't accept the finality of his words. "You talk like you've given up."

"I would never give up one moment with you and your sisters. I'll fight for every breath the Lord grants me."

"That's better." She managed a smile through the tears.

Daddy handed her his hankie. "Dry your eyes, Ruthie, and know that whatever trials come your way, you will persevere. Even if I'm not here, God will stay by your side. Never forget that. He will carry you through the rough patches."

Ruth bit her lip to still another flood of tears.

"Besides," Daddy said with a burst of humor, "I might live to be a hundred. After all, rumor has it that President Harding has a weak heart like mine. He even spent time at the Battle Creek Sanitarium some years ago. Now he's traveling all over the West, even to Alaska. That's not for the faint of heart."

Ruth had to smile at her father's humor.

He wasn't done. "Every day brings new opportunity, Ruthie. Open your heart to where God is leading and be willing to step into the unknown."

Ruth bowed her head. Daddy always exhorted her to take risks, but Jen had inherited all the spirit for adventure. Ruth was more the homebody.

Jen burst into the living room. "Ruth! Come to the kitchen door. You have a visitor."

"At the back door?" She stood. It must be a friend. No stranger would come to the kitchen. "Who is it?"

Jen fairly trembled with excitement. "It's *him*."

Ruth's feet nearly went out from under her. After all Sam Rothenburg had done, he was paying her a call? Her heart raced. What would she say? "I can't."

"Open your heart," Daddy said from his chair.

Ruth didn't dare upset her father. She mouthed to her sister to watch over Daddy and headed for the kitchen. She would tell Mr. Rothenburg never to come here again.

The moment she entered the room, Mother and Minnie slipped upstairs.

That left Ruth alone to face Sam.

He stood just inside the door, hat slightly askew and jacket unbuttoned. The usually impeccable man looked disheveled.

"Ruth." He pulled off his hat. "Please forgive me for barging in on your family, but this is urgent. There's no time to waste if we're going to prevent disaster."

Ruth couldn't stem the swell of anger. Instead of apologizing, he wanted to drag her away from the people who needed her most. Father would still be in the hospital if not for Sam. "Disaster has already happened, thanks to you."

The accusation smacked Sam hard. He'd already endured his father's scorn, but that pain didn't come close to what Ruth had just inflicted.

She stood ramrod-stiff. Unyielding. "I think you should leave."

"But you don't understand. I'm here to help." He didn't even care that he sounded desperate.

"I don't need your kind of help."

Her bitter response echoed too closely the scorn Lillian had tossed at him before she left with Ned. *I don't need your kind of love.* It was happening all over again. He'd opened his heart to a woman, only to have her stomp on it.

He crushed his hat between his hands. "Maybe I should leave."

"I think that would be best."

But then she averted her gaze, much like the day they'd met. At that moment he realized that she didn't believe her own words. And she couldn't possibly know how hard he'd tried to save the dress shop. After all, he'd insisted on anonymity. Perhaps he could win her over. His intentions were noble. He'd come here to help. Even if Ruth wouldn't let him into her life, she would accept help for her family.

He set his hat on the counter. "Not until I've had my say."

She backed away. "I don't care to listen to anything you have to say."

"Hear me out," he pleaded. "I didn't come here to talk about you and me or the mistakes I made. I came here to help your family."

"My family is fine." She crossed her arms around her midsection like a shield.

"I also wanted to discuss the dress shop."

She turned her face, but not before he caught sight of the rush of emotion. "What about the dress shop?"

"I'd like to save your business, but I can't do it alone. It'll take time and effort and a willingness to try something new. You would have to give up the shop." Now was not the time to whitewash the truth.

"I thought you said you wanted to help."

"I do. But it will take time. And you would have to do something else for a while." He stepped toward her, longing to hold her close and tell her everything would be all right.

She backed away.

Only then did it hit him how badly he'd wounded her. She wouldn't accept any help from him without repentance and forgiveness.

He struggled to find the words. "I've hurt you. You can't know how much I regret that. I should have told you the truth from the beginning."

She turned to the window and offered no response.

He took a deep breath and continued the painful course. "But I couldn't. You see, my father insists on keeping the store's identity a secret until the grand opening. I couldn't tell you or anyone else that my last name is Rothenburg."

"So you lied."

"No, I didn't. The family used the name Roth during the Great War. Only after anti-German sentiment died down did most of us return to Rothenburg."

"It's still a lie."

"I just explained that it isn't."

She stared him down. "We are not in the Great War, and your name is now Rothenburg, isn't it?"

Sam gritted his teeth on the raw edge of truth. "Yes, but I was under orders from Father. My job was on the line."

"And that's worth more than our friendship?" Her eyes flashed. "You should have trusted me. You asked for my trust. You held me. You even…kissed me." She swiped at her eyes. "How could you?"

Sam floundered for words that would calm her down enough to see reason. "I should have. I know that now, but we barely knew each other then. I didn't know if you could keep a secret."

"Do you always kiss women you don't trust?"

So they were back to that again. "I did trust you. I do trust you."

"Not enough." Her chin jutted out. "I trusted you completely."

Oh, how that hurt. No woman had ever trusted him completely. Lillian certainly hadn't. The secrets she'd kept had nearly destroyed Sam.

"You're right." If he had any chance of success, he had to bare his soul. "My late wife took a lover. My best friend. I learned about it the night they died." He clenched his fist to maintain composure.

"I'm sorry," she said flatly.

He tried again. "I have trouble trusting people." He punched the counter, preferring the pain of flesh cracking against wood to the pain in his heart. "But I did trust you. I do still. More than anyone I've ever met." He choked on the words that must come next. "I have no excuse for not telling you everything. I can only beg your forgiveness."

Her shoulders hitched before she forced out, "It's too late."

Too late. The final verdict. Guilty as charged and sentenced to life alone.

"Maybe it is." The admission hurt. Worse than Lillian's betrayal. Her infidelity had bruised his ego but not his heart. Ruth's rejection uncovered what love truly entailed. *Love is not self-seeking.* Pastor Gabe had put it well in his sermon.

Love dictated what he must do. No matter if she forgave him or not, he must set aside his own desires to help her.

"Please leave," she reiterated.

"Not until I finish what I came here to do. Look at me, Ruth."

She shook her head.

"Then don't, but I'm still making you the offer." He then detailed the duties and wages for the head-of-alterations job. "No one would do better in the position. It would give you the money to pay for your father's treatment, and in time you could save enough to open another dress shop."

Her shoulders had stilled, but she wouldn't look at him. "I'd work for you?"

"No." That admission took a toll. He'd hoped to stay, to make a life here—one that would someday include Ruth— but that was gone now. "I will go to another store in another city. After the new employees are hired and learn their jobs, you won't ever see me again. Someone else will take over as store manager." He hoped it wouldn't be Harry.

She sniffled and wiped her eyes. "It's not the same as the dress shop."

"I know, but I can't stop Father's purchase of the property."

Her back stiffened as if shot. "Your father is the buyer? He's the one throwing us out?"

Technically, Father wasn't throwing the Foxes out of their shop, but technicalities didn't matter when the end result was the same. "I tried to stop him. I told him the property wasn't worth his while." He almost revealed how he'd made a higher offer including a large down payment, but it sounded too self-serving.

"But you never told me." She stared at him with red-rimmed eyes. "All this time you knew what your father was planning, and you never told me."

Sam struggled to understand why she kept harping on whether or not he had told her. Even if he had, nothing would have changed. "I tried to help. I gave you the idea about turning old dresses into new ones."

"But you never told me the truth." She shoved a lock of hair from her brow. "Don't you understand? Friendship isn't about business arrangements or who's right or wrong. It's about trust. You didn't trust me enough to tell me the truth."

Sam stood speechless. Nothing he could say would change her mind. Ruth felt exactly the same as he had the moment he learned Lillian had betrayed him. Nothing he could do would save their relationship. He ought to be grateful to turn his back on this mess, but instead he ached. Deep, deep inside. And, as he took his hat and bid a silent Ruth farewell, he doubted he'd ever feel joy again.

Chapter Sixteen

Ruth held back the tears until Sam closed the screen door. He didn't slam it. He didn't yell at her. He left with dignity. And in pain. She'd seen the hurt on his face and couldn't watch him walk away. Turning, she spotted her sister in the doorway to the living room.

"What happened?" Jen asked.

How could her sister invade such a private moment? "I thought I asked you to watch over Daddy."

Jen crossed her arms. "No need to throw a conniption. He's asleep."

Ruth glanced around the room for something to do. Anything. She did not want to discuss Sam with Jen. She did not want to break down or lash out. Spotting the dirty breakfast and luncheon dishes, she drained hot water from the stove-top tank into the washbasin, donned an apron and grabbed a rag.

"I'm washing dishes, if you care to help." That ought to send her sister running. Jen detested any kind of housework.

"I think I hear Daddy waking up." As hoped, Jen darted off to the living room.

Ruth took a deep breath. She needed time to sort out

her jumbled feelings. Part of her wanted to yell at Sam and have nothing to do with him. Another part ached for him and the opportunity lost. She had cared for him, or at least for the man she'd thought he was.

The creak of footsteps on the stairs meant she wouldn't be alone long.

"I'll help you with those." Mother crossed the room and pulled a clean drying cloth from the cupboard.

"There aren't that many dishes. I can do them myself."

"Perhaps, but I'd like you to explain what's going on with that young man. Mr. Roth, is it? Minnie didn't make a bit of sense."

Ruth shaved some lye soap off the bar. People with more money bought liquid soap. She had to scrimp even on this. Anger drove the knife deep, slicing off a thick curl of soap. Too much. It dropped into the water. Why was everything going wrong? Ruth fought tears of frustration.

Mother lightly touched her arm. "Ruth, dear? We've always been able to talk about things. I can see something is bothering you. Let me help."

Mother had an uncanny ability to untangle difficult emotions. What she lacked in business sense, she more than made up for in relationship sense. But talking about Sam would unleash the tears Ruth struggled to hold inside.

So she shifted to an equally painful yet somehow easier subject. "Daddy isn't any better, is he?"

Mother did not reply for some time. "This isn't about your father. You've been avoiding the topic of Mr. Roth."

Ruth scrubbed at the residue of dried oatmeal ringing a bowl and considered how to dismiss her mother's concern. "I've only known him less than two weeks. Since you left. It's nothing."

"It didn't sound like nothing."

"Well, it is." Ruth used her fingernail to scrape off a

particularly stubborn spot. "It turns out I didn't know the man at all." She dunked the bowl in hot rinse water and hurried to the next dish. As the water cooled, the soap would form a film on the surface and stick to the dishes.

"I see." Mother took the bowl from her and wiped it over and over, as if she couldn't get it dry enough. "Did I ever tell you that your father and I had a falling-out early in our courtship?"

Ruth shook her head, though she remembered the story well. The sicker Daddy got, the more Mother clung to the memory of their earlier days.

"I thought he had eyes for another girl." Mother chuckled. "I should have known better. Your father was kind to everyone, but especially to those girls who were ignored by the rest. He'd see a girl sitting by herself and go talk to her. He'd compliment the girls who had to wear patched dresses."

That was the kind of man Ruth had hoped to meet. Poor but kind. A man whose heart was so filled with the Lord that love overflowed onto everyone around him. Instead, she'd let herself fall for Sam Rothenburg. "It's not the same."

"Isn't it? A little misunderstanding can lead to a terrible rift."

Ruth stopped scrubbing the next bowl. "It's not a little misunderstanding. He lied to me."

"About what?"

"He claimed his name was Sam Roth when he's actually Sam Rothenburg. And he never mentioned that he was opening a department store next door."

To her surprise, Mother didn't look shocked. "Did he tell you why?"

"Does it matter?" Ruth braced the bowl against her left hand and put her weight into scrubbing off the dried oatmeal. "He said he couldn't tell me the truth because his father insisted he keep his name and the store a secret until the grand opening."

"You don't believe him?"

"I do." Ruth dunked the bowl in rinse water. "And I don't. I thought after all we'd shared that he would trust me."

"The way you trust him?"

Ruth shoved away a twinge of guilt. Sam didn't need to know about Jen's silly marriage idea when it hadn't amounted to anything. "That's not the point. He didn't trust me."

"Because he wanted to obey his father. Children will go to great lengths to please and even protect their fathers."

"I don't think Sam's doing that."

"Maybe I'm not talking about Sam." Mother picked up the bowl and wiped it. "Did you tell us about the sale of the dress-shop property?"

Ruth sucked in her breath. "I didn't want to worry Daddy."

"I see. So you made that decision for us."

Ruth bowed her head. "I did what I thought was right." But she felt terrible.

"Is it possible that Sam also did what he felt was right? That he didn't want to worry his father?"

The gentle reprimand hurt. "I suppose so."

"Then you will grant him the same forgiveness your father and I grant you?"

Ruth scrubbed the bowl with vigor. "It's too late."

"You'll wear through the bowl, dear." Mother stilled her hands with a touch. "It's never too late for an apology, especially when that person loves you."

Something leaped inside Ruth. "Love?"

"I could see it in his eyes." Mother smiled softly. "Your

father looks at me like that sometimes." She squeezed Ruth's shoulder. "I treasure every time, knowing it might be the last."

Ruth's throat constricted. "It won't be."

"It might. That's the truth, dear. None of us knows the number of our days here on earth, but thanks to Our Lord Jesus, we know eternity awaits us."

Ruth's hand shook as the errors of the past two weeks mounted. "I've failed, Mother. I tried so hard to save the dress shop and pay the debts, but it's all come to naught and now Daddy had to come home and he won't get the treatments he needs and he'll die because I failed."

The bowl slipped from her fingers and thudded against the bottom of the washbasin. Mother enveloped her as the sobs came.

"Hush, hush now." Mother rubbed her back. "It's all right. Everything's going to be all right."

"I don't see how."

Mother kissed the top of her head before holding her at arm's length. "We seldom see how, but the Lord knows, and He's right here beside those of us who love Him. He's here with us this very minute, and He's with your father."

Ruth took off her tearstained glasses. "I know, but it's hard sometimes."

Mother cupped her chin. "Of course it is, child. This life isn't meant to be easy, but God will see us through. Remember, He will never give us more than we can bear."

Ruth wiped her glasses on her apron. "What if Daddy doesn't get better?"

"Then we will press on until we join him one day. You must believe this, Ruth. You must hold it dear in your heart. Your father loves the Lord and is ready to join Him when his time comes. We must be strong for him."

"And the dress shop?"

"Ah, dear child, what is a shop compared to our love for each other? We must fix our attention on the Lord and our loved ones, and all else will fall away."

Mother's grace in the face of loss humbled Ruth. "Maybe you're right."

Mother lifted Ruth's chin. "God has a plan for your life, Ruth, a great and glorious plan."

Ruth averted her eyes. "If He does, I don't know what it could be."

"Then we will pray for God's guidance. He will show us the path He has chosen. Do you believe that with all your heart?"

"Yes, Mother."

"Will you trust in the Lord's plan for your life?"

Ruth hesitated before whispering, "Yes, Mother."

"Even if He tells you to go where you're afraid to tread?"

Was Mother suggesting Ruth risk even worse pain to work for Sam? She must apologize to him, surely, but work in his store, the one that had destroyed the dress shop and forced her father to leave lifesaving treatments? She couldn't.

"Ruth?" Mother caught her attention. "Only God knows the best path. You must trust Him."

Ruth wanted to. Truly, she did. As long as that path didn't include Sam.

Sam couldn't return to the store to face Father. The boardinghouse offered no comfort, and he had no one to talk this out with. Sam had to deal with Ruth's dismissal alone. Not only did her words sting, but he'd also managed to lose his only friend in this town. His best friend.

He wandered the streets, oblivious to those who greeted him. No store window could suggest an answer. He glanced at the church. Years ago he would have found consolation there, but he'd stopped believing in God's grace after Lillian's betrayal and death. Today, the prim little church beckoned, and for a moment he considered crossing the street to slip inside its doors. But then Pastor Gabe opened the door. Embarrassed, Sam hurried down the street, hands in pockets and face averted, before the minister spotted him.

The street ended at the little park where he'd picnicked with Ruth and her sisters. The warmth and love of that family had woven so thoroughly into his heart that tugging a single thread had ripped open a gaping hole. He had wanted this above everything. This love. This concern for each other. This closeness. He'd dared to hope he could get it, but Ruth had shoved him away. Just like Lillian. Both times he'd tried so hard to please the woman he loved. Both times he'd failed.

He hurried across the freshly mowed grass and past the ball field. The crack of a bat connecting with the ball sent up shouts and cheers from the kids participating. A double, if the center fielder got there quickly enough. Sam paused long enough to see the skinny boy throw the ball in a great arc to the second baseman, who let the ball bounce past his glove. Cheers turned into jeers. Just like life.

He ducked around the pavilion and away from the boys' cries. Here, tall trees filtered the hot sun. Dapples of sunlight danced upon the undergrowth. A cool breeze blew up from the river. The path leading to the water was deserted in the heat of midday. He walked to the platform overlooking the river without seeing a soul. The water below passed at a steady clip. It burbled over and around scattered rocks and ran deep black at the center.

Black as his heart. The blinders fell away, and he could see every fault clearly. So many deceptions. He'd filled his life with them. Ruth was right. He'd lied by omission. And he'd lied to himself, thinking it didn't matter. So many excuses, and not one of them was valid. What a mess he'd made of things. Again. Hadn't he learned anything in eight years?

How could I, Lord?

He tossed a dead birch leaf into the water. It bobbed up and down as it made its way downstream. Could he throw away his faults and wrongdoings that easily? Baptism was supposed to wash away sin, but Sam had been baptized years ago. Yet he still floundered and failed. A whole tree couldn't supply enough leaves to account for his mistakes. What could wash away that mess?

Jesus can.

Pastor Gabe had said that on Sunday. Sam knew the truth of the minister's words. He'd heard it often, but until this moment he'd never really wanted it. That kind of gift came with a price tag, and he didn't want to pay what God was sure to demand. Sam could get by on his own terms. He did not surrender control. Pastor Gabe insisted that was the way to peace. Turn over the reins to God. The idea had sounded ludicrous until Ruth had cast him off. When he'd lost her, he'd lost the most precious thing this world had ever brought into his life. With Ruth beyond reach, he no longer cared about the price. He had nothing of value left to lose.

A narrow path led down the bank to the water's edge. Fallen leaves lined it. Plenty for his sins. If he could reach the water, he could throw every wrongdoing away. Sam plowed down the path, braving the overhanging branches that whipped his face and arms. At last he stood in the spongy soil at river's edge. He grabbed a handful of leaves off the ground.

"God, forgive me for getting angry at Lillian." He tossed the first leaf.

"And for hating her." Another leaf.

He recalled his late wife's contemptuous rebuke. *You only care about your precious company.* Was that true? Had he been cold and unfeeling in his quest to prove himself? But he'd done what any man would do. What Father had done. And he'd done it for her. He'd given her diamonds and the most expensive gowns. Yet she threw it all in his face and left with Ned. What did Sam's best friend have that Sam didn't? Time. Ned had treated Lillian like a rare flower, while Sam had been engrossed with earning his father's approval.

Sam tossed another leaf into the swirling water. "For not being the kind of husband Lillian needed."

The admission brought only a moment of relief. He'd done the same to Ruth. In both cases, he'd tried to be what he thought they needed, not who he truly was. He'd played the role of rescuer instead of entrusting them with his heart.

"Forgive me for hurting Ruth." He tossed an entire handful of leaves into the water but felt no relief.

Surrender everything.

The pastor had said it in his sermon. Sam knew the man was right. But how to do it?

As the water gurgled past, an idea came to mind. He kicked off his shoes and stepped into the stream. The cold water made him gasp. But water could wash away stains.

"Lousy place for a swim." Pastor Gabe's comment seared through Sam.

Why would God let anyone interrupt this moment?

"Rocky bottom, but the boys like to swim here anyway," the minister said. "They're the ones who made this path." Judging from the crackling of branches behind Sam, Pastor Gabe was coming down that path.

Sam did not want company. "I'm not planning to swim."

"You're in the water."

"I'm wading." Sam refused to look at Gabe, hoping he'd get the hint and leave.

"Must feel good on a hot day." The pastor splashed in behind Sam.

Apparently Pastor Gabe was not the sort who took a hint.

"I wanted some time alone to think things through." In case the pastor missed the point, Sam repeated, "I think best when it's quiet."

"Me, too." The pastor drew up beside him. "Nothing like a bracing swim to sort things out."

Sam hazarded a glance. The minister wore dark trousers and a white shirt rolled up to the elbows. No hat. No jacket, but still formal enough for the office. "In street clothes?"

Pastor Gabe shrugged. "Felicity will probably have my head, but sometimes it's worth the risk." Without waiting for Sam's reply, he plunged beneath the water in a clean dive and popped up midstream. "Care to join me?"

Sam hadn't dived since he was a boy. He recalled with intense clarity the mountain house at Lake Minnewaska, the lake clear as glass. How he'd loved to run down to the water, race out the dock and dive off the end.

"Come on," the pastor urged. "See if you can beat that dive."

"Are you challenging me?" Sam countered. "Because if you are, I have to tell you that I could beat any boy at Lake Minnewaska."

"Prove it."

Sam couldn't resist. He ripped off his jacket and hat and tossed them on shore. Then he crouched and sprang through the air, the old form coming back. The cold water slammed into him like a rock. Every muscle tensed, but he was going to beat the pastor's dive. With three strong kicks, he pushed through the water. Eyes open, he scanned

for his opponent, bubbles trailing past his face until his
lungs ached. He popped to the surface and gasped for air.

"Good one," Pastor Gabe said. "With one more kick,
you would have beaten me."

Sam swiped the water from his eyes. He couldn't believe
it, but the pastor stood an arm's length distant in chest-
deep water. Sam struggled to his feet. "How did you get
so far? You're shorter than me. I should have been able to
outkick you."

Gabe grinned. "Maybe I'm not carrying such a heavy
weight."

"Heavy weight? I took my jacket off."

"Not in there. In here." Gabe pointed to his heart.

Sam stiffened. "Why would you think something's bothering me?"

"It's not every day I see someone standing in the river
throwing out leaves and asking for forgiveness."

Sam cringed at the thought of what the pastor must have
heard. "That was private."

"And it'll stay that way. I'm a pastor, remember?"

Sam had to concede that point, but he still felt uncomfortable knowing he'd revealed his wretched past in front
of the man. At least, as Gabe had said, he was a minister and would keep this between them. And now that the
damage was done...

Sam couldn't hold on to the pain any longer. "My late
wife died in a motorcar accident. She ran off with her...
lover." The word sat bitter on his tongue.

"I remember it from the newspapers."

That caught Sam by surprise.

"I was still in New York at the time," Pastor Gabe added.

"Oh." Sam stared at the river. "I know that I should have
gotten over it by now, but I can't seem to stop remember-
ing that night."

Gabe nodded. "Maybe that's why God urged me to come here today. I'd just returned to the office after lunch and felt this overwhelming need to take a walk along the river."

"God told you?" Sam found that tough to believe.

"More like a nudge."

The water tugged past Sam. "I thought maybe I could get rid of all my mistakes."

The minister nodded. "If you want to talk about it, I'm a good listener."

It had been years since Sam trusted anyone with the deepest darkness in his soul. Other than Ruth. And look how that had turned out. But he had no idea how to fix things with her...if he could fix them.

"It's not really about Lillian." He hesitated. It was one thing to tell Pastor Gabe about someone the man didn't know personally but quite another thing to reveal the mistakes he'd made with one of Gabe's parishioners.

The minister stared across the river. "It's never simple, is it?"

Hours ago, Sam would never have unburdened himself to a minister, but now he had nothing to lose. "I've made a lot of mistakes in my life, but now I've hurt the person I care for most." He wiped the dripping hair from his eyes. "Trouble is, I was trying to help her." Then he told the pastor everything that had happened since arriving in Pearlman—everything except the kiss.

Pastor Gabe nodded from time to time but let Sam get out the whole story.

"I don't know what to do to make things right," Sam concluded.

"Hmm. Reminds me of the rich young man who came to Jesus looking for approval for the way he'd lived his life."

Sam groaned. He didn't want a sermon.

Gabe grinned. "I know. I could find a better example,

but this is the one that came to mind. Indulge me. Seems this man had followed every commandment all his life and wanted to know if he'd done enough to get into heaven. Do you remember what Jesus told him?"

How could Sam forget? He'd never understood this story, for it made entry into heaven impossible. "To sell all he owned and give it to the poor."

"But the rich man couldn't do that, so he left saddened."

Sam felt sick. "You're telling me to give away all I own?"

"Do you think that would have made the man happy?"

Sam tried to sort through the story. "No, because he enjoyed his wealth."

"He held on too tightly to earthly things," the young pastor said. "You see, no one can get to heaven on our own efforts, not even me. I can't earn it or buy it or do enough good. All of us have made mistakes. All of us have failed. And all of us have been offered an amazing gift. We just have to accept it."

Sam knew all this in his head, but until that moment it had never made sense in his heart. Now, as if the water had washed a film from his eyes, he could see clearly.

"I want that."

Pastor Gabe nodded. "It means you'll have to let go of everything, including the things you want most desperately."

Ruth. Pastor Gabe was asking him to let go of Ruth. But Sam had never truly had her. No, she was as airy and soft as silk. Hold on too tightly, and it ripped. Let it go, and, like a butterfly, it revealed its full beauty. "I will let go."

"Then ask Jesus into your heart. Put your trust completely in Him."

"How?"

"Just ask Him the way you'd ask me."

Standing in the middle of the river, Sam struggled to

find the words. "Will you accept me, Jesus?" he began haltingly. "I've made a mess of things on my own, but I want to make things right, and I know now that I can't do anything without You. Please come into my life. Please take over. Please show me the way You want me to walk. And please help Ruth."

Pastor Gabe smiled and then grasped Sam's hand. "Welcome to the family of God, Sam Roth."

"Rothenburg." It felt good to say his full name. "Sam Rothenburg." Sam flexed his shoulders. The weight that had crushed down on him for years seemed to have disappeared. "Now what?"

"Race you to the other side?" Pastor Gabe motioned across the river.

"You're on."

On the count of three, the two men splashed and kicked their way across the river, and by the time Sam reached the other side, he knew exactly what he had to do.

"I have to go," he said as soon as Gabe surfaced two strokes behind him. "I have to take care of something, and there's not much time."

Gabe nodded. "Godspeed, then."

Sam would need God's help to seize the only chance left to make things right.

Chapter Seventeen

For as long as Ruth could remember, family life centered on the dress shop. Each of the girls had grown up there. At first they'd been under Mother and Daddy's feet. When they got a little older, they learned to pin seams. After they'd mastered that skill, they could cut inexpensive fabric and baste. Jen had never graduated to that stage, but the rest of them got at least that far. Ruth had always wanted more. She spent every Saturday in the shop. Sometimes she didn't return home until after supper.

Now Fox Dress Shop was closing. It hurt to pack up the fabrics and ribbons, the dress forms and sewing machine, the needles and pins. Everything, great and small, had to go into boxes. Those boxes then had to be carried across the alley to their house and up into the attic for storage.

"It's not right," Minnie sniffed as she threw a tangled bolt of muslin onto the worktable. "How can mean Mr. Vanderloo kick us out after all these years?"

Ruth had struggled with the same wrong thoughts until Mother's talk. She rewound the muslin so it wouldn't wrinkle. "We can't blame Mr. Vanderloo for making a simple business decision. You or I would do the same in his place."

"No, I wouldn't," Minnie insisted.

Jen concurred. "We wouldn't kick out a perfectly good renter just to make a little extra money."

"We're not renters. Daddy was buying the property." Ruth couldn't explain it all. She didn't fully understand what had happened herself, except that Daddy wanted to let go of the shop. Since he was head of the family, she must accept his decision even when she didn't like it.

"Then how can he force us out?" Jen asked.

"Because we didn't make the payments." Ruth wound a measuring tape.

"What?" Jen and Minnie said at nearly the same time.

"Why didn't Mother and Daddy tell us?" Jen gripped the edge of the worktable. "I would have given all my wages to the family rather than save up for flight lessons."

"And I wouldn't have lost my job," Minnie added.

"Stop this, you two. It's no one's fault." Ruth picked up the pincushion they'd held when they'd vowed to help each other find husbands. Why had she ever gone along with such an outlandish plan? "I should have known better."

"How?" Jen's eyes widened with realization. "Are you saying that you knew we were going to lose the shop?"

Ruth bit her lip, caught in her error of omission. "I didn't want to worry you. I never thought it would come to this." If she'd had only a little more time, her dress-redesign concept might have worked.

Jen braced her hands on her hips. "Stop acting like our mother. We needed to know."

"I know, and I'm sorry." Ruth pushed the pins flush into the cushion. "But I wanted you to keep your dreams."

"By giving up yours?" Jen snapped. "Or didn't you realize that none of us would have had to give up our dreams if you hadn't sent Sam away?"

"I had to." Ruth squeezed the pincushion. "He lied to us."

Jen's gaze narrowed. "You mean about how rich he is?"

"Money doesn't mean a thing."

"Except you would have dismissed him out of hand if you knew he was rich," Jen said.

"No, I wouldn't have." But even as Ruth said it, she knew that Jen was right. "It doesn't matter. He's gone. Or soon will be."

Both Minnie and Jen stared at her now. "Gone where?"

Ruth squeezed the sides of the pincushion until the pinheads pushed up a tiny bit. "To another store in another town." Though her throat constricted until it ached, she would never let her sisters know how much that hurt.

"You have to stop him," Jen urged. "Put up a fight."

Ruth recoiled. "Fight?"

"Yes, fight. He loves you. I know it."

Minnie joined her sister in a chorus of encouragement, but Ruth couldn't forget the look on Sam's face when he left. Anything that might have blossomed between them had been crushed. Even the job offer came with assurances that he would soon leave.

No, her sisters were mistaken. Sam didn't love her. After the way she'd treated him, he wouldn't even like her.

"I don't care how he feels." Ruth shoved the pincushion into a box. "It doesn't matter. What's happened has happened, and there's no use wishing things had turned out differently."

"How can you say that?" Jen exclaimed. "You're acting like your whole life is set, like you have to accept whatever happens because there's nothing you can do about it."

Even though Ruth recognized the truth in her sister's words, she couldn't bear to admit it. "Maybe I don't want to see Sam again. Have you considered that?"

"A moment ago you were practically in tears over him."

"A moment of weakness." Ruth turned to gather the fabric remnants off the cubbyhole shelves. Each had been carefully rolled and arranged by color. She began with the yellows. "Closing the shop is painful."

"Saying farewell is always difficult." Mother's calm voice made Ruth hesitate. When had she arrived? "But we will always carry a part of what we love with us."

Ruth resumed placing the yellow scraps into a carton, unsure if Mother was talking about the shop or Sam.

Will you trust the Lord's plan for your life?

The thought came into Ruth's mind so loudly that she turned to see if Mother had said it. But Mother was walking out the door with one of the smaller boxes. Ruth pondered her mother's advice. Did she trust the Lord? Ruth had always thought she did, but she was no longer certain. She certainly couldn't see the path He wanted her to walk.

Even if He tells you to go where you're afraid to tread?

Mother's words echoed in her head as Ruth finished the yellows and moved on to the reds. Surely He didn't mean for her to chase after Sam. Apologize? All right. She could write him a letter. But not chase him.

"I won't throw myself at any man," Ruth murmured.

Jen quirked an eyebrow. "Why not? Your namesake did." That was her way of referring to the biblical Ruth. "She lay at Boaz's feet on the threshing floor while he slept. Can you imagine the scandal?"

"That was thousands of years ago. Their culture had different customs than ours."

Jen refused to let go of her point. "An unmarried woman sleeping in the same room as an unmarried man? I can just imagine what the other girls said the next day. The gossip would have spread like wildfire."

"Thank you for proving my point. Chasing after a man is scandalous."

"Except that Ruth won." Jen acted as if her point was obvious to even the simplest soul. "She risked everything and gained a husband. A good husband. One worth fighting for."

Ruth tried to swallow the lump in her throat. "She could have lost."

"Maybe." Jen shoved the whole shelfful of blue fabric into a box. "But to win big, you have to take a chance."

Could Ruth do the same? Once before she'd risked her heart. She'd chased after Blake Kensington only to discover he'd used her to get Beatrice. Pursue Sam Rothenburg? Until she'd discovered his lie, she'd thought him good and kind and moral. No, Jen was wrong. Sam had used her for his own purposes.

"I don't—" Ruth began, but before she could counter Jen's proposal, the front door of the shop burst open.

Mr. Vanderloo stepped inside. "Where is your father?"

"He's—" Jen began before Ruth cut her off.

"Not here. You may speak with me." She would not subject Daddy to a tirade.

"You?" Mr. Vanderloo surveyed her with disdain. "What can you do?"

Ruth swallowed hard. "I can promise that we will have everything out of here by dark."

"Out?" Mr. Vanderloo scoffed. "You have no idea what's happened."

Ruth froze. "What do you mean?"

Vanderloo's lip curled into a sneer. "I don't know who bailed you out, but you tell that father of yours that the moment he falls behind on the payments again this property goes up for sale."

Then, before she had time to fully take in what Mr. Vanderloo had just said, he left, slamming the door behind him.

Jen and Minnie stared at her.

"Does he mean what I think he does?" Jen whispered, wide-eyed.

"Impossible." Ruth mentally calculated the account balances. "There's not enough money. Anywhere."

"But Mr. Vanderloo said we don't have to close the shop," Minnie said.

"It makes no sense." Ruth hugged a bolt of muslin. "Who would have done such a thing?"

"Beattie," Jen said. "It has to be."

Ruth's older sister was the only one in the family who had access to that much money. "I don't know. She told me that she couldn't pay anything. Besides, why would she keep it secret from us?"

"If not her," Jen mused, "then maybe that's why Mother and Daddy came home."

"But Daddy insisted we close the shop," Ruth countered before a horrible thought occurred to her. Had he done this for her? Had he seen her distress and spent money he didn't have in order to save the shop? "I don't know where he would have gotten the money."

Jen voiced what Ruth couldn't bear to think. "Maybe he used money that should have gone elsewhere."

Such as for his treatments.

"Oh, Daddy. What have you done?" Ruth whispered into the dead silence.

Sam secured Mr. Fox's approval of the alteration manager's contract before the sisters returned home. Once Sam told him that the contract stipulated Ruth take the position, Mr. Fox promised he would talk to Ruth about it. The man had been surprisingly understanding and genial. Sam anticipated success.

After taking care of business at the bank, Sam headed for the store, a copy of the contract in hand, and braced himself for the storm that was bound to occur when his father discovered what he'd done. His father's choice for the position, Miss Tinderhook, would have to stay in Cleveland.

At this late hour, pedestrians and automobiles clogged the sidewalks and street. Only when he paused at the corner opposite his store to wait for a break in the traffic did he see that Father had already struck.

A huge banner proclaimed the new Hutton's Department Store was opening August 1st. Tomorrow! But the ball gowns hadn't arrived yet, and he hadn't oriented the Chicago sales staff. All the advertising copy specified August 3rd. How dare Father change the date of the grand opening without consulting him? This was a grand mess.

Sam stormed across the street, where a curious crowd had gathered beneath the banner.

"Then the rumors are true?" Beatrice Kensington stopped Sam on his way to the back entrance.

Sam nodded and hustled past. Soon enough she'd learn about the rift between Ruth and him, but he didn't want to be the one to explain it.

Other people accosted him with similar questions. To each he either nodded or shook his head, keeping his gaze on the alley and the door that would free him from the throng. It took ten minutes to get there, only to see the rumpled newspaper editor blocking the door.

"Care to make a statement?" Devlin asked. The stump of an unlit cigar hung from the editor's mouth.

Sam offered a smile, hoping charm would pry the man away from the door. "I think the banner says it all. Hutton's offers excellent merchandise at an affordable price." The company motto rolled off his tongue with practiced ease, but this time he heard the crass commercialism behind it. Yes, the words he'd staked his career on still held true at face value, but it didn't account for those small-business owners who'd been crushed by their giant competitor.

Devlin scribbled in a notepad. "Why wait until now to announce that you're opening a Hutton's Department Store?"

That was always the question, and Father was nowhere in sight to answer to the rule that he had put into place. Sam chafed that he always had to fend off questions while Father hid in the office. Yet this time Sam felt his culpability. He'd gone along with the plan. He'd withheld the name of the store from everyone, including the one person who'd trusted him with all her heart.

"Do you have an answer, Mr. Rothenburg?" Devlin tapped his pencil against the pad.

Sam started to spout the usual response that he was following standard procedure, but Pearlman deserved a better answer. Pearlman deserved the truth. "Hutton's executives believe that the speculation generated by withholding the store's identity will generate interest and spur business on opening day."

Devlin's jaw dropped, and the cigar fell to the ground. "I can quote you on that?"

"Quote away." Father would be furious, but spilling the truth would put an end to this tactic. It also freed Sam from the shackles of untruth. His spirits soared, and an uncanny peace settled over him. This was the way God intended man to live.

Devlin hurried off to the newspaper, and Sam entered the store, where Father shattered that newfound peace. The man stood behind the front window display, whose backdrop had been pulled aside.

Father pointed at Ruth's ball gown. "Where did you get that? It's not one of ours."

Sam shoved the copy of the contract in his jacket pocket

and set his jaw. "No, it's not, and if you'd bothered to consult me, you would have learned that the evening gowns have not yet arrived. That's why I didn't intend to open early."

Father brushed off Sam's comment. "Where did you buy this gown and how many do we have in stock?"

"None." Sam felt a surge of pride in Ruth's work. "It's a designer original."

Father's gaze narrowed. "How much does it sell for? Or are you planning to have it produced?"

Produced. Of course. That was the answer to Ruth's dilemma. Her design was exquisite. All her sketches were. With his industry connections and her creativity, she could succeed beyond her biggest dreams. What was a little dress shop in Pearlman compared to a glamorous shop in the New York Fashion District?

"Well?" Father demanded. "Answer me."

"I'll have to ask the designer." This idea would save Ruth's family. Maybe it would even bring Ruth back to him.

"Why did you do it?" Ruth sat down next to her father, determined to somehow convince him to retract any funds he'd spent on the dress-shop loan. Just hours ago that shop had stood as her future, but she would give it all away to save her father's life. "You need to get well."

He gently patted her hand. "Now, Ruthie, you know as well as I that healing is in God's hands."

"And those of the doctors."

He smiled weakly. "That's my Ruthie, always needing a solid answer. I had hoped you would understand why I needed to make this decision."

"No, I—"

"Just hear me out. Do you agree that as head of the family, my decisions are not to be questioned?"

"Yes, but—"

"But this time you are." He winced and rubbed his shoulder.

"You're hurting." Ruth hopped up. "I'll fetch a warm compress."

"Don't baby me like your mother. It's just a little spasm, probably from lifting the luggage. A little honest pain never hurt a man, especially when he's helping his family."

"You always help us, Daddy."

The corner of his mouth ticked upward as she sat back down. "Except in the case of this decision."

"I didn't mean—" Ruth began before he cut her off with a raised hand.

"A father must make decisions for the good of his family. Do you trust me, Ruth?"

"Of course." *Unlike Sam.*

"Hmm." He didn't look convinced. "Then you'll accept my decision and work at Mr. Rothenburg's store?"

"What?" Ruth stared. "I thought you were talking about the dress shop. Work at the store? I already refused the position."

"I know. I heard you."

Her cheeks heated at the memory of her strong words. Had Daddy overheard everything? "I'm sorry. I didn't mean for you to hear."

"Then you shouldn't have spoken so loudly."

Ruth averted her eyes. She'd tried so hard to keep all stress away from her father, but in the end she'd brought it right into their home. Or rather, Sam Rothenburg had. "He should not have come here."

"Now, listen to me, Ruthie." He waited for her to look

at him. "Mr. Rothenburg is a generous man. He wants to help."

She fisted her hands on her lap. "How do you know?"

"He spoke with me a little over an hour ago."

"You?" Ruth choked. "Here? About the job I already turned down?"

"He thought you might be a little too overwrought over the dress shop to see things clearly."

"Overwrought, indeed." Ruth's outrage built. No wonder Jen preferred to make her own decisions. No wonder she'd rallied with the suffragists prior to the passage of the 19th Amendment and now fought for equality of wages. Jen wouldn't let the men in her life make decisions without her say-so. This time, neither would Ruth. "Samuel Rothenburg has no right to speculate on either my emotional state of mind or my ability to make a rational decision."

"He only wants what's best for you. As do I." Ruth's father rubbed his left arm. "After all these years you must know that I would never recommend anything that would hurt you." The last words came out a bit strained, and he leaned back in the chair, eyes closed.

"I know, Daddy, but I am a grown woman now. I ran the shop while you and Mother were gone. And I spent enough time with Sam Rothenburg to know that he doesn't always reveal the whole truth. He's manipulating us. He manipulated me."

"Now, Ruthie."

She had to make her father understand. "He told me his name was Sam Roth, and he withheld the name of his store. He let me think he was a friend when he…he—" she could barely spit out the words "—he intended to destroy our dress shop."

"Don't you think you're overreacting a bit?"

"No! You should have heard him."

"I did hear him out, child," he wheezed. "He confessed that he hadn't been up front with you. He laid bare every mistake. If anything, he was a bit too hard on himself."

"I don't believe that." Ruth had heard Sam's manipulations. "He can be quite convincing when he wants to. What I don't understand is why he's so desperate to hire me. To ease his guilty conscience?"

"Maybe he wants to…" Daddy gasped and clutched his chest. His lips blued, and bit by bit he leaned forward.

It happened slowly, like a moving picture shown at the wrong speed. Ruth heard herself scream. She saw her arms reach for him. She felt his dead weight. His cold and clammy skin. Odd gasping sounds issued from his lips.

"Daddy! Daddy! Help!" Her voice sounded so far away, as if from behind the other side of the mirror.

She held on to him. She screamed for help. But he fell silent, even the gasps gone.

Chapter Eighteen

"Call him," Sam's father demanded, still pointing at Ruth's dress. "I want more of these. Buy all he has in stock."

Sam stifled a grin at Father's assumption that the designer was a man. His father would be speechless if he learned that Ruth had made that gown. Sam was tempted to tell him but couldn't put Ruth through the ordeal of dealing with Father. "I'll do what I can."

"Get through to him by morning." Father glanced one last time at the display. "Get everything he has on the first train out of New York. We'll promise the customers new arrivals by the end of the week. It'll build anticipation after the opening. Now, that's the way to run a business."

Satisfied, Father headed upstairs to the office.

Sam could hardly wait to tell Ruth. Now that Fox Dress Shop had staved off closure at the expense of his bank account, anything extra Ruth earned could go directly to her father's medical treatment.

"Whew, that was close." Miss Harris ducked out from behind the backdrop before pulling it back across the display window. "I was adding a necklace to the female mannequin when your father showed up."

Sam tried to recall if Ruth had worn a necklace that night. Maybe. He wasn't sure. He'd been too drawn to her stunning eyes and gentle manner.

"Walk me home?" Without waiting for an answer, Miss Harris snaked her arm around Sam's and flashed one of those sultry smiles that would have enticed him years ago.

Today, it set Sam on edge. He wanted to talk to Ruth, not Miss Harris.

"You still owe me lunch," she said.

Sam bit back his impatience. Ruth was still fuming. Maybe he should give her a little time to cool down. Meanwhile, he would come up with a plan of attack that Ruth couldn't turn down. Maybe he'd place a call or two to some fashion contacts to tout Ruth's designs and test the possibility of sending them to production. "All right."

Miss Harris widened her smile. "I understand there's a cozy little place behind the drugstore."

Sam couldn't swallow the bitter taste. He'd seen men duck into the speakeasy, but his carousing days were long over. They'd died with Lillian.

"I don't partake," he said simply.

"Oh. Fine. It was just a thought." Any disappointment didn't stop her from clinging close once they left the building.

Cars chortled, wheezed and hummed past. One horse and wagon rumbled toward the feed store, a reminder of bygone years. The sidewalks were equally busy. Dresses in every hue of the rainbow dotted the boardwalks in front of the stores. He closed his eyes partway, and the scene jumbled into ever-moving colors, much like the old kaleidoscope.

"Penny for your thoughts," Miss Harris said once they started for the restaurant.

"I was just thinking about how pretty small towns are on a summer day."

Miss Harris wrinkled her nose. "They're small. Absolutely nothing to do. Give me a city any day. You know what I mean. You're a man of the city."

"I'm beginning to think I'm more of a small-town man at heart."

"You?" She playfully punched his side and then looked at him oddly. "What's that?" She pulled something from his pocket.

Sam recognized it at once. The contract for the head of alterations. "That's private, Miss Harris."

"Private?" She pulled away and affected a look of shock. "Are you keeping secrets from your secretary, or is it your father you're trying to avoid?"

He grabbed for the paper, but she snatched it away and unfolded it.

"Odd," she mused. "It is the Hutton's letterhead, but I don't recall typing anything for you."

"You didn't. Nor do I need to explain anything to you." Sam had paid the typist at the local attorney's office a healthy fee to type it quickly. "Please give it back."

"In a minute." She proceeded to read the document. Not two sentences in, her brow knit. "I thought your father was sending for Miss Tinderhook."

Sam gritted his teeth. This woman had no right to read the document. "Miss Harris, it would do you well to remember I am your employer."

But the woman's eyes widened, and her red lips formed a stunned circle even as the hand holding the contract dropped to her side. "Her? You're hiring her? Didn't you hear one word your father said?"

"My decisions are not your concern, and they certainly are not your job."

Miss Harris jerked her head in that odd way some women did when trying to fight off disappointment. "You love her, don't you?"

Sam looked down the main street of this charming town. Until today, he wouldn't have had the confidence to answer. Now he knew beyond a doubt. "Yes, I do."

Miss Harris went very still. "I didn't want to say anything. It's none of my business, really, but I can't stand to see you fall victim to another woman like Lillian."

Miss Harris must have worked in the New York offices when his wife was still alive. They hadn't inhabited the same social circles, but gossip ran rife in New York, fed by eager society columnists. Miss Harris had no doubt heard plenty.

"Ruth is the opposite of my late wife."

"Perhaps in wealth." Miss Harris set her hand on his arm.

He shook it off. "In every way."

"Except ambition." She sighed and examined her perfect manicure, handbag dangling from her wrist, the clasp slightly open. "Like I said, I didn't want to tell you this. I'd hoped I wouldn't have to."

"But?" Sam steeled his jaw. Nothing Miss Harris could say would change his mind. Ruth embodied perfection. Humble, lovely and compassionate. She was everything a man could ever want in a wife.

To her credit, Miss Harris looked uncomfortable. She even cast her gaze downward before going on. "She's been manipulating you."

"Impossible. I don't know anyone less capable of deceit."

"I know it seems that way—"

"Not seems. Is. Ruth Fox would never, ever manipulate

me. I am the one who needs to beg her for forgiveness. I'll do everything in my power to win her back."

"Didn't you hear me?" Miss Harris shook her handbag at him like some self-righteous interfering matron. "That's exactly what she wants you to do. You'll fall right in her trap."

Sam crossed his arms. "Who told you this nonsense?" Miss Harris stayed out late most nights. If she was going where he feared she was, she could have heard almost anything—none of it true.

"It doesn't matter who told me." She leveled her gaze at him. "What matters is that I know for a fact that she and her sisters plotted and planned to lure a wealthy man into marriage. You."

"They would never…" But even as he said it, he recalled how Ruth had tried to match him with Jen. Several times the sisters had tried to point out Ruth's best features. He'd thought it sisterly love, but could it be more? The thought that Father might be right made Sam sick. Lillian's bald statement flashed through his mind: *I only married you for the money.* But not Ruth. Impossible. "Why would they?"

"For your inheritance," she said. "For the money."

No words could have skewered him more cleanly. Lillian had deceived and manipulated him for her own purposes. She'd liked high living. Not so Ruth, but the need was even greater. Would she pretend to love him simply for the money?

His gut told him no, but his head said she would do anything for her family.

"I'm sorry." This time when Miss Harris touched his arm, he didn't shrug her off. "I hoped it wouldn't come to this."

He felt sick. He'd given everything away for Ruth. For a lie.

* * *

Ruth did not join her sisters on the porch. Sobs and sniffles might help some people. In a crisis, Ruth needed to work. So when Doc Stevens suggested a warm compress might help, she went to the kitchen to prepare it.

Naturally the stove had gone out. Wasn't that just like her sisters? Minnie was supposed to keep the fire burning, but she and Jen had complained the stove generated too much heat in hot weather. So they'd conveniently forgot to add coal this afternoon, and the fire had died. That meant the water in the hot-water tank was cold.

"Selfish children," she grumbled under her breath as she pumped water into a pan.

After stirring the ashes, she found a few embers. By opening the dampers and encouraging a flame with a bit of newspaper, she was able to relight the stove. It would take long minutes for the fire to grow hot enough to warm the water.

Most likely a mild stroke of apoplexy stemming from his weakened heart, Doc Stevens had said. Ruth's father was fortunate it hadn't been a severe one. If it had…

"Selfish girls," she said aloud. "Never thinking of anything but your own comfort."

"Don't be too hard on Jen and Minnie. They already blame themselves." Beatrice entered the kitchen, her steps so light that Ruth hadn't heard her approach. She unhooked the pearl buttons on her lace gloves and slid them off. "What can I do to help?"

Ruth shook her head. Beatrice had never done any of the heavy housework. By far the most beautiful of the sisters, she had been pampered with pretty dresses and few chores. After marrying Blake Kensington, she enjoyed the services of a housekeeper.

Beatrice settled onto one of the kitchen chairs, looking completely out of place in her expensive dress and hat. "Are you certain?"

"I'm just heating water for a compress."

Beatrice smoothed the soft cotton pad that Ruth had set on the table. "How does he look?"

"Weak. Pale." Ruth brushed away a tear that ran down her cheek. "I don't like seeing him like this."

Beatrice looked at her hands. "Me, either, but he wants to see us. You know how deeply he cares for us. He would do anything to ensure our happiness."

Such as spend money intended for treatment on the dress shop. Ruth fought a wave of guilt. She bit her lip and eyed her sister. "Tell me you're the one who paid the overdue loan payments."

Beatrice's brow furrowed. "I told you I couldn't."

Ruth clutched at dwindling hope that Daddy hadn't done what she suspected he had. "Would Blake's father have done it?"

"You're saying the loan was paid off?"

"To date."

Beatrice took it in. "I can't imagine he would have. Blake refused to ask his father. He said the mercantile is struggling, and with the new department store, business is only going to get worse."

Ruth fisted her hands. Their troubles always came back to Sam. "As if it wasn't enough to put all of us out of business, he stressed Daddy with that horrid contract."

"Who? What contract?"

"Sam Rothenburg." Never had his name tasted so bitter. "He waited until the rest of us were busy packing up the dress shop and then called on Daddy and talked him into approving a contract that would make me the head of alterations at his store. Can you imagine the gall?"

Beatrice's brow puckered. "Giving you a department-head position is bad?"

"I'd already turned it down."

"Why would you do that?" Beatrice prodded, her brow still knit. "The position must pay well."

Ruth hadn't bothered to ask the wage. "It doesn't matter how much it pays. I will not work with him." She dipped a finger into the pan of water. Lukewarm.

"Ah, I see."

"No, you don't." Ruth did not like the tone of her sister's voice. "It's a matter of principle."

Beatrice smiled. "Then you and Mr. Rothenburg have a romantic attachment."

"We have no such thing," Ruth snapped. "I don't want to talk about him. I don't want to ever see him again. I'm done with Sam Rothenburg."

Thankfully, a slight scraping sound from upstairs stopped further questions. Beatrice rose. Ruth listened. Another scrape. That was a chair. Maybe the doctor had finished. She looked to her sister, who appeared worried.

"Maybe Daddy's condition has improved." It might be wishful thinking, but Ruth had to shake away the memory of her father's strangled gasping and ashen face.

The floorboards above them creaked under heavy footsteps.

Beatrice crossed the kitchen to stand by her side. Both watched the empty stairwell. Would it be Dr. Stevens or Mother? If the doctor, he'd done all he could. If Mother, Daddy might be asleep. If both, then hope was lost. Mother would never leave Daddy's side unless he'd died.

A tremor shimmied up Ruth's spine. Beatrice slipped an arm around her waist. Ruth tried to will herself to remain calm. Mother didn't need another hysterical daughter. Minnie produced enough histrionics for the entire family.

Mother needed someone to help, to remain sensible in the face of calamity. Mother needed her.

She squeezed her eyes shut. *Please, Lord, save Daddy's life.*

The footsteps stopped at the head of the stairway, and Ruth resisted the urge to rush to the foot of the stairs.

Heavy steps descended the staircase.

"Do you understand my instructions?" Doc Stevens said as he thumped down the last steps and entered the kitchen, black bag in hand. His gray hair still stuck up from when he'd removed his hat upon arrival. His rumpled gray suit looked as tired as he did.

Mother, on the other hand, appeared unnaturally energized. "Warm compresses until the tightness eases. Aspirin for the pain. What else?"

"Digitalis once per day, beginning this time tomorrow."

"That's right." Mother filled a glass with water and hurried back upstairs.

Upon her departure, Doc Stevens glanced at Ruth. "Do you want me to write down my instructions?"

"That's not necessary. I understand." She squeezed Beattie's hand. "We understand."

Beatrice nodded. Slipping her arm from around Ruth, she extended gratitude to Doc Stevens. "We can't thank you enough for coming so quickly."

"Fortunate I was in town. The Highbottoms called me out to the farm earlier."

"Anything serious?" Beatrice asked, filled with concern.

"Little accident with the youngest. He'll be fine in a day or two. Your father, on the other hand, needs rest." Doc Stevens looked Ruth squarely in the eyes. "You'll want to keep him from all stress. No disagreements or disputes, however mild. Do you understand?"

Ruth felt the weight of the accusation. Doc Stevens wasn't telling Sam to prevent any arguments. He didn't look at Beatrice. He must have heard about her argument with Daddy and was placing the full responsibility on her. "I do."

"Good. His life might depend on it." He plucked his hat from the table.

Ruth trembled at the doctor's words. Sam might have started the incident, but she had protested Daddy's decision right before the seizure. In her anger, she hadn't seen the signs that he was struggling. By the grace of God, he was still alive. "If we keep all stress away, will he live?"

Doc looked at her. "It's too early to tell. These seizures sometimes repeat themselves."

Ruth drew in a shaky breath.

Doc's bushy eyebrows eased as he gave her a gruff smile. "He stands a better chance if he makes it through the night."

A whole night. Never had the hours seemed so long.

The sun slipped below the trees, casting the porch of the boardinghouse in deep shadow. Still, Sam sat in the corner. He hadn't eaten. He couldn't even drink the glass of lemonade that Mrs. Tzerchanovic—Mrs. Terchie or Mrs. T., to the boarders—had brought out to him an hour ago. Miss Harris had kindly offered to postpone their supper at the restaurant.

Sam could only think of how Ruth had deceived him. Wasn't it true that those doing wrong tended to criticize that very flaw in others? That would explain why she'd lambasted him for not telling her his name and that he was opening a department store. She refused to listen to his explanation. When he managed to get one in, she dismissed it out of hand.

Yet she had withheld the truth also. The sisters had played a game and put him at the center. His empty stomach churned at how he'd been duped.

Over the next few hours, boarders came and went. Sam barely noticed them. A group played whist on the far side of the porch, but after dusk settled and the mosquitoes arrived, they headed into the parlor. Sam had never reacted to the annoying pest's bites. Tonight he wished he did. Better a misery he could scratch than one buried deep inside.

Father hadn't arrived yet. Hopefully, he and Harry had taken rooms above the drugstore. With the speakeasy below, it was more Father's kind of establishment than the squeaky-clean boardinghouse run by the stout Polish widow. Father would have balked at Mrs. Terchie's insistence on thanking God before each meal.

The stout proprietress pushed open the screen door and approached, empty tray in hand.

"Now, Mr. Sam," she scolded. "No food. No drink. You waste away."

"Missing one meal won't kill me." His voice sounded flat, hollow, even to his own ears. "I'm not good company tonight."

Instead of taking the hint, she settled in the chair next to his and said...nothing. The tray dangled from one hand and rested against the worn planks of the porch. Her head tilted back. She breathed in deeply. "This is my favorite time of day."

At least she didn't ask what was bothering him. The hours and the weather, he could handle. "Because your day is almost over?"

"Ah, no." She chortled and slapped her leg with her free hand. "Still need to make sweet rolls for breakfast and tidy up here and there."

Sam had never thought of that. The woman was truly amazing. "Your day never ends."

"Wouldn't want it any other way." She sobered. "Since my Casimir passed, I don't much like being alone."

"Your husband?"

She nodded. "Good man. Godly man." She crossed herself. "I'll see him again one day."

That was the kind of faith Mother had. And Ruth. Sam stirred uncomfortably. For the space of an afternoon, Sam had felt that heady certainty, only to have it dashed by Miss Harris's revelation.

"Sounds like you trusted him," he said.

"Ya."

"He never let you down."

Mrs. Terchie turned to look at him. "Ain't a soul on this earth that doesn't let someone down from time to time. Is that what's botherin' you?"

Sam stared straight ahead.

Mrs. Terchie chuckled. "Must be a girl."

Sam tensed his jaw and gripped the arms of the chair. "I'd rather not talk about it."

Mrs. Terchie didn't take a hint. "What she done? Told you goodbye? If it's that Miss Harris gal, a handsome fella like you can do better'n someone like her. She's something to look at but no good."

"It's not Miss Harris. This lady is much more beautiful, even though the world wouldn't think so."

"Doesn't matter what the world thinks. Beauty ain't what's on the outside." Mrs. Terchie jabbed a finger into her chest. "It's what's in here."

"I know. Believe me, I know." Lillian had taught him that much. "I just found out something disturbing." He hadn't intended to tell anyone, but Mrs. T. was so easy to talk to. "I found out she and her sisters devised a plan to trap me."

Mrs. T. burst out laughing.

It did sound ludicrous. After watching Mrs. T.'s mirth, Sam cracked a tiny smile, too.

"My, my." She wiped her eyes with the corner of her apron. "There ain't a girl on this earth don't find a way to attract the man that catches her eye."

Sam could only stare at the rosy-cheeked doughball of a woman.

"Take my Caz, for example. He thought he liked my cousin Rose. Even asked her to the church social, but Rose didn't think much of him. She knew I was sweet on Caz, and since we looked like twins, we traded places."

"You did what?" Even Sam hadn't faced that much manipulation.

Mrs. T. laughed heartily. "I tell you, that boy never noticed! Took two socials and a buggy ride before I had the heart to tell him. By then—" she winked "—he'd forgotten all about Rose."

"But didn't he think you were Rose?"

She shrugged. "What's a name? Rose. Polonia. They're spelled different. Caz had fallen in love with me." She pinched his forearm. "Trust me. If this gal's gone to the trouble of getting her sisters' help, she's sweet on you. That's the one you want, Mr. Sam, not some floozy who's only lookin' for a fancy house and a big name."

"But how do I know if she likes me for who I am or for what I can give her?"

"What's she willin' to give up? My Casimir didn't have much learnin' or prospects. That's why Rose wasn't interested. I saw something in him that she couldn't."

"What was that?"

Mrs. Terchie grinned and hefted her bulk to her feet.

"It's different for everyone, but once you find it, you'll know deep in here." Again she jabbed at her heart.

Sam leaned back with a frustrated sigh. That was the problem.

Chapter Nineteen

Every sound, every creak or cough, woke Ruth. A dozen times that night she tiptoed to her parents' bedroom door. Lamplight streamed from the crack beneath the closed door, and she could hear Mother talking and singing so softly that her words could not be discerned. Each time Ruth crawled back to her bed, taking care not to wake Minnie. But she could not sleep, and though she prayed without ceasing, no comfort came.

Only dawn brought hope, for its arrival meant her father had survived the night.

"He's weak," Mother said as she prepared chicken bouillon.

Minnie wrinkled her nose at the smell. "I don't know how anyone can drink that at this hour."

"Dr. Stevens suggested it." Mother poured the liquid into a bowl and set it on a tray. "Ruth, dear, will you bring this up to your father? Then I suggest you take a nap. You look like you didn't sleep a wink all night."

"Yes, Mother." Ruth had learned her lesson yesterday. Never again would she dispute her parents. But that vow did not erase the trepidation.

Mother handed her the tray.

Ruth must face her father. He wouldn't chide her. Daddy never scolded, but his disappointment cut deeper than a sharp tongue.

She carried the tray up the narrow steps, taking care not to spill any liquid. With each step her nerves increased. At the top, she turned to the left and walked past the linen closet. The door to her parents' room was shut. She balanced the tray on her arm and rapped lightly.

Not a sound. Maybe he'd fallen back asleep.

"Breakfast is ready," she whispered. If he didn't answer, she'd leave the tray on the bedside table and scurry back downstairs.

"Come in."

Daddy's voice sounded weak, and when she pushed open the door and saw how pale he was, she nearly dropped the tray.

He managed a wan smile from his position propped against the headboard. "I must look awful."

"No, Daddy." She set the tray on his lap while avoiding eye contact.

"I know better." He sniffed the broth. "Your mother wants to baby me. I asked for eggs and bacon. She gives me broth."

"Dr. Stevens said it would be good for you."

He leaned against the headboard and ignored the broth. "Doc Stevens has his opinions. I have mine. But I'm glad you're here. Have a seat."

Ruth gingerly sat on the bedside chair.

He patted her hand. "I imagine you're blaming yourself for this little episode."

Ruth ducked her head. "I'm sorry I upset you yesterday."

Something sounding suspiciously like a chuckle came out of him. "You can never upset me by speaking your mind."

"I can't?" Ruth met his gaze and found affirmation there. Just like Sam. He'd said the very same thing.

"I'm proud of you. You've grown into a courageous young woman. You managed the shop all on your own."

"Not on my own." Nor did she do a good job of it.

He shook his head. "No false modesty, now. I know your sisters aren't much help. Jen isn't suited to sewing, and Minnie is still growing up. Ruthie, I wish you realized how talented you are. Your mother showed me some of your sketches. They're beautiful. And your idea to refurbish old dresses is brilliant."

"It wasn't completely my idea," she admitted.

"Ideas are seldom completely ours. The point is you took the kernel and developed it. That takes vision and imagination."

Tears rose to her eyes. "Not enough. If I'd thought of it sooner, you wouldn't have had to leave the sanitarium and spend that money saving the shop."

"Saving the shop? What are you talking about? First of all, I left the sanitarium because I wanted to be with my girls. Secondly, I did not spend a cent on the dress shop."

"But Mr. Vanderloo said the payments were brought up-to-date." She couldn't tell him the rest—that any future delinquency would bring the same result. "If you didn't make the payments, who did? Beatrice said she didn't, and she's sure Mr. Kensington wouldn't have paid."

"To be sure." Daddy stroked the corners of his mouth, which threatened to inch up into a grin at any moment. "I wonder who would do such a thing. It would have to be someone who cared deeply. Maybe even someone who loved one of us. Do you have any ideas?"

Ruth couldn't fathom her father's levity in the face of such a serious matter. "It must be the bank. Mr. Shea seemed very sympathetic."

"I doubt very much that Mr. Shea loves any of us enough to pay off our debt."

"I suppose you're right." Ruth twisted the corner of her apron between her hands. He thought Sam had done it, but how was that possible after the way she'd treated him?

"Whoever it is, we'll need to repay him."

"I will," Ruth vowed. "I mean, we will. We're a family, and we'll figure this out together."

A faint smile creased his lips. "Then you'll take the job that nice young man offered?"

Ruth swallowed hard. "I'll talk to him."

"Good girl." He patted her hand. "I like that Sam Rothenburg. Good man. Heart's in the right place." He grinned. "And he's partial to you, which shows good sense."

"You must be mistaken. What could a rich man like him see in someone like me?"

He cupped her chin. "Beauty, kindness, goodness."

Ruth saw none of that in herself.

But Daddy did. "Mark my words, Ruthie. If you give that man a chance, there will be a wedding in the future."

"I don't think so." Still, she couldn't hold back the rush of heat to her cheeks.

"I do. It's not every day that a young man spends his fortune helping a young woman's family keep their business."

"Sam?" Ruth choked. What had Sam told Daddy yesterday?

"It's the only explanation."

She felt a measure of relief. "Then you don't know for sure that he's the one who did it."

"Do I have proof? No. But I'm a pretty good judge of character, and he displayed every indication of a man so smitten that he would do anything to win your approval. Trust me. Sam Rothenburg loves you." He coughed and sank back against the pillow. "Now let me rest."

Ruth set the breakfast tray on the bedside table, kissed her father and left the room. Her mind reeled at the thought of Sam paying off their debt. If so, then he must have done so yesterday afternoon—*after* she'd unceremoniously told him to leave.

That meant Daddy was right. Sam did love her.

Her knees threatened to give out, so she sat on the top step of the stairs and rested her head in her hands. Which was the real Sam Rothenburg? The one who would go to great lengths to help others or the one who kept secrets from those he should trust most?

By any measure, the grand opening was a success. Customers streamed through the store all day. Sam mingled, welcoming them and answering questions. He matched Mrs. Evans with the perfect boudoir gown and helped Mr. Amos select a pressure canner. The sales staff reported brisk sales. It was everything Sam had dared to hope. Except for one thing: no Ruth. Despite the gnawing concern that she might have pursued him strictly for the money, he'd still hoped she would come over and see the crowd of ladies admiring her gown.

The store bubbled with excitement. Even Father should have been pleased, but he scowled as he brushed past the customers on a beeline toward Sam.

"Report to my office at once," Father snapped before heading upstairs.

Sam steeled himself. Whatever had upset his father, it wouldn't be good news for Sam.

"Was that your father?"

The familiar voice of Beatrice Kensington caught Sam off guard. "Yes, it is."

The pretty woman exuded sympathy and something

more. Sadness? "I won't keep you." She looked left and right. "I wanted to tell you that you have a lovely store."

"Thank you." It must have taken courage to come here against Ruth's wishes and to offer a compliment to the man who'd nearly destroyed the family's livelihood. "I'd hoped Ruth would stop by to see her dress on display."

Beatrice ducked her head, so much like Ruth that it made Sam's heart ache. "I don't believe she will." Her shoulders heaved and a hand fluttered to her throat. When she lifted her gaze again, pain replaced the sympathy. "Daddy suffered a seizure last night."

Sam reeled. "But he seemed fine when I spoke with him."

"Doctor Stevens said it could happen at any time."

"Is he...?" Sam couldn't get out the rest of the question.

"He survived the night, which is a good sign, but he's very weak."

Relief flooded over Sam. "Thank You, God." God? Since when did Sam turn to God? Since yesterday at the river. "Let me know if there's anything I can do."

"Thank you." Beatrice nodded. "I simply wanted you to know. It hit Ruth particularly hard. She could use a friend." She lightly touched his sleeve. "I must return home."

"Good afternoon." Sam watched her leave with a growing ache in his heart. This was the last thing the Fox family needed.

"Why, God?" he whispered. Life made no sense. Ruth's beloved father hovered near death while Sam's cantankerous one wrecked lives without regret.

Sam reluctantly left the crowded floor and climbed to the mezzanine. The long walk to the office seemed even longer after what he'd just learned.

"Your father is inside," Miss Harris said without stopping her typing. Despite her unwelcomed flirtation, she was a valuable employee. She would have to work in a different store than him, but he would not fire her as Father had suggested and he'd considered last night.

The office door was ajar. When Sam pushed it open, he saw Father seated at his desk, scowling like a gargoyle.

"What took so long?" the man snapped. Never a kind word. Never a moment of consideration.

"I was talking to—" Sam paused. Father would not understand anything but commerce. "I was talking to a customer. Sales have been brisk." Sam closed the door behind him. "I wouldn't be surprised if we outsold Cleveland on opening day."

"Sit." Father motioned to the chair across the desk from him.

That couldn't be good. At least his brother wasn't here. "Where's Harry?"

"Headed back to college," Father growled. "Apparently he wasn't ready to take charge yet."

Sam considered that a victory. In previous sibling battles, Harry usually came out on top.

He sank into the chair. "What's bothering you?"

Father leaned forward. "I think you know."

A knot slowly formed in Sam's gut, but he struck a casual pose. "I can't imagine what you mean."

"The property deal fell through." The older man looked ready to snap off Sam's head. "But I suspect you know that already."

Did Father know about Sam's involvement? How? By bullying Shea? The banker had promised confidentiality. Sam had to trust the man would not break his promise.

"How would I?" Sam hedged. "I thought Harry was handling the details."

"Harry," Father said, fuming. "I thought the boy had more smarts than that. Outmaneuvered, that's what happened. What I want to know is who. Vanderloo claims Fox did it. That's why he came back yesterday. But the man hasn't got the funds."

Sam gritted his teeth at the callous way Father referred to Mr. Fox, especially after what he'd just learned. "Mr. Fox suffered a seizure last night."

Father didn't display the slightest degree of concern. When had he lost the smidgen of compassion he used to possess? Sam recalled his father putting money in the collection pail for the poor that Christmas they'd been stranded in Pennsylvania.

"That takes care of one competitor," Father said.

Sam stared at the man he'd spent so many years trying to please. Why? So he would end up cold and embittered, too? If that was what power and success bred, Sam wanted no part of it.

"But not all of them." Father banged his fist on the desktop. "Someone swooped in behind my back and cut me off. I suspect Kensington. The man's livid that we opened a Hutton's next to his paltry mercantile."

"I rather enjoy the charm of the general store," Sam countered.

Father glared at him. "Are you going soft on me? I've been counting on you to take over the business."

Sam didn't believe that for a second. Father had pitted him against Harry for years. For what? A handful of department stores? A wife who languished at home hoping to see him from time to time? Children forced to compete for affection? That future had never looked so unappealing.

Father leaned even closer, his voice low. "I want you to find out who is behind this."

"Why?"

"Why? Because whoever it is, I intend to crush him to dust. Find out who paid that note. If it's Kensington, I'll see to him." The man's eyes gleamed at the prospect. "Find out who did it, and I'll publicly name you my successor."

Sam battled revulsion and a thread of desire. As president of Hutton's he could turn the callous firm toward philanthropy and goodwill. Father's vile legacy could be reversed. He would lavish every moment of affection possible on a woman like Ruth.

At last Father had given Sam the chance he'd fought for his entire life. All he had to do was name the man who'd paid down the loan. Unfortunately, he couldn't. Sam was that man.

For the next two days, Ruth watched the crowds pass by her dress shop and throng outside the new Hutton's Department Store. Though the dress shop had staved off closure, business had dwindled to nothing. Worse, half the promised orders she'd received at the Women's Club meeting never materialized. Oh, they each had an excuse, but the true reason was obvious. They could get a new dress at Hutton's for less than Ruth could redesign an old one. By the end of the year, they'd face expulsion again.

"He's so handsome," Minnie sighed as she basted two skirt panels together.

"Who is?" Ruth lifted her attention from the sewing machine. "Is there a new man capturing your interest?"

Minnie made a face that indicated there wasn't and pointed a finger toward Hutton's. "I meant your Sam."

"He's not my Sam." Still, her pulse accelerated. "Tell me he's not coming this way."

"Why would he come here when you were so awful to him?"

Ruth swallowed hard. She had treated him coldly, but Minnie didn't realize the extent of his interference in their lives. If Sam hadn't gone behind her back and talked to

Daddy about that contract, he would never have had the stroke. Paying down the loan—if Sam had done that— salved the ache, but it didn't excuse his lack of trust in her. Or did it? Daddy seemed to think so.

Minnie left the table to press her face to the glass. "He's looking at the window display of your dress. Everyone's talking about it."

Ruth concentrated on feeding the fabric under the presser foot of the sewing machine and keeping a steady rhythm on the treadle. That was another reason she couldn't walk next door. Her dress on display in the Hutton's window? She'd thrown it together so quickly that she'd probably forgotten to snip all the thread ends. What if a seam puckered? Still, she was curious. How had they displayed it? On a hanger or a mannequin? What type of shoes and millinery? Maybe one evening after the store closed she'd take a look. "I'm sure no one is talking about it."

"Yes, they are." Minnie bobbed back to her stool. She could not work and talk at the same time, so Ruth usually tried to keep chatter to a minimum. "Kate says all the girls want a dress like that."

"Kate?" Ruth paused, stunned. "Kate Vanderloo?"

"Do you know any other Kate?" Minnie grinned. "If she only knew you made it from her mother's dresses."

"Whatever you do, don't tell her that."

"I won't, silly. It is rather difficult keeping a straight face, though, when she goes on and on about it."

Ruth shook her head. "I can't believe she doesn't recognize it from the dance."

"It was dark, and she wouldn't have been looking at you. She was too busy watching Reggie." Minnie's disgusted tone and wrinkled nose told Ruth she was completely over the man. "Like everyone else."

Girls Minnie's age would not have noticed Ruth. Only

bachelors and competitors mattered, and she didn't fit in either category.

Ruth lifted the presser foot and snipped the thread. "I understand that the matrons noticed the dress, but that Mrs. Vanderloo didn't recognize it. I wonder if she does now that she can see it in the light of day. If she was even considering coming back to our shop, she won't now."

"Don't worry. She doesn't recognize it," Minnie said. "Kate says her mother is going to ask Hutton's to order one for her."

"Really?"

"Really." Minnie grinned. "You ought to see the display. It's fabulous."

Curiosity stopped Ruth's foot on the treadle. "Do you think I should?"

"Absolutely."

Ruth smoothed her hair. "But I can't while Mr. Rothenburg is there."

"Why not?"

"He might think I want to talk to him." Ruth paced to the door, spotted Sam and hurried back out of sight. "I'll wait until evening."

"Maybe he's out there because they're taking down the display."

"Already?" Ruth bit her lip. She really did want to see how Sam had displayed her dress. "They wouldn't take it down the second day the store is open."

"Sam said he was only keeping it on display until his order arrived."

Ruth worried the knob on the door. "Maybe I should go now." Except she wasn't ready to confront Sam. Emotions still warred inside. One moment she was mad at him. The next she wept that he would spend his own money to save the dress shop. Seconds later, she doubted he would do such a thing. Nothing made sense except that she couldn't face Sam yet. "I hate to seem prideful."

Minnie let out a disgusted groan. "You are the least prideful person on earth. Go, or I'll fetch Jen and we'll drag you out there."

"Oh. All right." Ruth grabbed her plain straw hat, squared her shoulders and marched out the door. The tinkle of the bell died away as the door slipped shut behind her. Out on the sidewalk, she felt very much alone. Sam stood in front of the display window with that pretty woman who worked for him. Miss Harris. He said something to her. She was not happy. In a huff, she turned and stalked away. The distance and the noise of the street swallowed their words, but the conversation was clearly private. Ruth should go back to the shop.

Then Sam turned toward Ruth, his expression unreadable. No one else stood outside the store. Fifty feet separated them, but she felt a surprising tug. The thread that had once stretched between them had returned. How could that be? She'd cut it that day she told Sam to leave. But no, there it was, terribly fragile yet straining to draw them together again.

Ruth's feet would not move. She could not blink, could not breathe.

Sam stared, arms at his sides. No smile. No encouragement.

The world around them stopped. Sounds, pedestrians and cars all slipped away. Ruth saw only Sam, felt him as intensely as the night he'd kissed her. The brush of his lips. The love in his expression.

You're beautiful, he'd said. *With or without glasses.*

Something changed inside her. The dam she'd worked so hard to build bulged against the flood of memory and emotion. Sam represented all she'd ever wanted. A good and caring man. He'd encouraged her in every way.

Go to him.

But her feet would not move.

He'd lied to her. How could she trust him?

They might have stared at each other for seconds or an hour. The thread stretched taut, tighter than the thinnest piano wire. Strike it too hard, and it would break. Ease the tension, and it might last. Could she? Could she find the strength to rebuild what they'd once had?

She drew in a breath and willed her feet to move. One little step would do it, but before she did, he nodded curtly and returned to his store.

The thread snapped.

Ruth mechanically followed Sam, stopping shy of the door. Her chance was gone. She wrapped her arms around her midsection.

Go back. The voice inside her urged retreat before someone saw her standing outside the door. Laughter. Fingers pointing. Derisive taunts. *Who does Ruth Fox think she is? She's not beautiful like Beatrice or vivacious like Jen or romantic like Minnie. She's plain and dull and unattractive to men.* Ashamed, she turned back toward the dress shop.

But something stopped her and made her look at the department-store window. Pride? Curiosity?

The display stole her breath. There they stood. A silvery moon and stars twinkled over beautifully painted male and female plaster mannequins that looked so much like… She closed her eyes against the rush of emotion. The night of the dance. He'd re-created it in every detail. There they stood, just like that night. The intimacy of the moment returned with such force that the dam burst.

He loved her. He loved her. And she'd sent him away.

Dear Lord, what have I done?
Blinded by tears, she stumbled back to the dress shop.

Sam returned to the store with a heavy heart. Telling Miss Harris that she was being transferred to the Pittsburgh store was tough enough, but seeing the look on Ruth's face hurt far worse. She'd looked terrified of him. A woman in love was not afraid of the object of her affection. A guilty woman might fear being discovered. That meant Mrs. Terchie was wrong, and Miss Harris was right. Ruth had pursued him only for the money.

That made his decision easy. Tonight he would pack his bag.

Chapter Twenty

Ruth couldn't eat a bite of supper or sleep a minute that night. Unable to turn on a lamp lest she wake Minnie, she sat on the windowsill in the light of the full moon and called to mind every Bible verse she'd ever memorized.

Mother had urged her to rely on God's direction for her life, but Ruth couldn't see the path. Confusion muddled her thoughts, and the events of the past few days had left her emotionally spent.

Please help me, Lord.

She could think of no other words to pray.

Moments later, her thoughts drifted to Sam and the moonlit night that he had so lovingly re-created in the window display. Even by moonlight, she had seen the love in his eyes. She had felt the tenderness in his embrace. His strength had lifted and protected her.

Maybe that was why the betrayal had hurt so much. She'd thought she knew him, but he wasn't who he claimed to be. That bit about shortening the name during the war? She did know German families who had done that, but it didn't erase the fact that he no longer went by that shortened surname. *A man must be completely honest with the woman he loves.*

Like you were with him?

Mother's gentle prodding had revealed the flaw in her carefully constructed argument. She hadn't been completely honest with Sam. She hadn't told him about Jen's marriage plan. What if he'd found out? That would explain the cold stare he'd given her this afternoon and the wall that had grown between them.

Please, Lord, help me.

She stared at the moon and squeezed out prayer after prayer. Nothing helped. Nothing could erase the doubts and fears that crowded the nighttime hours.

Only when the moon set and the sun lightened the eastern horizon did drowsiness lower her eyelids. She slipped into bed, grateful for rest. In what seemed only seconds, Minnie's departure jolted her awake. Sunshine streamed through the window now, gilding the new day with promise. The verse about the vine and branches came to mind.

Abide in Me.

Abide. Wait and listen for His voice. Dwell in His love. But how?

Abide in Me, and I in you.

Was that it? Had she been so busy protecting her heart that she hadn't let God inside, either? The stark truth shamed her. Instead of relying on God, of abiding in Him, she had put all her trust in her own abilities. God hadn't pruned her from the life-giving vine. She had cut herself off.

She knelt. "Forgive me, Lord. I have sinned against You by trusting only in myself. What a foolish, selfish thing to do." Tears flowed with the words, but tears cleansed, and in the stillness of morning she felt the gentle rain of His forgiveness.

Forgive us as we forgive others.

She must forgive Sam—not just in the quiet of her room

but face-to-face. If she hurried, she might catch him at the boardinghouse or walking to work.

She dressed quickly and descended the stairs to the kitchen. Mother prepared eggs while Minnie sipped a cup of coffee.

"Are you feeling all right, dear?" Mother said. "You don't usually sleep this late."

Ruth glanced at the clock and gasped. "It's after nine o'clock!" The department store would have opened already. "The dress shop…"

"I sent Jen to open it." Mother flipped the eggs over to lightly cook the top, just the way Daddy liked them. She must have given in to his demands for real food. "Minnie is on her way, aren't you, dear?"

Minnie grumbled but rose from her chair. "I don't know what's the rush. No one stops in anyway."

Yesterday, Ruth would have chided her sister, but not after this morning's answer to prayer. "I'll be there shortly. I have an errand to run first."

Before she could fetch a hat, the screen door banged open, and Jen burst into the room waving a newspaper. "He's dead! I can't believe it. He's dead. Just like that."

Ruth froze, her thoughts immediately shifting to Daddy. But no, Mother wouldn't be calmly cooking him eggs if something had happened. If it was in the newspaper, the person must be local and an acquaintance. Sam. *Please, Lord, not Sam.*

"Who is dead?" Mother turned to Jen, still holding the spatula and egg. "Slow down, Genevieve, and take a breath before answering. The world won't stop in the next minute."

Jen's shoulders heaved as she set the newspaper on the table and opened it to display the headline: President Harding Dead.

Ruth took a breath of relief. This was terrible news, but at least it wasn't Sam. "How?"

Jen looked stricken. "A stroke of apoplexy."

Minnie stared. Mother dropped the spatula. Egg splattered all over the floor. Ruth grabbed the counter for support.

"The same as Daddy," Jen stated. "His staff said he was feeling weak and unsteady the whole trip. And then last night in his hotel room in San Francisco, while his wife was reading to him, he died."

What had at first seemed wholly unrelated to their everyday lives now shocked them into silence. The president's symptoms were just like Daddy's. Their father could die at any moment.

Mother dropped into a chair. "My heart goes out to Mrs. Harding."

Jen hovered over the newspaper. "Apparently she's already on her way to Washington with the body."

"Jen!" Ruth admonished when she saw Mother press a handkerchief to her face. "Take care what you say."

"It's all right." Mother wiped her eyes and squared her shoulders. "Mrs. Harding is only doing what must be done in times of hardship. With the Lord's comfort, we can endure any difficulty on this earth, for we know our place as believers is with Him in eternity."

Ruth had forgotten how strong her mother was. She had been trying to tell her daughters this since their return from the sanitarium. Preparing them for the worst. Praying for the best. And holding fast to the Lord.

"Oh, Mother," Minnie sobbed and threw herself into their mother's arms.

Mother rubbed Minnie's back. "Nothing in this life is certain. We can only live each day we're granted and love those around us. Remember that, my dear daughters."

Love. Abide in Him. If Ruth had needed further confirmation of what she must do, she'd just gotten it.

"Love can't be held inside or saved up," Mother said softly. "To truly flower, it must be given away."

"Even when undeserved?" Ruth whispered.

"Especially when undeserved. That's when love can truly change lives."

Beatrice loved Blake despite his faults. Ruth saw it in her eyes, in the way she looked for him and smiled when he appeared. That deep well of love gave her unending hope. It also fortified Mother to face an uncertain future. That was the sort of love Ruth wanted. But to have it, she must open the heart that she'd clenched so tightly closed and give that love away with no hope of return. It would hurt. Perhaps terribly. But she must, and even if Sam tossed her apology back at her, she would be able to continue on, for not only did God ask her to abide in Him, but He also promised to abide in her.

She squeezed her eyes shut to stop sudden tears.

"Ruth?" Mother gently asked. "Are you all right?"

"There are no guarantees, are there?"

"No, dearest. None but God. His love never fails."

That would be enough.

"I suggest you explain this." Father stabbed a finger at the document lying on the desk.

Sam halted in the doorway to the office. He'd barely gotten the sales staff on task and opened the doors of the store when his father had breezed past and demanded his presence upstairs.

Father had once again appropriated Sam's desk. The man's fury was unmistakable. His thick eyebrows had been drawn together like the prow of a warship. He leaned forward, ready to make the kill, and Sam stood in the cross-hairs.

Father shook a piece of paper, his agitation escalating. "Imagine my surprise when I found this lying on the desk last night. I thought I'd made my directions clear. Everything—and I mean everything—must pass through me. You're not president of this company yet."

Sam puzzled through what paper Father could possibly be waving in his face. He didn't recall leaving any paperwork on the desk, and he hadn't seen anything there when he'd dropped off his portmanteau this morning. Best guess? The loan paperwork, even though Mr. Shea had promised to keep Sam's involvement confidential. Father had been obsessed with the dress-shop property, as evidenced by his directive that Sam find the person who had paid off the loan.

"I was too busy with the grand opening to look into the property next door." Calm facts worked best in the face of fury.

"I don't care about that property," Father snapped.

"You don't? Just two days ago you insisted I discover who made the loan payments."

"Unimportant in the face of this." Again Father stabbed his index finger at the paperwork. "Surely you recognize the contract you drew up."

Oh, no. The contract for the head of alterations. But he'd put that… No! He'd never gotten it back from Miss Harris. He'd been so upset by her revelation of Ruth's plan to marry into wealth that he'd completely forgotten about the contract. This must be the woman's revenge for transferring her away from both Pearlman and him.

Father glared at him. "You signed it."

"I did," Sam said as calmly as he could manage, considering his building anger at Miss Harris's actions.

"First of all, we do not offer contracts. Secondly, you offered it to *that* woman," Father sputtered with distaste.

Sam's hackles rose. "That woman has a name. Ruth Fox."

"That woman is no one. I told you to stay away from her. That's the type who is only interested in your inheritance."

When Miss Harris said it, Sam had believed her, but the same words from Father's mouth sounded wrong. Shy, self-effacing Ruth would never pursue a man strictly for his money. She was nothing like Lillian. Sam would not give his father the satisfaction of knowing he'd doubted Ruth for even one moment. "What if she is? There's plenty to go around."

Father's gaze narrowed. "Don't get smart with me, boy. If you even think of marrying that low-class woman, I'll cut you off without a penny."

"Ruth is not low-class. She might not have money, but she has more important qualities. Faith, love, compassion. Like Mother." With every word, the last wisps of doubt blew away. Ruth was all of that and more, so much more. She was worth fighting for.

"Don't throw your mother into this," Father growled. "We're talking about your future, about the family line, about your inheritance."

"Maybe I don't want this inheritance." Sam swept an arm around the room, but what he really didn't want to inherit was the cutthroat business practices of his father.

"What?" Father's face turned dark red as he rose to his feet. "After all the effort I put into molding you, you're throwing it away?"

"Push me on this point, and I will." Sam crossed his arms. Father might be strong, but through faith, Sam was now stronger.

"For a woman?" Father laughed derisively. "You're a

fool when it comes to women. You let that wife of yours run around and disgrace you publicly. Do you have any idea how many favors I had to pull to cover up that episode?"

In the past, that kind of accusation would have sent Sam into a black temper, but not today. Ever since that dip in the river with Pastor Gabe, he'd put Jesus in control of his life. And he knew in his gut that he was making the right choice. Sam had forgiven Lillian, Ned and even himself. The past had been washed away, and all he wanted now was to carve out a future with the woman he loved. No matter how long it took to earn back her trust.

"I'm not hiding any longer," he told Father. "Let my life be an open book. Let the gossips chatter away. God has forgiven me."

"God? What good is that going to do in the business world? You have to play the game."

Instead of bowing to his father's tirades like he'd done in the past, Sam saw the path ahead with utter clarity. "No, I don't. I won't blindly obey your dictates any longer. I'm done with secrets and pretending. I won't hide my name or what I'm doing ever again. If that means I lose my inheritance, so be it."

To emphasize the point, Sam picked up his luggage and walked out, past Miss Harris, who stared openmouthed, and onto the mezzanine.

"Where are you going?" Father yelled behind him.

Sam kept walking.

"Come back here. I'm not finished."

"I am."

Judging by the raised faces of the shoppers below, Father had followed him onto the mezzanine. In the past, Sam would have gone back. No more. He walked away, into a future without security of any kind apart from God. He'd never felt so free.

To his surprise, he heard his father cackling behind him. "That's my boy. Finally got some gumption."

Sam stared at the man who'd become a stranger to him.

Father crossed the distance between them. "Now you're ready to preside over this company."

Preside? Sam shook his head. After all this, Father was handing over the presidency to him? He didn't believe it. "Even if Miss Fox agrees to marry me one day?"

Father's face darkened. "Never!" He shook a finger at Sam. "That woman is a gold digger."

"She's no such thing. I will not allow anyone to malign Ruth. She's the finest woman I know."

"Is that why you covered the delinquent payments on her family's loan?" Father's grin showed that he thought he'd won. "Yes, I figured out what you did. Our bank back home confirmed you drained your account. You've got nothing left. Walk away, and you won't be able to afford one night at that boardinghouse. You talk about God forgiving you?" He snorted. "I'll show you forgiveness. If you cancel this contract and break all ties with that woman and her family, I'll give you the presidency. You'll get everything."

Instead of rage, Sam felt pity. His father was trying so hard to hang on to his vision that he couldn't see what was truly important. Poor Mother. Sam would do all in his power to give her the family she so richly deserved. And he'd pray that one day Father would see the truth.

"Please try to understand." Sam made his words very clear. "I don't want the company. I don't want your money. Give it to Harry. He's wanted to run the company his whole life. My path leads in another direction—one that I hope one day includes Ruth Fox. I love her, and I intend to keep loving her no matter what you say or do. I will give you my written resignation this afternoon."

Father was dumbfounded. "You're walking away from all this for a floozy?"

"No," Sam said, an unnatural yet unshakable calmness coming over him. "I'm walking away from all this for the woman I love."

The moment Ruth entered Hutton's Department Store, the old doubts returned. The store was crowded, and she knew every woman shopping there. Many had been dress-shop customers at some point. The way they turned their faces away told her they would never come back.

No wonder Sam had offered her the alterations posi-tion. He'd seen what she couldn't. The dress shop would fail. Her family needed an income, and he had provided, but she had stubbornly turned him down. Such unwar-ranted generosity!

Tears threatened, but she blinked them back. No man liked a blubbering woman. To change his mind, she must keep her composure and present her case rationally. An apology, of course. Then acceptance of his offer. Grati-tude. Hope for the future.

Her mouth had gone dry as paper, and her heart pounded in her ears. The last time she saw him, she'd frozen and he'd walked away. What if that happened today? It couldn't. It just couldn't.

Abide in Me.

Ruth took a deep breath. No matter what happened, God's love could not be shaken. He would remain faithful.

She looked around the store but didn't spot Sam. He could be anywhere. Back in house furnishings or help-ing someone in men's apparel. Where to check first? Or should she come back later? No. She would lose what little courage she'd mustered. Another look still didn't reveal him. What if Sam hadn't come to work at all? What if at this moment he was heading to the depot to catch the morning train?

Opportunity could pass her by if she didn't ask for help. Someone must know where Sam was. She wandered into the accessories department, with its shelves of gloves and hats and suspenders and belts.

"May I help you, Miss Fox?" Mrs. Highbottom smiled at her from behind the department's counter. It was the perfect position for the pretty woman, who'd never struck Ruth as much of a farmer's wife despite her marriage to Charles Highbottom.

"No, no." Ruth turned to head in the other direction and then realized this was her chance. She pressed close to the counter. "Is Mr. Rothenburg here today?"

Mrs. Highbottom's eyebrows lifted for a second. "I assume you mean the younger Mr. Rothenburg?"

Ruth nodded and swallowed hard. This wasn't going to be easy. If Mrs. Highbottom knew about her relationship with Sam, then everyone did.

"He was here a quarter hour ago or so," Mrs. Highbottom said. "He's probably assisting in another department."

Of course the employees wouldn't know exactly where to find Sam. Ruth would have to do it herself.

She walked out of the accessories department. Ahead, the everyday dresses hung in every imaginable color. Headless mannequins modeled the most stunning outfits. The displays took her breath away. Sam's store was beautiful. No wonder women wanted to shop here. *She* wanted to shop here. She'd be proud to head up the alterations department, if the offer still stood.

First, she must find Sam. She turned slowly, surveying the store from her new position. To her left a staircase led to the upper mezzanine, and on that staircase stood a man. Sam! She started toward him, but then her heart sank.

He was descending the stairs, a portmanteau in one hand and a hat in the other.

No! He couldn't leave now. Not before she apologized. Not before she had a chance to retract every cruel word she'd spoken and beg for the alterations job.

Why would God snatch him from her now, when she finally understood that love must be given with no hope of return?

Ruth sucked in her breath. That was it. That was the answer God had been trying to reveal all along. Love was all about giving. She must give with no hope of return. She couldn't expect a job. Nor Sam's love. Not even forgiveness. She must expect nothing and be willing to walk away empty-handed.

Pain sliced through her heart.

Sam had nearly reached the bottom of the stairs without once looking in her direction. Soon she would lose sight of him behind the displays. With his long stride, he could be out of reach in seconds.

She raced toward him, but a woman with two toddlers blocked her way. She darted around them, only to come face-to-face with a towering display case on a long counter. Left? Or right? Which would get her there more quickly? By now he must be on the floor, striding toward the door. The door! She'd cut him off there. She spun, but Mrs. Grattan stood before her.

"Ruth, I've been meaning to speak to you."

"Not now." She tried to look around the large woman. "I'm in a hurry."

"But I'm bringing you business," Mrs. Grattan said.

"Thank you, but this is urgent."

Her pulse pounded in her ears. Sam was leaving. He

would be gone if she didn't do something to stop him. He couldn't leave. He couldn't. But she couldn't stop him. Or could she? One avenue remained.

Cupping her hands around her mouth, she yelled with all her might, "Sam Rothenburg! I love you!"

The din of shoppers quieted as eyes turned toward her. No doubt they thought her crazy. Well, let them. She was crazy in love with Sam. The whole world could know it.

But he didn't answer.

"I love you," she yelled again. When she saw no motion and heard no response, her courage faltered.

God's love never fails.

Even if it cost her every scrap of pride and Sam paid her back only with pain, she must give her all.

"I will always love you."

Chapter Twenty-One

The moment Sam heard Ruth's voice he tried to find her. He wanted to sweep her into his arms and kiss away the trace of doubt that lingered behind each word. Unfortunately, he'd never been good at direction. When Father had tested Sam and Harry on their camping trip by making them find the source of his duck call, only Harry had found the way back. Father had been forced to mount a search party for Sam.

Now the sweetest voice in the entire world was uttering the finest words he'd ever heard, and he couldn't find her. She must be hidden behind something. Though he had the advantage of height, he wasn't tall enough to see past whatever was blocking her. He needed more height, and that meant returning to the staircase.

He sprinted up the steps two at a time.

Then he heard her shout again, this time filled with confidence. "I will always love you."

"And I you," he returned.

This time, he saw her threading her way around the displays and customers. Mrs. Evans stepped aside with the widest grin he'd ever seen. Every customer watched and waited, collective breath held. Ruth disappeared behind the shelves of knitwear, and when she reappeared, Miss Grozney pointed the way.

"Sam." Ruth halted at the foot of the staircase, her expression anguished. "I must apologize."

"No." He hurried down the few steps separating them. He couldn't let her suffer even one instant of pain. "The fault is mine. I should have told you what I was doing. I should have trusted you."

"And I you," she echoed. But her lip quivered, and she blinked rapidly. "I didn't really mean it when I said I didn't want you to help me...us, that is. I—I—I—"

He reached for her but she waved him away.

"Let me say what I must." She drew a shuddering breath. "I needed to let go of the past. A wealthy man once hurt me, and I foolishly measured you by the same standard. It was wrong."

"But I did hurt you by not telling you who I am. Nothing can make up for that."

"But you did." She ducked her head momentarily before lifting it. Fierce determination lit those pale blue eyes. "I know all you did to help us. The dresses. The loan. The job offer. I want to accept that job if it is still available."

Sam did not want her working for his father, even if Father would have her, which he wouldn't. "I resigned from the store."

"Resigned?" The tough edge melted away. "But I thought…"

"That's right—I gave up my inheritance. I'm as poor as you now." He pulled out his trouser pockets. "Poorer, it seems. I'll have to work off my room and board at Terchie's." He gave her a wry smile. This was the point when a gold digger would make excuses and scurry away. Lillian certainly would have.

Ruth's shoulders actually relaxed. Her gloved hands covered her mouth. "Y-you did? Why?"

"For you," thundered Father's voice from above. "He gave up a department-store empire for a dressmaker. If you have any sense, you'll tell him to come back."

Instead, those beautiful eyes of hers welled with tears. "For me? You did this for me?"

"You taught me what's truly important, Ruth." Sam went to her, cupped her chin his hand. "Family. Love. Working hard to help each other. Laughing and crying and praying together. That's what's been missing all these years. That's what I want in life, and if you would someday give me a second chance, I'd like to earn back your trust."

Warmth surged through Ruth. Sam Rothenburg was everything she'd ever dreamed of in a man. He loved her. He loved her family. He loved the Lord. The sights and sounds of the store faded away. She saw only Sam, felt the gentle strength of his touch. His scent welcomed her like a cup of afternoon tea. In the depths of his eyes she saw everything good: honesty, loyalty, love. The thread between them grew stronger, twined so it would not break.

"You have my trust already," she breathed.

That little-boy smile of his flickered into place. "I do?"

"Will you forgive me?"

"There's nothing to forgive. But I do have something important to ask you."

"I'll ask Mother and Daddy if you can sleep in the parlor."

"Ruth!" He rolled his eyes just like Jen. "Let me speak. That's not even remotely close to what I wanted to ask." He swallowed, the mirth replaced by seriousness. "I would like to ask your father's permission to court you, fully and for a proper length of time, if you are willing."

"No."

He stiffened.

She did feel just a tiny bit guilty for that, but her grin should have given the joke away. "I've waited my whole life for you, Sam Rothenburg. I don't want to wait a full and proper length of time. If I've learned anything these last two weeks, it's that every day is precious. I don't want to waste a single one. Do ask Daddy for permission, but please make the courtship as short as possible."

The smile returned, and oh, how he could draw her in. "I think I can manage that."

Then he kissed her. Not soft and gentle like their first kiss, but with the firmness and strength that a lifetime commitment deserved. This kiss acknowledged that though they'd made mistakes and would continue to do so, their love would always forgive.

Ruth drank in his secure embrace and the future she'd always wanted. Only after he broke the kiss and wrapped her in his arms did she realize that the customers, those dear citizens of Pearlman, were clapping.

Sam gazed deeply into her eyes. "You are the most beautiful woman I know, Ruth Fox."

"Glasses or no glasses," she laughed. For the first time in her life, she truly believed it. She threaded her arm through his. "Shall we go see my father?"

"I'm at your beck and call, my lady." Plopping his hat on his head, he picked up his portmanteau and walked her to the door of the store. "After that, I must look for employment. Your father will never approve my suit if I can't provide for you."

She laughed as the perfect solution came to mind. "Funny thing. My family happens to have a little dress shop, and we might be able to use a man of your abilities."

He pulled open the door and waited for her to exit. "Speaking of dresses, did I tell you that I contacted a couple clothing manufacturers who are interested in producing your designs?"

"You did?" Ruth halted. "My designs?"

"Yours."

She nearly burst with excitement when he detailed the efforts he'd made on her behalf.

As they stepped into the sunshine, the path ahead had never been so obvious.

"I wonder why I never saw it," she murmured.

"Saw what?" Sam held her close. "Do you need stronger glasses?"

She smiled up at him. "Not at all. For the first time in years, I can see clearly."

Epilogue

Two months later

Ruth smoothed the batiste flouncing on the ivory satin gown for the hundredth time. Though she had no doubts about marrying Sam, she couldn't help but worry about their future. They had yet to receive a definitive answer from Sam's contacts in clothing manufacture, so they hadn't been able to lease an apartment of their own. Instead, they would have to impose on her parents. The concern for her father also remained. Though Daddy had not recovered much of his strength, he insisted on walking her down the aisle at her wedding. She worried that he would not be able to manage the fifty feet to the front of the church. Why, this very morning, after Sam had helped him downstairs, he had sunk to the sofa, winded. Would she be able to support him if he faltered walking down the aisle?

"May I come in?" Mother poked her head into the tiny bedroom Ruth used to share with Minnie. After the wedding, Jen would move in here, while Ruth and Sam squeezed into Jen's room. The house would be full to overflowing.

"Of course." Ruth managed a tremulous smile. "Is Daddy feeling better?"

Mother shut the door behind her. "Now, don't you worry about your father. He simply had to rest a spell. He wouldn't miss this for the world. Blake is driving him to the church right now, and then he'll come back for you and Beattie." She frowned. "Where is your sister? Your matron of honor should be here."

"She forgot the veil. I told her I didn't need it, but you know Beatrice. She insisted on going home to fetch it. I thought she was going to ask Blake to drive her there, but if you didn't see her leave with him and Daddy, then where did she go?" Ruth pressed her hands to her cheeks. "Oh, dear, why is everything going wrong?"

Mother hugged her. "Everything is going the way it always does on wedding days. Did you know that your father was late to the church? My mother distracted me by saying the minister wanted to pray with the groom." She chuckled at the memory. "I actually believed her. Only later did I learn that your father hadn't secured the buggy properly and his horse took off without him."

Ruth recalled that her father had grown up on a farm well outside town, but she'd never heard this story before. "How did he get to the church?"

"He walked. What a dusty sight he must have been, but I never noticed. All I saw was the look on his face when he first saw me." She squeezed Ruth again. "You'll forget everything else when you see Sam standing at the front of the church."

"I hope so."

"You will." Then Mother looped her strand of pearls around Ruth's neck. "I want you to wear these today."

"Grandmother's pearls." Ruth touched them with reverence. Mother seldom let any of them see the heirloom necklace, much less wear it. "Are you certain?"

"Yes, dearest." She dabbed her eyes with a handkerchief. "How beautiful you are."

Instead of deflecting the compliment like in the past, Ruth accepted it. The pearls, the gown—it all made her feel like a princess. "You did such a wonderful job altering Beatrice's wedding dress to fit me."

"And you look just as lovely as she did." Mother smiled. "I hear the car. It's time to go."

Ruth's nerves multiplied during the short ride from her house to the church. The sun shone brightly, and the maples were turning scarlet and brilliant orange. The colors of this time of year always took her breath away. Today they lined Main Street in glorious celebration. But she couldn't help fretting. What if Beatrice didn't return in time? What if Daddy felt ill? Had Sam's brother arrived? The list went on and on.

When Blake stopped the car in front of the church, Ruth saw to her relief that Beatrice waited outside with the veil and Ruth's younger sisters. Everyone else had already gone inside. Blake helped Mother and her out of the car before going inside himself.

"You look so pretty," Minnie gushed.

"Scared?" Jen asked while Beatrice fussed with the veil.

"Not at all." Ruth looked up the steps leading to Sam and their future together. Now that she was here, she felt confident that all would turn out well.

"My darling Ruth. I need to take my place inside," Mother said and gave her one last kiss before going into the church.

Then Beatrice began to pin on the veil. It seemed to take forever.

Ruth winced as a pin poked into her scalp. "Aren't you done yet?"

"It's not quite straight," Beattie insisted yet again.

Jen rolled her eyes, looking uncomfortable in the autumn-red cotton voile dress. "How straight does it have to be? Let's get on with this before we all turn into old maids."

Ruth stifled a snicker. At least Jen had managed to take her mind off all the details of the wedding for a moment. If not for her sister's crazy marriage idea, she might not be standing here today.

"Thank you." She embraced Jen, who, like an abashed child, shrugged off the gesture.

"Let's get this ceremony under way," Jen said.

"All right, all right," Beatrice conceded with a wave of her hands. "I give up." She gave Ruth a big hug. "I love you, sis." Like Mother, she dabbed at her eyes with a handkerchief. "You're so beautiful."

Her younger sisters also gave Ruth a hug, though neither of them teared up.

Hendrick Simmons poked a head out the door. "Are you gals ready yet?"

Ruth took a deep breath and nodded. In minutes she would become Mrs. Samuel Rothenburg Jr. She had never dreamed such a marriage possible, yet here she was, following her sisters up the steps and into the church.

Inside the vestibule, Daddy sat on a chair, while the groomsmen stood around him laughing at something he'd said. At the women's entrance, the laughter died, and the couples paired off. Minnie walked up the aisle with Peter Simmons. Jen took Hendrick's arm, and Beatrice was paired with Sam's brother, Harry. In the two months since Sam gave up his inheritance to his brother, the two had become close. Harry sought Sam's opinion on everything. Sam generously helped his brother. Though Ruth's family held out hope that Sam would regain his inheritance one day, she knew his heart lay elsewhere.

One thing could make this day complete. Ruth looked for Sam's father at the front of the church. He was not there. Her heart sank. That bridge had yet to be crossed.

The organist began playing the wedding march, drawing Ruth out of her disappointment. Her pulse accelerated as the guests stood. This was truly happening!

"Ready?" Daddy asked.

Ruth held out a hand to help her father stand, but he waved off assistance and used his cane to push to his feet.

"My lovely Ruthie," he whispered, his eyes soft with tears. "You will always be my precious little girl."

She felt the tears well, too. "Daddy. You'll always be the most important man in my life."

He shook his head. "No, child. From this day forward, Sam must be most important."

"But you're my father, and you'll always be a part of my life."

"Yes, but Sam must take the lead now. That's as it should be." He patted her hand. "Are you ready to become Mrs. Rothenburg?"

How grand that sounded, almost intimidating. She swallowed the nerves that resurfaced and managed a nod. Then she took his arm and slowly they walked down the aisle past all of Pearlman—friends and neighbors, customers and competitors. Today they stood as one, smiling and encouraging her forward.

Then she saw Sam, and every trace of nerves vanished. The look on his face—marvel and wonder and love all mixed together—strengthened her. With him she could face any hardship and conquer any trial. Her feet itched to dance toward him, but she measured each step by her father's pace. When Daddy released her into Sam's arms, any sadness for what would be lost was overwhelmed by anticipation for the new life she and Sam would stitch together.

Their future gleamed as brightly as the autumn colors. Their vows came straight from the heart, wrapped in love. When at last Pastor Gabe pronounced them husband and wife, Sam bent to seal their union with a kiss. Ruth's heart could not possibly hold one more ounce of joy.

Then everyone in the church clapped and cheered, and she knew deep down that no matter where life took them, she and Sam would always be members of the greater family of Pearlman.

* * * * *

Dear Reader,

Like Ruth, I developed poor eyesight as a child and let other children's taunts define my impression of myself for many years. Today, the media is filled with advertisements and products that continually tell girls and women that they are not pretty enough, thin enough and so forth. It breaks my heart! In God's eyes, every single one of us is beautiful beyond compare. If only we could see ourselves the way He sees us. Yet we look in the mirror and dwell on each blemish and imperfection.

When a dear friend was in the last stages of ovarian cancer, her body was terribly ravaged by the disease. Yet God's Spirit radiated from her so strongly that I could see only exquisite beauty. The frail body was cast away and the true woman of God revealed. That is who we truly are, sisters!

Ruth's story imagines how an ordinary woman might take those insecurities so much to heart that she closes off any avenue to the life God has in store for her. Sisters in Christ, I pray every one of you looks in God's mirror and sees the true beauty you are. Step forth in the knowledge and security that you are His treasured daughter.

In Christ Jesus,
Christine Johnson

Questions for Discussion

1. Of the three sisters, Jen seems the least likely to come up with the plan to marry into wealth. Why do you think she is most interested in this?

2. Ruth constantly averts her face. Why? What is she afraid people will see?

3. Minnie has a crush on a rich, handsome playboy who is several years older than her. Did you ever have a crush on a man who didn't seem to notice you? What happened?

4. Why doesn't Sam tell the people in town his real name? What do you think is the real reason he withholds his full name from Ruth?

5. Illness both dictates the Fox family's financial troubles and their actions. Have you ever faced devastating illness? It could be in family or friends. How did it affect everyone around the person who was ill? What or whom did they turn to in the dark hours?

6. At the picnic, Ruth plans to try to match Sam with Jen, yet she allows herself the indulgence of a walk with Sam. When he comforts her, she pulls away. Why?

7. Ruth fears dances above any other social function. What reason does she give for avoiding them? What might have happened in her past that would increase her fear of them?

8. Ruth focuses most if not all of her energy on running the dress shop and trying to make changes that will help it survive. What changes are taking place in society at large that threaten the dressmaking business? Why does Ruth invest so much energy into the shop? What does it represent for her?

9. All his life, Sam has tried to please his father, even going so far as to accept his father's orders to hide his identity. Why does he desire his father's approval so much? Why does his father pit the brothers against each other? What scars would come out of such a battle?

10. Ruth's father chooses to return home rather than pursue expensive medical treatments. If you were placed in such a situation, what would you do? What would be the repercussions on your family?

11. At first, Sam doesn't understand Ruth's anger over his not telling her his full name. Why? How does Sam see the situation differently from Ruth?

12. Ruth's mother shows uncommon strength in the face of her husband's failing health and the family's dire financial straits. What gives her this strength? How would you imagine she will cope as events continue to transpire?

13. Why does Sam create the window display to match the night of the dance with Ruth?

14. Ruth has trouble speaking in public. Fear overwhelms her, and the words disappear. Fear of public speak-

ing is one of the top fears. Have you ever spoken to a group? If so, how were you able to overcome that fear? If not, how do you think you would cope?

15. Sam gives up a great deal at the end of the book. Do you think it was wise? Should he have worked out a compromise with his father? If so, why? If not, why not?

COMING NEXT MONTH FROM
Love Inspired® Historical

Available August 5, 2014

THE WRANGLER'S INCONVENIENT WIFE
Wyoming Legacy
by Lacy Williams

Forced into an unwanted marriage to save Fran Morris from a terrible fate, cowboy Edgar White finds that his new bride just might be exactly what he needs.

THE CATTLEMAN MEETS HIS MATCH
by Sherri Shackelford

Moira O'Mara is determined to find her long-lost brother, and John Elder is determined to leave his suffocating family behind. Brought together by a group of orphans in need of rescue, can Moira and John find hope for a future together?

PROTECTED BY THE WARRIOR
by Barbara Phinney

When new midwife Clara is accused of hiding a Norman lord's son, duty commands soldier Kenneth D'Entremont to find the child. But as his feelings for Clara grow, will he honor his duty... or his heart?

A MOTHER FOR HIS CHILDREN
by Jan Drexler

A young Amish spinster accepts a position as housekeeper for a widower and his family. She never expected he'd have ten children...or that she'd fall in love with the single father.

REQUEST YOUR FREE BOOKS!

2 FREE INSPIRATIONAL NOVELS
PLUS 2
FREE
MYSTERY GIFTS

Love Inspired
HISTORICAL
INSPIRATIONAL HISTORICAL ROMANCE

SPECIAL EXCERPT FROM

Love Inspired

Don't miss a single book in the
BIG SKY CENTENNIAL *miniseries!*
Will rancher Jack McGuire and former love
Olivia Franklin find happily ever after in
HIS MONTANA SWEETHEART by Ruth Logan Herne?
Here's a sneak peek:

"We used to count the stars at night, Jack. Remember that?"

Oh, he remembered, all right. They'd look skyward and watch each star appear, summer, winter, spring and fall, each season offering its own array, a blend of favorites. Until they'd become distracted by other things. Sweet things.

A sigh welled from somewhere deep within him, a quiet blooming of what could have been. "I remember."

They stared upward, side by side, watching the sunset fade to streaks of lilac and gray. Town lights began to appear north of the bridge, winking on earlier now that it was August. "How long are you here?"

Olivia faltered. "I'm not sure."

He turned to face her, puzzled.

"I'm between lives right now."

He raised an eyebrow, waiting for her to continue. She did, after drawn-out seconds, but didn't look at him. She kept her gaze up and out, watching the tree shadows darken and dim.

"I was married."

He'd heard she'd gotten married several years ago, but the "was" surprised him. He dropped his gaze to her left hand. No ring. No tan line that said a ring had been there

LIEXP0714

this summer. A flicker that might be hope stirred in his chest, but entertaining those notions would get him nothing but trouble, so he blamed the strange feeling on the half-finished sandwich he'd wolfed down on the drive in.

You've eaten fast plenty of times before this and been fine. Just fine.

The reminder made him take a half step forward, just close enough to inhale the scent of sweet vanilla on her hair, her skin.

He shouldn't. He knew that. He knew it even as his hand reached for her hand, the left one bearing no man's ring, and that touch, the press of his fingers on hers, made the tiny flicker inside brighten just a little.

The surroundings, the trees, the thin-lit night and the sound of rushing water made him feel as if anything was possible, and he hadn't felt that way in a very long time. But here, with her?

He did. And it felt good.

Find out what else is going on in Jasper Gulch in
HIS MONTANA SWEETHEART by Ruth Logan Herne,
available August 2014 from Love Inspired®.

The Wrangler's Inconvenient Wife
by
LACY WILLIAMS

With no family to watch over them, it's up to Fran Morris to take care of her younger sister, even if it means marrying a total stranger. Gruff, strong and silent, her new husband is a cowboy down to the bone. He wed Fran to protect her, not to love her, but her heart has never felt so vulnerable.

Trail boss Edgar White already has all the responsibility he needs at his family's ranch in Bear Creek, Wyoming. He had intended to remain a bachelor forever, but he can't leave Fran and her sister in danger. And as they work on the trail together, Edgar starts to soften toward his unwanted wife. He already gave Fran his name…can he trust her with his heart?

WYOMING
Legacy

United by family, destined for love

Available August 2014
wherever Love Inspired books and ebooks are sold.

LIH28274